TIER 2

CINDY GUNDERSON

Button Press

"The disadvantaged have structural interests that run counter to the status quo, which, once they are assumed, will lead to social change. Thus, they are viewed as agents of change rather than objects one should feel sympathy for."

—Alan Sears, *A Guide to Theoretical Thinking*

1 / ERIC

"Hey Dad, check this out!" Tal calls from across the room. I quickly lay the freshly rinsed zucchini in the bottom of the fridge drawer, then walk over to him.

"What is it?" I ask, leaning over the back of the sofa, trying to determine what he's working on.

"I finished the problem!" he says excitedly, looking down at his tablet. "I think it's right. Is it right?" he asks, suddenly unsure. I swiftly scan his work, primarily making sure his steps are correct. The numbers are too large for me to calculate in my head, but I assume they're solid. They have been every other time I've checked.

"The formulas look right to me," I congratulate, giving him a fist bump. "Great job. How long did that take you?"

"About...25 minutes," he says, glancing down at the timer in the corner of his display.

"Not bad." I ruffle his hair. "I mean, I would have definitely done it in ten or less, but I guess that's a decent time for a kid."

Tal grins and rolls his eyes. "Dad," he complains, then hesitates, looking away.

"What is it, bud?"

"Nothing," he retorts, shaking off his previous thought.

"I'd really love to hear it," I gently prod, moving around the couch to face him. I know he must be concerned about something important or he wouldn't have let it slip to the surface. He's been like a closed book these last few months.

"It's just—do you think I'll ever make it to Tier 1?" he looks up, eyes blue and pleading. So hopeful that a little part of me dies inside. My shoulders slump slightly and I drop onto the thin cushion next to him. In his mind, he's too old to be hugged, but I pull him close anyway, stalling while I contemplate my next words.

"Tal, you are abnormally smart. I am sure you've noticed that your capacity far exceeds that of your peers."

His head moves slightly against my shoulder, encouraging me to go on.

"I'm not saying that to compare or make you feel like you are somehow better, it's just a fact. So, no need for that smug smile," I say, poking his ribs. Tal laughs and playfully shoves me back. He settles his head against my chest, and I rest my hand on his head, his hair soft and boyish.

"It's just...it's not that simple."

"How?" he asks quietly, his hopeful energy visibly deflating.

"We've talked about this before, but maybe you were too young to understand."

Tal sits up and his eyes sear into mine, his attention unwavering. My mouth goes dry and I clench my fists to hide my trembling fingers. How am I in charge of this growing human? I don't even have a semblance of mastery over my own life yet.

"People in Tier 1, they aren't like us. And before you take that in a way that it wasn't meant, let me explain," I say hurriedly. "In a lot of ways, they *are* like us. We both have plenty of markers that qualify us for Tier 1 and, more importantly, we *don't* have the worst markers that would *dis*qualify us. But, we've also been through some things that have left us a bit...well, a bit scarred."

Tal's eyes don't leave mine for a second. Has he even blinked? I wave my hand in front of his face, causing his eyes to flutter.

"Good, just making sure you didn't pass out while I was talking."

"Dad, I'm listening. Seriously?"

"Ok, sorry," I smile. Sweat has begun to form along my chest, and there aren't any other obvious distractions I can shift my attention to. Tal stares at me expectantly.

"What I'm trying to say is that our brains have been dramatically affected by the—the events that have...occurred in the last couple of years," I stammer, stumbling through the inadequate words I am able to conjure.

"Dad, you can say it," Tal says, his tone indignant. "Mom died. We both know what happened and it's okay to talk about it."

A defeated sigh escapes my lips. "I know. And I am a terrible example of all of the things your mentor has taught you to do. I try, Tal, but—"

"It's okay, Dad," he interrupts apologetically. "I didn't even know her."

I imagine her then, the familiar image flashing in my mind's eye. Kate, on hands and knees, her hair pulled into a loose bun through her sunhat, turning to smile at me while she plants seeds in the garden. Her gaze meeting mine, a playful smile on her lips, her kind eyes full of excitement. She loved making things grow. Creating things out of nothing.

"That's why it's so hard!" I blurt out and Tal flinches. "I have thought about it a lot and I think the reason I hate talking about Mom is that I have this—this whole thing. This whole big thing that you don't have. I have a full, beautiful, strong, nuanced person in my brain and all you have is a name. How do I convey that? Do it justice? And, on top of that, I somehow feel like I'm flaunting my closeness! Something that you'll never have—" I pause mid sentence, my face flushed. "Does that make any sense?"

"It does," Tal says, pondering. "But, I would rather know what you know. Even if it makes me sad that I didn't get to have those experiences with her first-hand."

My head cocks to the side involuntarily, my eyebrows furrowing. Even the air seems to stand still as I assess my son, really taking him in. His chin is set stubbornly, arms crossed against his chest.

Something catches my eye, and I glance down to see his mismatched socks. An affectionate smile curls the corners of my mouth and I have to work to hold it back. I haven't been fair to him. I've kept him from having a mother in more ways than one.

"You're right," I exhale slowly. "As hard as it is for me, I promise I will do a better job of talking about Kate. Starting now."

"Now?"

"Right now. What do you want to know?"

Tal fiddles with his stylus and doesn't speak for a few minutes. I wait purposefully, letting the silence fully settle on both of us.

"Did she love me?" he mumbles finally, his voice cracking.

I place my fingers gently under his chin and turn his face to mine, relieved. This. This I can talk about.

"Oh, she loved you," I say, my heart swelling. "She loved you so much that I thought she might not need me anymore. I was a second thought after you were born!"

Tal laughs and shrugs my hand away. "Dad, c'mon."

"I am being honest!" I insist. He looks down, his eyes not focusing on anything in particular, and his arms relax to his sides. Intently, he looks up.

"Will you tell me about when I was born? But this time, tell me what Mom did, not what you did."

Breathe, I remind myself internally. Here we go.

2 / ERIC

I REACH into the muslin bag slung across my shoulders, pulling out a handful of knobbly tubers, each approximately two inches long. Sunchokes. We grow them all year round, but try to stagger the plantings so that our supply is always replenished, while minimizing waste.

It's magnificent here in the morning. The only sounds breaking the calm, dawn air are bird songs and the soft rustle of leaves, displaced by the starlings flitting between branches. Their vibrations seem to carry farther at this time of day, somehow more full and lively. Sunlight has barely begun pouring over the horizon and the warm light bathes everything in orange hues. The trees seem hazy in the morning mist, the ground fresh and cool on my skin as I create a series of planting holes with my trowel.

Having been one of the coordinating growers here since Kate died, I know these fields almost better than my own home. Out here, my mind often wanders to life before she passed—to who I was then.

That day became a veritable milestone in my service. Before it, I worked exclusively in the lab on hybridization. After, I couldn't stomach the thought of going back. I needed a change. Working early allows me to be home with Tal after conditioning, and the physical labor keeps my mind from wandering. Well, most of the time. I rarely have a day when something doesn't remind me of her.

I gently press the pieces of root into the craters I have prepared and cover them with the displaced soil. Then, moving on to the next section, I begin the entire process over again. My eyes glance toward my sensor regularly, reminding me to pick up the pace. Movement near the fence catches my attention and I squint to get a closer look. A head is bobbing toward me.

Kip waves as he gets closer. He has on a wide brimmed hat and, if it weren't for his tell-tale saunter, I wouldn't be able to recognize him under the deep shadow it creates.

"Hey, Eric," he drawls.

"Kip, how are you?" I ask.

He nods and points to my bag. "You have the rest of the sunchokes in there or are there more back at the storage facility?"

"Yep, this is all of them. I plan to get them in today and then work on planting the greens," I answer, moving my hips to the side to stretch my lower back. Kip is technically more experienced than I am, but he is arguably more concerned with getting the job done than doing it well. Nice enough guy. He lets me do things my way and I try my best to afford him the same courtesy.

"I'll go prep the rows for the greens then," he says, pulling up a long piece of grass and chewing on it. My eyes narrow. I've never quite understood the appeal of that particular behavior.

"That would be helpful, thanks," I say, leaning down to replace more soil.

"Val is here today," he says provocatively, gauging my reaction. I resume planting, not allowing my body or facial expressions to stray from their current positions.

"Oh?" I ask, nonchalantly, continuing to fix my gaze on the dirt below me.

"She will be here for the next week to assess our November planting needs," he states, drawing out the words and leaning on his shovel.

"Perfect timing. I have some requests I was planning to send to the Committee. It will be more efficient to pass them on to her directly. Thanks for the heads up." I glance up at him then and smile calmly.

His face embodies disgust as he tosses the masticated grass shoot to the ground. "I don't understand you, Eric. Val is beautiful, has great numbers, and is into you—despite the fact that you already have a kid and trauma baggage to boot."

I stiffen, but shift my focus to placing the next sunchoke.

"I haven't even paired once and you are turning down second offers. Maddening," he finishes, waving me off like he doesn't want to catch whatever I've got. Not knowing how to respond to that, I let him walk away, my blood beginning to pulse heavily through my temples.

As he disappears over the hill, I find it difficult to breathe. A pit of dread has settled in my stomach and I want to curl up on the ground until it passes. Forcing myself to stay on my feet, I close my eyes while my heart continues to race. Breathe in for four. Hold. Out for four. I do this continually until my heart rate finally returns to normal. How much time has passed? I glance around, ashamed, despite the fact that nobody is near or would likely be able to sense what had happened even if they were.

My mind flashes to the countless meditation sessions I have attended and, while I recognize they have helped, I have yet to get these panic attacks under control. I understand what the trigger is, but the problem lies in the fact that I can't predict when someone will approach me about it. Re-pairing certainly wasn't a topic I was expecting to be confronted with this morning, during my service assignment nonetheless. My nostrils flare.

I shrug it off and return to the task at hand. Pressing my trowel back into the dirt, I allow myself to process the information about Val. She and I met last month when she arrived to restock our seeds and irrigation supplies. That visit had lasted only a few days, but we spent a fair amount of time together. I would be lying to myself if I didn't acknowledge that I enjoyed the company. Val is soft-spoken and has a kind smile. Objectively, she is beautiful, but my brain didn't initially register this until Kip brought it to my attention. I assumed he was interested in her, and really, I wasn't wrong. When she didn't return the sentiment, though, he naturally backed off.

On her last day, she asked if I would like to run our numbers and possibly get together outside of work. I was completely taken aback, and my response obviously hurt her feelings. I didn't get a chance to explain, but the thought of doing so now...I quickly shut that down, hoping to avoid another bout of anxiety.

Matt is constantly reminding me that I need to move on. That there are plenty of opportunities to do so. That I have a responsibility to Tal. I get it. But the idea of getting to know someone new on that level makes me want to vomit. Nausea is rising in my chest from just envisioning a potential romantic situation. Beyond that, being compliant and doing what my mentor or Berg *wants* me to do nearly gets the same reaction. I am more than slightly horrified at my current frame of mind and want to be a better version of myself, I just—well, I haven't figured that part out yet.

At least I am still a good dad. I hope. And I am serving in my assignment, so there's that. If I go through the motions long enough, maybe some of my past idealism and flexibility will be unearthed.

With my bag empty, I head back to the storage facility for the mesclun seeds and azomite. My empty water bottle bounces against my leg. Since most of the storage facility is underground, the portion of the building that is visible from the fields looks like a glorified shed. Sunshine glints off of the corrugated metal roof, and the concrete walls seem vastly out of place in the middle of the growing fields. I give the heavy metal door a tug and walk into the office. After using the washroom, I walk to the kitchenette to take a snack from my lunchbag, when a sound startles me. Turning, my eye catches Val climbing the last of the stairs, returning from the cellar. She notices me immediately and seems startled.

"Eric," she says, startled, "I wasn't expecting to see you until this afternoon. Is there anything I can help you with?" she recovers, greeting me warmly.

"I don't think so, thanks. I am ready to get going on the next planting, so I came back to pick up the seeds. I figured I may as well take my break at the same time instead of having to walk back in another thirty minutes," I explain, unzipping my lunchbag and pulling out a small container of berries.

"Good thinking," she replies, smiling again. This time, seeming more relaxed.

I motion to the stairs. "I'll be on my way, then. It's good to have you back," I say, trying to express gratitude without seeming flirtatious. Moving past her, I exit down the stairs. As I descend, the air grows damp and earthy, the wild scent of the soil hitting my nostrils. Groping the roughly cast stone on the wall, my fingers eventually find the switch. A thin strip of light is triggered, illuminating the path ahead of me.

Walking past rows of wooden seed boxes, I scan for the one I need in the alphabetized line of labels. Finding it, I lift it from the shelf and attempt to remove the top, but it doesn't budge. Adjusting my grip, I wrench the left edge, only to have my hand slip, liberating a long shard of wood that splinters underneath my left index fingernail. Cursing under my breath, I move toward the light and gingerly remove it, being careful not to leave any fragments.

Pressing my finger against my thigh to stop the stinging, I search for a crowbar.

With the lid to the crate finally on the floor, I remove ten seed packets, replace the crate, and assure that the new quantity has been noted on the shelf display. Once I confirm that everything has been recorded correctly, I make my way back up the stairs toward daylight.

Val is still in the office, brows furrowed, looking very intently at information on her display.

"Is everything okay?" I ask, slinging my bag into place.

"Oh? Yes, sorry. I tend to look a bit upset when I am working like this. Numbers tend to consume me."

"I'm the same way," I laugh and her shoulders relax. "I'll be back after I get these seeds in—I have a couple of things I am hoping you could pass on to the Committee for me. Will you be here when I get back?"

She straightens in her chair. A little too eager. "I will likely be the last one to leave this afternoon, but I may be over at the main office by then. We could meet there?"

"If I don't see you here, I will stop by on my way out. Thanks," I say, trudging back toward the main door.

"Happy to help."

As I grip the handle, her voice calls out, "Hey, is your hand okay?"

Lowering my gaze, I see blood dripping from my finger. "Oh, I didn't realize it was bleeding. Just a small casualty from my attempts to open a seed crate," I chuckle.

"Let me help you," she offers, rising from her chair.

"No, it's alright," I say, pressing my finger again to my pant leg. "These need to be washed anyway." I give her a wave as I pass through the door, and my body is enveloped in the bright afternoon sunlight.

3 / ERIC

LEANING BACK against the wooden chair, I wait for Val. She wasn't at the storage facility when I finished my shift, so here I am, true to my word. Being in such a formal greeting area makes me acutely aware of my dirty apparel and the dried sweat in my hair. I self-consciously notice the tracks of dirt that my boots left behind when I entered. I assure myself that this can't possibly be the first time a field hand has come here to get a fresh drink after a shift. The glass in my hand feels cool and inviting, and the lemon floating on top of the water is fragrant. Still, I find myself hoping that Val turns up sooner rather than later.

A few long minutes later, the door opens at the other end of the room and Val walks toward me. My shoulders relax to their normal position as I stand to greet her. We awkwardly shake hands and she sits across from me, nodding to the attendant when he offers to bring her water, as well. She really is beautiful, and I can't help but notice her long, strawberry-blonde hair flowing over her right shoulder and along her collarbone. I hastily clear my throat.

"Thanks for meeting me," I start, all business. "I had a few requests and thought it would be easier to explain in person."

"I avoid digital communication whenever possible," she laughs and I notice small creases springing up along the corner of her eyes. "What can I help with?"

"Over the last few planting seasons, we have seen an increase in powdery mildew, specifically on our squash and pumpkin plants. I am worried we may be seeing another adaptation in the fungus. When I was at the lab, we were specifically working on genetic resistance in cucurbit crops. I wondered if there have been any viable seeds produced that we could have access to? I would be happy to run a trial here if it would be helpful." I hesitate to go on, noticing her growing confusion. Then a flash of understanding crosses her face.

"You used to be in the hybridization lab, I forgot about that," she says, clearly impressed. "I was expecting complaints about seed variety or something. That's typically what I hear when I visit growers."

"Sorry to take you off-*gourd*," I blurt without thinking. She snorts and heat rushes to my cheeks. "That—was a really lame joke," I say apologetically. "I blame it completely on my mental exhaustion after a full workday." Am I flirting? Is this what flirting is? I chastise myself, but the energy is intoxicating.

"Well, luckily, I am also coming off a long day, so I found it funny," she laughs. The emptiness comes fast, without warning, and nearly bowls me over with its intensity. I take a drink of water, trying to conceal my shaking hands. She notices, nonetheless.

"Hey, are you all right?" Her voice is tender, concerned. It only serves to make me keenly aware of my own convalescence.

I stand up abruptly. "Yes, I just need to get some rest. If you could pass that along to the Committee, I would really appreciate it," I request hastily. "We will also need increased amounts of potato and onion starts next quarter, though I am sure they are aware of our population growth. Thanks, Val," I finish, moving to go. Her hand reaches out, stopping me, and remains frozen on my forearm.

"Eric, you don't have to punish yourself," she pleads quietly.

I look at her, bewilderment apparent on my face. "I'm not—"

"Yes, you are," she asserts. "Somehow you think that forcing yourself to be a martyr is going to serve some purpose, bring gravity and meaning to Kate's life and death."

I shudder involuntarily when I hear her name and look away.

"You don't have to continue to suffer," she continues. "I am not saying that you need to pair right away or even that you need to be interested in me, but for goodness sake, sit and have a drink and allow yourself to have a good time! You can have a conversation with an adult who is interested in you without it taking anything away from your past."

The cognitive dissonance is overwhelming. My learned synaptic responses to pain scream at me to escape—to avoid ever getting close to another human again. The familiar void permeates my being, and my skin becomes clammy with cold sweat. Yet, I crave connection and logically understand that I will be better for it. For the moment, those enlightened desires are not winning.

"I—"

My throat closes and nothing else comes out. Patting her hand is the closest I can come to finishing my sentence. I walk out the door without a backward glance.

4 / KATE

THEY'RE ASLEEP. Both of them. At the same time. I sit down, not quite knowing what to do with myself. My headache is nearly nonexistent, Bentley is at conditioning, and the girls are sleeping. This has never happened before and I am elated. I can't decide if I want to frantically clean the house, or lie down and take a nap myself. Nap. Definitely nap. Tip-toeing to the bedroom, I lie down on the bed and pull a light blanket over my legs. Allowing my head to luxuriously settle into the pillows, I sigh contentedly. Just as I am drifting off, the sound of the front door opening jolts me back to the present, disoriented. My heart rate skyrockets as I move quickly into the hallway, throwing the blanket on the floor behind me. Could Bentley be home early?

Nick laughs when he sees the expression on my face, barely visible as I peek around the corner.

"Were you napping? Did I scare you?" he asks, amused.

"Shhh!" I say hurriedly, reaching for his hand. "This is a miraculous moment and you are ruining it!" I rush in a whisper, pushing him quickly to the bedroom and shutting the door.

"What is going on?" he says softly, mirroring my tone and setting his messenger bag gently on the floor by the closet.

"You are witnessing the first moment *ever* where both girls are asleep. At the same time. And I am not responsible for any children." I give a dramatic bow. "And yes, I was napping and you woke me up. What are you doing home so early?"

He stifles a laugh, but humors me by gently lowering himself to the bed and stretching out slowly, resting on his elbows.

"I am so sorry, I thought you would be excited to see me! I had no idea I would be interrupting your incredibly rare and valuable time." He gets points for at least attempting to be apologetic.

I sigh. Walking over to him, I climb onto his lap, wrapping my legs around his waist. "I guess I am a little happy to see you," I say, kissing his brow. His surprised response is exactly the reaction I was hoping for. A thrilling tingle shoots up my spine as his hands find my back.

"Are you...are we...I mean, I know your body has been all over the place since having the girls. I don't want to assume—"

"Oh, you better assume," I say, pushing him onto his back. He grips my arms and I fall with him. His chest presses against mine, the pulsing of his quickened heart rate mimicking my own. It's been too long.

.   .   .

My legs drape over his, both of us exhausted, halfway between sleep and consciousness. At least one of the girls should be waking up any moment, so I soak in the quiet relaxation.

A few moments later, as predicted, desperate protests emit from the bedroom down the hall. I reluctantly move from the bed and throw on the closest items of clothing I can find, my cotton pants and Nick's shirt. When I open the door to the bedroom, the crying halts and Leah whips her head toward the sound. Somehow, after all of her sister's commotion, Beth is still fast asleep. Leah's face lights up when she sees me peek over the crib railing. I lift her into my arms and tip-toe back to our room, giggling at her efforts to find food by rooting on my neck. Nick is propped up in bed waiting for us. He greets Leah excitedly and she responds with frantically kicking legs. He isn't able to distract her for long, though. She whimpers and I hurriedly latch her to my breast. I trace her smooth, perfect forehead and her eyes flicker in response.

"So what instigated your early return today?" I ask Nick.

"Oh I see, now you're interested in my life when there aren't better options," he teases.

I laugh and smack his arm softly.

"I wasn't able to begin any more trials this afternoon— the machine was updating, so I prepped everything for tomorrow and came home," he answers, reaching over and rubbing Leah's foot.

"What trials are you running right now?"

"I'm still entrenched in the amygdala."

"Of course. A completely normal thing to be entrenched in," I laugh. "Any luck?"

"Yes and no. I think I have found another specific point that tends to store particular memories involving fear. It's just really difficult to isolate every location where the brain has harbored those responses during an incident. When we reverse a patient's trauma, the findings still show that people are continuing to respond irrationally to similar stimuli. The response is significantly lessened," he sighs, "but not completely eliminated. We are getting closer."

"That's great, Nick. You are definitely the man for the job," I flash him a cheesy grin and he rolls his eyes.

"Thanks for the vote of confidence," he remarks, slipping on lounge pants and a new t-shirt, eyeing mine suspiciously. "I think I hear Beth, I'll go get her," he says, a smile playing at the corner of his lips.

When both girls are fed, we move out to the living room and lay them on their blankets with a few favorite toys to keep them busy. Nick helps tidy up in the kitchen while I prepare vegetables and fruit, in case Bentley needs a snack upon arriving home from conditioning.

Nick's hand brushes my hips as he moves to the front door, on his way to pick up Bent from his meeting point. Leah and Beth continue to coo to each other while I clean up my prep area. So much of my time goes into feeding and entertaining these tiny humans. At the end of the day, I often look around and wonder what exactly occupied all of my time, having nothing to really show for myself. I have to be satisfied with full bellies and smiles. And when there are no smiles, to trust that they will come.

Moments later, Bent runs through the door, energetic as always, and throws his bag and shoes across the floor.

"Nope!" I correct good naturedly, "where do those belong?" He huffs, quickly hanging up his bag and scooting his shoes to the mat with his foot.

"Better, thank you," I say gratefully, giving him a kiss on the forehead. "How was your day?"

"The best!" he answers excitedly, and I can't help but absorb some of his enthusiasm.

"What made it the best?" I ask, sitting him on the couch beside me.

"We were studying plants. It was all in the greenhouse. I *love* the smell in there. And then we got to eat things that were ready to be picked."

"Wow, that does sound like an amazing day. I guess I didn't need to make you a snack, though."

"Yep, I'm not hungry yet," Bentley says, hopping to the floor and playing with Beth. Her face erupts into a gummy grin and her eyes widen when he moves his face close to hers.

"It's ok, we can save it for later." I turn to see Nick coming through the door. "What took you so long?" I tease.

"I was talking with Pat. Apparently her sister is debating reversal therapy and she had some questions about it."

"Oh? What about?"

"Just pros and cons. I told her what I could."

I nod. "Hey, do you want to do something together before training tomorrow night? I could ask Shari to come over a bit earlier to watch the kids. I am kind of in the mood to be alone with you right now."

"Gross, Mom," Bentley grimaces, but I know he secretly likes our flirting.

Nick laughs. "Whatever, Bent! You're just jealous." He playfully tackles and pins him to the floor, giving the girls a wide berth. Bent tries to wriggle out of his hold, but ends up collapsing in a fit of laughter instead.

"That's a solid yes on tomorrow. What did you have in mind?" Nick says, letting Bentley go free.

"Maybe we could walk to training? Go through the gardens?"

"Perfect," he agrees, and I tap my sensor to message Shari.

5 / KATE

"Wait up!" Bentley yells, chasing after Tal down the trail. "Tal! Wait!" he pleads. Tal doesn't look back. Regardless of whether he is legitimately not hearing his calls or purposefully ignoring him, it results in Bentley halting abruptly mid-trail and bursting into sobs. Eric scoops him up and whispers something in his ear while I jog past them down the trail.

"Hey!" I shout, causing Tal to finally turn around. He pauses, allowing me catch up. "Hey, did you hear your brother back there?" He doesn't answer. "That made him really sad," I say, hoping to stir some empathy in him.

Tal sighs. "I know, I'm sorry. I just wanted to go fast and Bent always complains when I do that."

I put my arm around his shoulder as we continue on. "Tal, someday Bent will be bigger and you're going to wish he still wanted to keep up with you. I know it's hard to be the older brother, but if you can have some perspective—what I mean is, you and Bent have the chance to be great friends. But it will take effort from both sides to make it happen."

"So I always have to go slow?" he whines.

"No, but you could communicate with him. Find a compromise."

"Okay, I'll try," he promises glumly, and I ruffle his hair.

I hear Eric and Bentley approaching behind us and turn to greet them, but it's only Bent.

"Where's Dad?" I ask.

"Dad? Who's that?" Bentley questions, looking puzzled. Panic rises in my chest.

"Dad. Eric. He was holding you back there."

Bent turns to look. "Nobody was holding me, Mom."

I run a few steps back, my throat swelling, making it impossible to speak. The boys stand there watching me, clearly confused, and completely—abnormally—still. My entire body begins to shake and tears spring to my eyes.

"Who can help me!?" I desperately shout into the trees, realizing that no words have left my lips.

My eyes fly open, my cheeks and pillow soaked with tears and my body damp with sweat. I lay there, terrified. What *was* that?

It wasn't real, I think, forcing myself to breathe deeply. It wasn't real.

Nick stirs beside me. I flick off the sheet and leave the bed open, allowing it to dry while I use the washroom. Sitting longer than I need to, I stretch my neck and attempt to shake the vivid images still lingering in my thoughts. My hair sticks to my neck. Standing up, I peel it from my skin, tying it into a loose knot. After splashing water on my face, I reach for a towel and use it to wipe my face and decolletage.

The soft, clean shirt I pull over my head feels wonderful. Though the sheets aren't completely dry, I slip between them and slowly press my body up to Nick's back for warmth. He turns toward me and I pull back. Though I didn't intend to wake him, my body relaxes in relief. As his face mirrors mine, I crush my lips to his before he gets a chance to ask. He quickly responds, despite his surprise. I know he can sense my desperation, but he doesn't require an explanation. Allowing the dream to fade against his strength, I lose myself. *This* is real, I repeat. This is real.

Nick doesn't mention anything all day, but I know he has to be wondering what prompted our middle-of-the-night soirée. I debate whether I should tell him the truth or not, considering that I have already opened up about the dream with my mom. That one came frequently when I was pregnant with the girls. This might tip the scales to full crazy. Now I am not only experiencing terrifying dreams, but I am imagining a child? An Eric that lived? What is wrong with me!?

I go through the daily motions, and eventually Shari arrives to watch the kids. Nick opens the door for her since I am nestled on the couch with both girls, topping them off before we leave. Beth, as usual, is taking longer than Leah. She frantically grips my breast when I try to remove her. I sigh, deciding to allow her a few more minutes, though I'm fairly sure she is only comforting herself. The cushion sinks next to me as Shari sits, forcing me to shift my balance.

"Are you excited for your night off?" she asks. Beth's eyes fly open and her head arches toward the newcomer. I shift so she can see Shari without taking my nipple with her.

"Hi, Beth," Shari laughs, stroking the soft, slender strands of hair resting on her forehead. On her blanket, Leah kicks excitedly, doing her best to get our attention. Shari drops down and greets her as well, amused at her antics.

"I am, in fact, very excited," I say, answering her earlier question. "Thanks so much for coming over. I am slightly ashamed that training has become our only date night—"

"That's not my fault! I've offered my services anytime," Shari asserts.

I laugh. "I know, I know, it's completely on me. I feel guilty leaving when I know the girls hate bottles so much."

"They'll survive," Shari coos to the girls. Beth whimpers in complaint as I finally unlatch her. Shari whisks her away, patting her back. For not having children of her own, she has taken on this new roll instinctively. Putting myself back together and adjusting my shirt, I call for Bentley. He runs into the room and I lay out the evening schedule for him. Thankfully, he commits to helping with the girls in exchange for some one-on-one game time with Shari after they go to bed. I kiss the kids and thank Shari again, then join

Nick in the hall. Slipping on my shoes, he holds my hand and pulls me out the door before any of the children can delay us. My heart races, almost like I'm getting away with something, and the feeling makes me giddy. We skip down the path like children, finally hitting a normal, age-appropriate stride halfway down the block.

Crossing the street, our feet eventually hit paving stones instead of concrete. Vines crawl along the rough bark of the trees, flanking the garden's entrance. There's no rush, since training doesn't start for two hours. The scent of wisteria makes me heady, and we walk in silence for a few moments, taking in the delicate flowers.

"These are my favorite," I say, pulling a delphinium spire closer and inspecting the vibrant purple blooms.

"Every flower is your favorite," Nick laughs. He isn't wrong.

"This is perfect—thanks for walking with me," I sigh. The air, thick with moisture, is calm and smells of warm honey. The scent seems to seep from the spongy flower beds, the soil coming alive with the heat of the late afternoon sun.

"My pleasure," he says, wrapping his arms around my shoulders. Feeling his breath rising and falling, I lean into him.

"I owe you an explanation," I whisper hesitantly, turning to face him. "For last night."

"I don't need one," he says, grinning. "That was probably one of my best nights ever."

I laugh. "It was pretty great," I agree, my cheeks flushing, "but I wasn't really being fair to you."

"Oh?" he responds, his eyes widening in surprise. "You should be unfair to me more often."

I jokingly hit his chest. "I had a really terrifying dream!" I say.

He looks at me, a smile still playing at the corners of his mouth. "If you want to talk about your dream, let's talk, but I don't want you to feel like you have to, on my account. I don't feel used in the least." I pull on his arm, taking a step along the path, and we move forward again.

"That is good to know," I say.

"Do you want to talk about it?" he asks tentatively.

"Yes?" I answer, questioning my answer almost instantaneously. "Maybe? I'm worried you might think I'm crazy," I admit.

"Not possible," he assures me.

"And...well, I worry that it will hurt your feelings. It was about...Eric." My hands nervously twist and I peer at the ground, unable to meet his eyes.

Nick is quiet for a moment. "It won't hurt my feelings," he eventually sighs.

"That was a long pause," I counter.

"I know. I had to process for a second, but I really do want you to be able to share your thoughts and feelings with me. Eric was a part of your life and I want to hear about it."

I squeeze his hand gratefully.

"So what was this dream?" he asks.

Pulling him off the path, I lead him to a bench and we both sit. I lay it out for him, finding that some of the details are fuzzy now, hours after it happened. Saying it out loud makes the panic I felt in the moment seem silly, so those emotions are minimized in my retelling. Nick's gaze doesn't stray from the path, even after I finish. Getting no initial response, I fill the awkward silence with explanation.

"I know it doesn't make any sense. I wondered if you might have insights on where those ideas are coming from. Why would my brain make up a child? And why would I be imagining Eric alive, years later, only to lose him again?"

Nick is ominously quiet and it makes me abnormally self-conscious. Not knowing what else to say, I cling to his hand as he stands and continues along the path.

"I honestly don't know, Kate. Even with all of the research that has been done on the brain, we don't have a lot of answers on dreams. Sometimes it's a way to deal with fears, as you know—"

"That's what confused me," I interject. "Why would I be afraid of losing him when I already have?" Nick flinches, and I realize that may have stung. *Why wasn't my dream about losing Nick?* I stop and pull him toward me.

"I love you, Nick. I am so sorry that I have baggage. Please know that it has nothing to do with you. You are amazing," I say, pleading for connection and acceptance, but he is in his own world. Again, staring off through the trees. I wrap my arms around his waist and lay my head on his chest, feeling the curve of his muscles under my cheek.

Our relationship is so solid in most moments, but then—in seconds like this—it suddenly feels tenuous at best. The space between us nearly a chasm. I question whether I truly understand anything he thinks and feels, especially when it comes to how he feels about me. The discomfort in this silence is fed by insecurities that normally lie dormant within me. Only to be yanked to the surface when Nick's warmth is withdrawn, even temporarily. After what seems like forever, he pulls away and meets my eyes.

"I'm sorry you had a bad dream and I'm sorry you lost Eric. I...wish there was more I could do to help," he says genuinely. I swallow, relieved that he isn't upset, but still unsure. Pain—or maybe anxiety?—is evident in his expression and it kills me that I can only guess where it stems from. Standing on my tip-toes, I lean in and kiss him gently.

"Thanks for listening," I say.

6 / NICK

When we split for training, I kiss Kate's forehead and walk in the opposite direction when she has passed through the auditorium door. Moving down a series of hallways, I scan my sensor to access the restricted area of the campus center. The door to the room is open, and everyone is already there waiting for me. My body jolts in surprise when I see Shari.

"Where are the kids?" I ask quietly.

"Don't worry, I got them all to bed. They are in good hands and won't know the difference," she assures me. I nod gratefully. Sneaking Bent into the lab to remove a negative babysitting memory is the last thing I need. My muscles are tense, a byproduct of my previous conversation with Kate.

"Take a seat," the Director orders. We find our places around the steel table, Shari next to me and Grace directly across. Our displays activate almost simultaneously, the pale light adding to the soft illumination overhead.

"I appreciate you all being here," he continues. "Grace, may we have your report first, please?"

"Certainly," she acquiesces. "Our pairings in this region are moving along well. I'm not sure what the reports look like in other areas, but we still have a one hundred percent success rate. So far, we have 623 children born to our new pairs. Almost half of these are multiples. We have 84 pairs that have requested the opportunity to procreate again—with and without fertility options—and we are currently processing those. Obviously they will all be approved, but we will be making a couple of adjustments. We have," she checks her display, "nineteen pairs that have not been able to procreate. We are continuing to work on those and believe that we should see results within the next month."

"Wonderful," Shari murmurs. "How are we looking in terms of relationships? Stability?"

"So far so good. The few pairings that we were struggling with last quarter have all gone through their additional treatments and are bonding again nicely. If you remember Paul, he is still in weekly testosterone therapy and it seems to be balancing. I am somewhat concerned about Shay and Jamie, but their mentors are heavily involved. I should have a better report when we meet next month. I—" she hesitates. "I feel odd reporting on Nick and Kate. Perhaps he can take over?"

The Director nods in my direction, and my heart rate increases.

"Things are going extremely well, considering. We are...continuing to bond nicely, as you say, and she seems to be recovering extremely well from having the twins." Heat rises under my collar, my neck flushing, and I clear my throat. "I am concerned about her reversal therapy," I say in a rush, and the Director focuses on me sharply.

"Go on," he says, motioning for me to continue.

"Her headaches are still coming more frequently than I would like...if you remember, I reported last time that she has been having dreams about her mom, which I wasn't initially concerned about. This week, however, she had an incredibly vivid dream about Eric, Bentley...and Tal." There is an audible, sharp intake of breath.

"I know," I continue. "It shocked me, as well. I let her do the talking and tried to be supportive, but here is what I know." Reaching down and entering a short string of commands on my display, I pull up an image and project it for the group. "This is a patient's brain that I have been studying. This woman is Tier 2 and has had extensive trauma in her life. She had reversal therapy multiple times. If you notice right here," I point to a section at the back of the brain, "the activity in the posterior cortical hot zone fluctuates dramatically during her sleep cycles." I move forward through the images to show the difference. "This is consistent not only with dreamers, but specifically with dreamers *after* reversal therapy. The brain activity in patients who have never needed reversal is fairly static in this zone, regardless of sleep cycle. As the number of reversals goes up, the fluctuation increases. This not only leads to more dreaming, but also to brain fatigue. The frontal cortex compensates during the day for the extremes experienced at night, meaning that executive function also tends to suffer."

Shari, Grace, and the Director are all staring at the images, eyebrows drawn together in concern.

"Don't get me wrong, I am not overly concerned about Kate," I continue, "though I haven't scanned her yet. I am hoping to wait until our regular scan days to avoid making her suspicious. Since she has only undergone one reversal procedure—" The Director flicks his eyes to Shari and it distracts me. "Correct?" I ask, suddenly concerned.

"Yes, sorry, her session was just so extensive," Shari answers, glancing between us. "I guess I worry that she might not be comparable to your other research subjects." Her answer is incomplete and doesn't satisfy the uneasiness that pricked at me when noticing the Director's initial reaction. Involuntarily, my thoughts return to the first day I met him in the hallway, before any of this began. That overheard conversation playing in my head, as if it happened yesterday. Still so many unanswered questions. Shrugging it off, I continue.

"The truth is, reversal was never meant to remove large sections of memory like this. The research we have didn't ever purport to cover such invasive use of the procedure. While I know Berg feels that it isn't a huge stretch to assume results would be similar, we are now seeing evidence that they aren't. I would like to request approval for research surrounding these types of reversal echoes" I say, taking in their expressions. "It would entail studying subjects in both Tier 2 and Tier 1, which I know is not typical, but we need answers. We are using reversal therapy so extensively these days, and these symptoms make me incredibly uncomfortable with continuing at such a high rate. At least until we know how to prevent this effect. We will not be able to continue healing in this way if we don't understand what the repercussions will be."

The Director's mouth is drawn into a thin line, but he nods his approval. "I will get you your subjects, but the study will have to be blind. I will likely be able to put a smaller group together quickly, but it may take some time for us to sift through records for a full patient base. Hopefully we can get another group ready by the time you are finished with the first lot. Expect a briefing this week—next week at the latest," he says, standing up abruptly. "I have more to discuss with Shari and Grace for a moment, if you don't mind stepping out. Your report is greatly appreciated."

I nod, removing myself swiftly from the room and back into the hall. Reasoning that Kate's group won't likely be finished yet, I make my way to the main foyer. My mind is reeling and a weight has, yet again, settled on my chest. How long will it take for them to trust me? Have I not proven myself loyal to the cause? I have sacrificed my time, my energy, even my self-respect in doing what Berg has asked of me. I haven't required answers to my questions up to this point, but I always assumed that I would get them. Here I am, paired—with children—embarking on a quest for knowledge that I fully anticipate to be groundbreaking, and I am still not deemed worthy of *all* the information that the Committee holds. Information about someone I care for deeply.

The Director's mannerisms were, frankly, worrisome. I have always known that Kate's experience was abnormal, but now I wonder if there is more to it. I don't wonder. Deep down, I know I am missing something. My eyes squint in response to pressure at the base of my skull, and I recognize tension in my shoulders and neck. Using my thumb and forefinger, I roughly massage the muscles, forcing them into relaxation and nearly sighing audibly in relief. My questions will simply have to wait.

"You're pretty quiet this morning, Bent," I comment, jogging through the rich hues of the damp forest to catch up with him. His feet seem to barely skim the ground as he hops down the path to his meeting point.

"Yeah, just thinking," he says, his voice choppy from physical exertion. He's thinking. So cute. Such a little human and already trying to work through his world.

"What are you thinking about?" I ask, watching the morning sun glint off of his dirty blond hair, miniscule flashes of color reflecting from each strand.

"I don't know. Just what it's like in other territories. We have big trees and lots of rain, but no mountains or oceans."

"We actually do have an ocean in this territory, did you know that?" I ask, my feet hitting the path in beat to his rhythmic scuffling.

"We do?"

"Yep, it's further west. I've only seen it once."

"Could we go sometime?" he asks excitedly. He pauses unexpectedly, causing me to skid to avoid running into him.

"It's not usually something we do without a purpose, but if an opportunity ever comes up, I will definitely try," I answer. He smiles.

"No rainforests, though, right?" he confirms.

"No rainforests. Sorry about that."

We have reached the meeting point, but are a little early thanks to Bentley's energetic pace.

"Do other people ever go beyond our territory?" he asks.

"Sometimes, but again, usually only for a specific purpose through their service assignments."

"What service assignment would I need to get to do that?" he asks innocently. I laugh, watching the wheels turn in his head.

"It changes all the time—just depends on what is needed. Sometimes people travel for research, sometimes for agricultural needs. I guess you will have to hope to get lucky in your selection."

His brows furrow and he pauses before responding, "Okay. Thanks, Nick."

I wave as he runs to greet an approaching friend, noticing his instructor moving toward us from the opposite end of the path. Once he arrives, I will begin the walk home, but I want to make sure Bent is accounted for before leaving. When they begin inter-acting, I catch Bent's eye and mouth, "see you later" as he grins, giving me a small wave.

A fine mist is falling as I trudge back up the hill to our house, and the miniscule points of cool moisture on my skin are invigorating. I can't say that I enjoy Idaho as much as Colorado, but I definitely don't miss the intense heat. Having a body of water close makes for much more temperate weather. If I could somehow have the lush foliage with more sunshine and be closer to the mountains. And keep the ocean. A sardonic chuckle at my own greediness escapes my lips.

Arriving home, I see Kate struggling to feed Beth mashed sweet potato while Leah is slamming her hands on the counter, desperate for more. I quickly kick my shoes off, dramatically running to her aid.

"Leah," I coo, "such an impatient lady." I pick up a spoon and give her a bite.

"Perfect timing. She is out of control this morning! So hungry!" Kate exclaims.

"She's just a growing girl, right Lee?" Leah slurps another bite off of the spoon. Beth gives her a disgusted look and Kate and I break into hearty laughs.

"Did you see that?" Kate asks between breaths. I nod, laughing too hard to answer. The girls think this is great fun and begin giggling and kicking in response. It doesn't take Leah long to complain, though, still apparently famished. I continue to give her bites until the entire bowl is clean.

"I'll go mash more for Beth," I say, moving to the fridge, taking the bowl with me.

"Just wait a minute, she may actually be done," Kate directs, and I pause. Sure enough, Beth refuses her next bite.

"You better gain an appetite, little one, or your sister is going to double your size!" Kate says, wiping her cherub face with a damp cloth.

Both fed and happy, the girls are content to roll on the floor, their arms shooting out in all directions, searching for something to grasp onto. Though neither of them has crawled yet, they both have have begun rocking on their hands and knees. It's only a matter of time.

"Do you have anything on your agenda that is particularly pressing today?" I ask, rinsing the dishes. "I am waiting for new patient records to come in, so there's not much I can move on at the lab. I may stop over for about an hour this afternoon to prep, but other than that, I am at your service."

"Well, that's a nice surprise," she replies, grinning. "I would love to take a shower and then I need to check in with Shari about my service assignment. It's time for me to pick up some hours."

"Yeah? You are feeling like you can take that on?" I ask, stacking the small bowls on the drying rack and moving next to her.

"I am. The girls are sleeping well at night and I am...good. I could easily do one session per week. And I think it would be beneficial for the girls to have some outside experiences. Practice taking bottles." She winks.

"That would be nice, give us more flexibility," I say, running my hand along her waist, turning her toward me. "I think that's great. Do you want me to take the girls on a walk after you shower so you can have some peace and quiet for your call?"

"I would really appreciate that, thank you," she says, leaning in to kiss me. A clip barely holds her loosely tied hair into a twist at the base of her neck. Her oversized cotton shirt hits her mid-thigh and there is little splash of sweet potato on one sleeve. She is beautiful. Our lips meet, short and sweet, but I pull her back in for a deeper kiss. She smiles and pulls away.

"Shower and phone call, remember?" she says.

"Sorry, I got distracted," I laugh.

"Don't spend too long at the lab and maybe I will be distracted while the girls are napping this afternoon. Though I probably just jinxed it," she laughs, retreating to the bedroom. I definitely won't be staying long at the lab.

I lie down on the floor next to the girls, pushing gently on their feet and watching them follow my hands. They love peek-a-boo, never tiring of it. Their eyes are brilliantly blue, sparkling like gemstones, and they light up each and every time they see my face emerge from my hands.

My heart swells at the thought of Kate feeling good enough to get back to her assignment. Maybe that means she would be ready to talk about having more kids? When we paired, our minimum goal was four. With fertility treatments, we could achieve that—and possibly more—with only one more pregnancy. She worries about her age, but she handled the last one beautifully.

A deep, familiar uneasiness rises through my stomach. As is my custom in moments like this, I methodically walk myself back through the timeline of events. I did what I was asked to do. Kate and Eric *both* wanted this, though they weren't properly conditioned to follow through. I was willing to take this on despite the acute pain of rejection that continues to linger. We are making our impact, as Kate would say, and *are* doing this together. The fact that she required adjustment initially is irrelevant.

Kate materializes from the bedroom, looking radiant, hair still wet. The apprehension eases slightly as I take her in, and I conclude that I need to broach the fertility topic. Worst case scenario, it's a no. Or she gets mad at me for bringing it up and I lose distracted naptime. That last possibility is compelling, but I ultimately decide in favor of the proposition. She can't stay mad at this handsome face for too long.

"Hey, good shower?" I ask, easing into it. Seems like a safe opener.

"Great, thanks. I was thinking..." She pauses and my heart leaps. Maybe I won't have to be the one to bring it up? "...do you think those dreams I am having could be telling me something?"

I blink, taken aback. "What do you mean?" I ask warily.

"Well, I was just wondering if they could be serving a purpose— pushing me toward something I am supposed to accomplish. Take the dream about my mom, for example. She had such a passion for serving in Tier 3. I have been working the same service assignment for years. Maybe I need to switch it up. Do what was important to her and find something I am passionate about. I want to make an impact, Nick, you know this. I know I'm probably wearing on you with always coming back to this internal struggle, but I am feeling that drive again: to create, to build," she looks at me questioningly, pleading for a response.

"I think that would be great, and I am all for experimenting. If this could potentially fulfill a desire *and* improve your sleep, seems like a no-brainer," I say, fully aware that I am pandering.

She smiles gratefully. "I'll ask Shari what my options are."

"You know," I postulate, "this obviously hasn't been approved, but maybe we could do a couple of scans for you before and after. Just see if there's any difference or improvement," I suggest and her eyes light up.

"You could do that?" she asks excitedly.

"You can't say anything, and I'd have to figure out a way to save your scans off of the main database, but...it might be fun," I caution, grinning at her enthusiastic response.

"Yes! Figure it out! I would love that. Do you know much about dreaming and the brain?"

I'm about to, I think.

"Not much, but we could poke around." She runs to me then, throwing her arms around my neck. I would do pretty much anything for this reaction. Holding her tightly, my eyes close in contentment.

"Hey, I was also thinking while you were in the shower," I start. She meets my eyes, interested. "Do you think you feel good enough—I mean, you mentioned you were feeling up to getting back to your assignment, so I wondered if you had considered...kind of the same thing you mentioned, creating, building. More kids?" I fumble through my words and her eyebrow raises in amusement. That's a good sign.

"Was that difficult for you to get out?" she teases.

"I was thinking about it, but I didn't want to make you feel like we *had* to go there. Or that I would be disappointed if we didn't—"

"Wouldn't you be?" she asks.

"No. If we never discussed it, that would be frustrating, but right now, I don't want to push."

"You aren't pushing, I have been thinking about it, too," she says, relaxing her arms to her sides. "I think we should talk about it more seriously in a couple of weeks. My only hesitation is the fertility part. I don't know if I'm ready for that again," she shudders.

"I know. I mean, I don't know, but—well, my part was easy." I shrug. She laughs, running her hands through her damp hair. This is right. All of this is right.

8 / ERIC

Sitting at the table, I rest my head in my hands, waiting for Tal to arrive home. The call I received hours ago plays on loop in my head.

"...Tal didn't show up to his last period of conditioning. Somehow, walking between the courtyard and the teaching kitchen he slipped away..."

If I thought there was any chance this wasn't his own doing, it wouldn't be physically possible for me to sit and wait. Even knowing this, if he doesn't walk through that door in another fifteen minutes, I won't be able to stop myself from going out to search.

My patience is rewarded when, a few minutes later, the doorknob turns and Tal saunters in. I take a deep breath, steeling myself for our soon-to-be conversation. The last thing I want to do is make it worse.

"Hey, Dad," Tal says nonchalantly, pushing his shoes onto the mat behind the door.

"Hey, Tal," I say evenly.

"I'm going to—" he starts.

"Nice try, bud. You need to come sit down so we can talk for a minute," I interrupt.

Tal gives a dramatic huff, but walks toward me nonetheless. He pulls the wooden chair out from the table and drops into it.

"They told you?" he asks.

"Yep."

"What did they say?"

"What should they have said?"

"That I'm not really learning anything at conditioning, so there's no point in me being there," he answers matter-of-factly.

"That is definitely not what they said. Why do you feel like you aren't learning anything?"

"Dad, the pace is so slow. I could easily learn what I need to learn in less than five minutes. The teaching kitchen? It's a joke. I've been making meals for two years now and today I think they were planning to whip up some incredibly difficult rhubarb sauce," he says sarcastically. I smile inwardly at his confidence, maintaining a somber expression.

"I am confused," I say. "I thought we had a discussion with your team at the beginning of the year and they assured me that they would be able to adjust conditioning based on your abilities."

"Dad, *this is* the advanced group. I'm in with kids three years older than me. It wouldn't be appropriate for me to be with the *way* older kids."

"Hmm. I guess I didn't realize how frustrated you were with all of this." I pause, thinking. What is this behavior telling me? "Have you considered—well, that it might not be solely about you?"

"What?" he asks reflexively, his head flinching, eyes narrowed.

"I mean, conditioning isn't there just for you to learn specific information or skills. It's set up to be interactive and experiential for everyone's benefit. You obviously find the requirements extremely easy, but what about the relationships? What about giving, tutoring, and mentoring? Being an example and a leader?"

"That's not really the point—"

"No, it is, though," I interrupt, attempting to maintain a gentle tone. "Think of all of those kids that find learning difficult. How much easier would it be to have a peer reinforcing those ideas? Or to have someone to practice with outside of regular conditioning? How much more successful would those kids be if they had you to help them?"

He looks down at the floor.

"And how much better and happier would you be to have friends? People you care about because you are serving them. And relationships with your leaders, learning from them how to be a leader yourself someday."

He mumbles something, but I don't catch it, so I ask him to repeat himself.

"What if that's not what I want?" he asks, slightly louder this time.

"What *do* you want, Tal?"

"I want to be away from this place."

"From home?"

"No, Dad. Not from you or this house. I want to be out of this system. It's outdated and we aren't being served by it anymore."

I cross my arms in front of my chest, forcing myself to ask more questions so that I don't jump immediately into a lecture.

"What do you mean?"

"How many years has it been that we have had enough resources for all Tiers?" he asks and, embarrassingly, I don't immediately know the answer.

"Approximately sixty," he answers for me, "with the last twenty being particularly abundant. If that's the case, why do we need to be limited? Why can't everyone have the chance to be Tier 1?"

"Everyone does have the chance to be Tier 1, Tal, there are just specific requirements. And remember, 'being Tier 1' doesn't mean that there is suddenly nothing required of you, it's exactly the opposite! Aspiring to be our best is one thing, but aspiring to take on responsibility that we are not capable of shouldering is another."

"I know, and that's precisely why I think our system is antiquated.

We have accepted that Tier 1 responsibilities would be too much, but what if they aren't? What if everyone were given the chance to continue to progress? What if we weren't limited by our Tier? How does anyone truly know that someone like me couldn't do something amazing with access to better resources? Make some discovery or invent new technology? But with the conditioning I am stuck with, I won't ever have the chance to try."

I purse my lips, processing his reasoning. "There's one flaw in your logic, son," I say gently, "and it lies in your usage of the term 'resources'. Your argument is that we have plenty of them at this point, correct?" Tal nods. "You are forgetting," I continue, "that resources don't solely include food and shelter. They include time, energy, abilities, and did I mention—*time*? We do not have *time* to condition everyone as if they were Tier 1."

"But if you had more training—"

"No, Tal. We don't have enough people to do said training! And, that would cause so much conflict. Everyone would be competing with each other. That is exactly what we are attempting to avoid. When we all work together, we see success. Not when we are trying to be better than our friends. And yes, to your point, I fully agree that a small percentage of individuals from any tier would be able to rise above their station, but it would be a very small group," I finish, and we sit in silence for a few slow minutes.

"I want to be the best," he says softly.

"That's a noble goal, but my follow-up question would be, why?"

"Because..." he trails off, not quite willing or able to answer.

"If it's because you want everyone to be impressed by you, I promise you won't be satisfied even if you do achieve your goal. If it's because you need to prove your value or your worth, again, you will be disappointed. If it's because you want to be the best you can be to serve others and contribute, you will find happiness regardless of whether you end up being the *best* at anything. You need to find your 'why', Tal."

He nods.

"In the meantime, I don't expect you to bore yourself to death at conditioning, but I do expect you to fulfill your commitments and serve. Maybe I can—I don't know," I sigh, running my hands through my hair. "Maybe I can take over a couple of your conditioning subjects here at home. I will set up an appointment with your team to discuss options."

His face lights up.

"Whatever is decided, I expect you to abide by it. No more skipping out," I hedge sternly, and he nods.

"Thanks, Dad. I'm sorry I—"

"It's ok, Tal. I love you. *I'm* sorry this has been difficult." He stands, patting my shoulder, and runs to change his clothes. I breathe a sigh of relief. I think that actually went okay. If I can't find a compromise with his conditioning instructors...Well, I'll worry about that when I need to. For now, I will simply send the message.

"Dad, want to go throw the disc around?" Tal calls from down the hall.

My muscles and joints are sore from planting all morning. A deep ache emanates from my lower back and my fingers are tight, swollen from the constant friction against my gloves.

"Sure, Tal, just let me put on a t-shirt."

"You realize that when I said I would arrange childcare for the girls, I meant I would utilize the outdoor nursery on campus, right?" I say teasingly.

"I know, I just didn't want the girls to have to take a bottle from someone new without even introducing them to the space," Shari argues. "This will be an easier transition, I think," she explains, making excited faces at the girls.

"Kids are resilient," I say, "but I admit, having you here makes today a lot less stressful. I'm tired and it's nice to have less to think about."

"You're welcome," she says dramatically. Then, to the girls in a sing-song voice, she adds, "Dreaming doesn't make for the most restful sleep, does it?" Leah smiles and kicks in response.

"What do you mean?" I ask Shari hesitantly.

"About what?" she says flippantly, still playing with Leah.

"About dreaming. What do you mean?"

Standing up, she turns around, looking confused. "Oh, I don't know, I just assumed you were still having dreams interrupt your sleep. You said you were tired—"

"Why wouldn't you assume it was because I have twin six-month-olds?" I ask accusingly.

"I—"

"The only person I've told about having dreams since the girls were born is Nick. Did he talk to you about my dreams?" I ask, irrational fear and anger bubbling up in my chest. I don't want anyone to know that I have dreamed about Eric. I trusted Nick. If he went directly to Shari—

"Nick only mentioned that you were still having them, I don't know anything beyond that. I'm so sorry, I didn't mean anything by it," she says soothingly, rolling her eyes at my apparent over-reaction.

"When would you have even seen Nick to even discuss this? Did he say it randomly in passing?" I ask, tempering my voice as I become aware that my reaction is, in fact, blown out of proportion.

"Kate, you are going to be late. Ask Nick about it later—or we can talk about it when you get back." She's right, I need to get going. But the sick suspicion of betrayal makes it difficult to focus.

"Okay, bottles are in the fridge. I'll be back around three."

"Perfect. I will take the girls to the nursery for about an hour after I feed them post-nap."

I swallow my frustration and thank her, then stomp to the car.

When I walk into the facility, I don't see anyone that I recognize. I am on a different shift now, but I thought there would at least be a couple of familiar faces. I have been assigned a rotating cubicle instead of a permanent desk, which makes sense. It's slightly inconvenient to set up my credentials each time on this display, and I don't love the chair, but it will do. After logging in, I quickly navigate to the batch for today. Though I envisioned participating in physical sessions again, I decided I didn't feel up to meeting in-person with patients during this initial transitional period. It's difficult to get into a groove with only a few hours a week, and besides that, I don't know exactly how jumping back in is going to affect me and my other responsibilities. Sorting and analyzing patient data seemed like a better use of everyone's time and resources.

Opening the files, I start from the top of the Tier 2 potential candidates. Female, twelve years old, impressive scans, looks like she has done some reversal therapy due to lack of parental involvement. She has been in a stable home for the last four years and has no behavioral or mental health issues. I run her numbers and it looks like she qualifies. Since she is so young, we will need to bring her in for an assessment before putting her through to initial testing. I make a note on her file and then sort her into the youth potentials. Within the hour, I find three more youth meeting the cut-off. This is insane. I have never seen so many qualifiers in one batch.

As I progress through the list, it suddenly clicks that this list is organized by age. Once I passed the eighteen year olds an hour ago, there haven't been any other obviously viable options. Though

I don't expect to find more at this point, I am inspired by the Tier 2 youth and am excited to meet with a few of these candidates in the coming months. Maybe it truly will be possible to move away from a tier system eventually. If we become successful enough at healing and transitioning...it isn't out of the realm of possibility.

As the scrolling and typing becomes habitual, my brain begins to wander. Being removed from my earlier conversation with Shari, I no longer feel angry, but I am still confused. Why and when would Nick have talked with her? And, why did that knowledge set me off? Shouldn't I be sharing these things with Shari anyway? If I'm honest with myself, I haven't felt as close with her since I paired with Nick, but that's probably to be expected. We have been working on our own relationship and he has been so support-ive. I guess I haven't felt like I have been lacking. Maybe this is my fault? He was probably trying to keep her in the loop and I went off like a crazy person. I resign myself to an embarrassing apology upon arriving home. Glancing at the display, I am shocked to see that my time is already up. After finishing up the current record, I collect my things and head out.

As I walk, I realize my sensor is still set on 'do not disturb'. Changing the setting, two new messages immediately pop up. One is from Shari.

'The girls love it here. I just tried to remove Beth from a swing and she literally held onto it with a death grip. Are you okay with me leaving them here for you to pick up at the end of your shift? I will assume yes (considering you were planning to do that initially) unless I hear otherwise. Plus...I don't think I could take Beth home if I tried.'

Grateful that I checked, I change my trajectory to head to the nursery, smiling as I imagine stubborn Beth in the swing. She isn't as outspoken as Leah, but when she makes up her mind about something, it is incredibly difficult to sway her.

After a short jaunt, I find myself passing through the greenery to the nature playground. Even from this distance, I can see that Beth is still in the swing. Getting closer, I find Leah sitting in the grass with dirt around her mouth, actively engaged in pulling apart a leaf. They are both filthy, but look absolutely thrilled about it. I call their names and their heads whip around excitedly. Even this simple connection makes my milk start to let down, and I groan. I don't think I remembered to put in cotton pads.

Scooping them up, I latch them on whether they are hungry or not. Luckily, they both seem more than happy to help me out. The nursery leader laughs.

"I've been there before," she says. "Is this your first time leaving them?"

"Not my first time ever, but definitely the longest. I expressed before I left, but I should have taken my portable pump with me."

"Live and learn," she says grinning. "The girls were a pleasure to have. I hope you'll bring them back again soon. You know you can drop them off regardless of your assignment? We are here to assist new moms whenever they need a break,"

"I know. I think I was just nervous about how they would take to being on their own. Apparently I shouldn't have been."

"There's something about nature," she says. "It draws in even the most reluctant child."

"I can see that. Thank you so much," I say sincerely. Looking around, I notice other children crawling through hollow logs, pulling on tree branches and watching them snap back into place, picking up bugs, chewing on sticks. Not one of them is upset or crying. They look completely enthralled. I will definitely be bringing the girls back more often.

After I give them some mashed vegetables for dinner and scrub them clean in the bath, the girls fall into an exhausted slumber. No begging to be held, no stealing each other's blankets. Just silence and heavy breathing. I should probably take them to the nursery every day.

The sound of the door opening announces Nick's arrival home, and I am reminded of my need to call Shari. I gently close the door to the girls' room and walk into the hall. He unexpectedly comes up behind me, spinning me around and embracing me tightly.

"I am so sorry I didn't tell you," he says. I wrap my arms around his back, concerned.

"About what?" I ask, my voice muffled by his shirt.

"That I was meeting with Shari and the Director each month," he says, pulling back to look at me. Tears shimmer in the corner of his eyes.

"What do you mean?" I ask, thoroughly confused.

"Shari told me that you were incredibly upset that I had mentioned your dreams to her. I should have told you about our meetings months ago, I just didn't want you to worry about it. Our first one was before the girls were born and I knew how over-whelmed you were—"

"Wait," I say, stepping back and attempting to remain calm, "let's get dinner and then you can tell me everything." I lead him into the kitchen and carefully remove the lid from the simmering pot. "I only had time to make risotto tonight. Sorry it's not very exciting."

He laughs. "I am starving and that smells amazing."

Our vegetable share this week included mushrooms and spinach. I don't have any cheese to add, but butter will hopefully suffice. I watch him inhale gratefully as I spoon it into his bowl. While it cools, I pull out some sliced turnips for us to snack on.

"Okay, start at the beginning," I say, crunching into one and leaning on the counter.

He looks unsure of himself. "You remember our initial pairing was suggested because of our TSG numbers?" he asks.

"Wow, that's way at the beginning," I quip, and he laughs.

"Yes, sorry," he says, relief evident on his face. "After we paired, I didn't really hear much from anyone. I initially wondered if we needed to report back, but when we got pregnant right away and we were doing well, I assumed they weren't really worried about us. The Director reached out to me about a month before the girls were born and wanted to meet. Shari and another woman, Grace, were both there. I've been meeting with them every month or so since then. They ask about how we are both coping, but they are also very interested in my research. We talk about both."

I process this. It makes sense that they would want to know about our progress. We knew that there may be more monitoring upon entering into this pairing, and I assume it's the same for other pairs in the program. I honestly hadn't really thought about it. And I do wish that Nick had mentioned it earlier.

"How did this never come up?" I ask. "When do you even have time to meet with them?"

"It's usually during training," he says.

"So when I ask you about how training went, it never occurred to you to say something?" I say less gently, my feelings hurt.

"I guess, since I hadn't told you initially, I felt like it would be hurtful for you to find out later, which it obviously is. And, I don't know why I thought it wouldn't come up eventually. I didn't make the right call, and I am so sorry."

I don't say anything, his eyes pleading with me to accept his apology. This resonates with me deeply and I have a moment of realization. Do I make him feel the same way I felt on our walk the other day? Is he as unsure as I am in moments like this?

"Kate, what can I do?" he asks in desperation.

"Did you tell them the content of my dream?" I ask.

"Why would I?" he says, looking down. I sigh silently in relief, realizing I have probably hurt him by asking.

"Nick, I wish you would have told me. It really isn't a big deal. It's frustrating that none of you thought to include me. I realize that I have been going through a lot, but it can be helpful to feel needed and useful. I would love to come to the next one, if that's okay?"

He nods gratefully. "I think that's a great idea. You may not be able to stay for the classified research portion, but I will definitely bring it up."

"Thanks," I say. The food has cooled and we eat in silence for a few moments. The butter definitely sufficed, bringing out the earthiness of the mushrooms.

"I'm really sorry, Kate," Nick says between bites. I reach across the table and squeeze his hand.

GUILT. I feel incredible guilt. I wasn't completely honest with Kate this week and it's eating at me. Never mind the fact that I am literally living with her every day because of false information that she's been given. Though that wasn't my choice, I feel like an accessory, and it's more difficult to live with than I initially anticipated. Every time I see grief pass across her face, I remember that I was a part of causing that.

I sit on one of three chairs in a hallway of the Tier 1 administration building. This being an off-time, the typical buzz of a normal workday is absent. My nail cuticles are unruly and I busy myself, gently pushing them back, as I wait.

Back to Kate. There was never anything I could do about it. I was crushed when she chose not to go through with our initial pairing, but realized almost immediately that it had nothing to do with me. She was in an impossible situation. Well, impossible for her. She wasn't prepared to make the sacrifices necessary, so Berg removed that responsibility from her. Knowing that piece allowed me to move forward after her reversal. She cared for me before and could do so again. I also knew that she cared deeply, even then, about making an impact. She is making it now, whether she fully understands her sacrifices or not. If I had refused, she would have lost Eric anyway, and for what? I needed to be here to justify that action. Right?

This last thought falls a little flat and nausea flutters through my stomach. The truth gnaws at me, and I can't escape the fact that I am rationalizing. I could have done more. I could have at least tried to find another solution, or advocated for her family to be kept together. I was the only one with a say that would have mattered, but I was too hurt and upset to consider it, and then? Then it was too late. But was it really? Is it now? If I said something today, couldn't we reinstate those memories and repair everything?

I know, even as I think it, that this would be impossible. Doable? Potentially, but it would never be approved. And...impossible in other ways. For me, this time.

"She lost her oldest child," I hear in my head, my own consciousness playing devil's advocate. "And don't you think that Eric felt what you are feeling? Is it easy for him to live without her?" I shove those last thoughts away, my sensibilities warring with each other. The soft sound of footsteps pulls me out of my internal debate, and I sit nervously at attention.

"Nick, sorry to make you wait," the Director apologizes as he draws closer.

"No, thank you for meeting with me last-minute," I say, relaxing slightly. "I really appreciate it." He motions for me to follow him and we each take a seat, this time in his office, which feels slightly more inviting than our typical concrete meeting room. The Director is dressed casually and it feels out of context, almost humanizing him.

"What can I help you with?" he asks.

"I wanted to discuss a few things with you in person," I begin, unsure of how this will land. "Kate is aware that we have been meeting and she wants in." The Director nods pensively. "I told her that we have been meeting to discuss the TSG program and my research. She didn't understand why she hadn't been invited and, hearing her perspective, I think she has a legitimate point."

"I agree. I think it would be helpful for her to feel valued and appreciated."

"She also, in response to the dreams she has been having, feels like it would be helpful for her to explore new service assignments," I add.

"Do you believe, based on your research with reversal, that this will help?"

"No. Not permanently, I don't, but it could buy some time. Act as a distraction."

"Sure, I think that sounds reasonable. What is she interested in?"

"Specifically, she wants to walk in her mother's shoes, so to speak. She would really like to serve with Tier 3." The Director is very still. He doesn't respond for a full minute. I am about to repeat my statement when he finally opens his mouth to speak.

"That won't be an option, unfortunately," he replies calmly.

"May I ask why? If it's a concern for her safety, I think it could be in a small setting and I would be happy to accompany."

"It's not that, we simply don't have any service assignments available. I can check to be sure, but I'm fairly certain."

"Surely in a situation like this—"

"They are extremely sensitive assignments, Nick," he cuts me off. "Don't presume to understand what you are talking about."

I clench my teeth. "You're right, I apologize. I only want to support her in whatever way I can."

The Director moves around his desk and places his hand on my shoulder as I stand. "You are doing wonderfully. I will look through some potential options and we can discuss with Kate when we meet in a couple of weeks. Will that be satisfactory?"

I nod. "Thank you," I say, shaking his hand and leaving the room.

"Nick!" he calls after me and I stop, turning back toward his office. He walks my direction. "I forgot to tell you that I have a new set of scans for you to analyze. They all have the symptoms you described, but the less discussion you have with them the better. Until you have solid results, I want to avoid starting any unnecessary rumors."

I nod.

"I have categorized them by Tier," he continues, "though I'm sure you would be able to deduce that on your own."

"It saves time."

"Keep me posted on how it goes," he requests, smiling warmly.

"That wasn't terrible," I think, beginning the walk back to the house, though it definitely didn't go the direction I anticipated. The results were exactly opposite. I assumed that the service assignment request would be a non-issue, but—something still isn't sitting right with me about how he responded to that. It wasn't what he said, per se. That all seemed reasonable, but his mannerisms changed slightly. He isn't an overly expressive person to begin with and I can't put my finger on it. Just a gut feeling that something changed in that moment. Reminiscent of the feeling I had the other day during our report. What is he holding back? This time, was it talking about Kate's mother that triggered it? Mentioning Tier 3? I can't remember exactly when the energy shifted. My brain chews on this for the entirety of my journey home, annoyingly not arriving at any concrete conclusions.

I walk in the front door to find Kate rocking Beth. She meets my eyes and puts a silent finger to her lips. I stop moving immediately and leave the door slightly open to avoid making more noise. She sways toward the bedroom, walking slowly through the door, and re-emerging a minute or so later, gently closing the door and waiting silently. I barely breathe. When she hears nothing, she turns toward me and silently celebrates.

With a goofy grin plastered to my face, I close the door and turn to find her already next to me. I kiss her deeply and she reciprocates. All of the thoughts and insecurities I have had over the past few hours bubble to the surface, and I am desperate to make everything up to her. To prove to myself that everything is as it should be. The brief moment yesterday where I thought I had lost even a little of her esteem was enough to bring me to my knees. I need her, and the depth of that need scares me.

11 / ERIC

MATT and I are seated on a bench at the park across the street from our house. Tal is old enough to be on his own at home when I am close by, and I needed to talk with Matt outside of Tal's eavesdropping zone.

Matt has been mentoring me my whole life. When I was a kid, we used to hang out regularly. He would help me with my completely unrealistic projects, memorizing facts about genetics, and even put up with my obsessive bird-watching. As we got older, those earlier interactions set the stage for us to become close friends and, besides Kate, he is the only one with whom I feel truly comfortable confiding.

We haven't talked much lately, mostly because I don't have anything new to report. He's sick of hearing about me missing Kate, so I spare him that. Today, though, I need someone. Someone who will listen and not judge.

"Fill me in," Matt says.

"I don't know where to start."

"I'll help you. 'So, I was thinking about Kate...'" he motions for me to continue, and I can't help but laugh.

"Has it been that bad?" I ask, slightly embarrassed.

"No," he chuckles. "Not quite that bad."

"Well, this time let's start differently," I say, updating him on my work assignment and the ideas I have to make our plantings more effective and efficient.

"Sounds like that is going really well for you," he comments, and there is genuine happiness for me reflected in his face. It gives me strength to move on.

"It is. And there's a woman—" I start.

"That's what I'm talking about," Matt teases, nudging me.

"No, it's not like that. I think she wants it to be, but I seriously can't even talk to her without having a negative, visceral response. I have most definitely hurt her feelings already. And Tal is really struggling."

"How so? Are those two things related?" Matt looks concerned.

"No, he doesn't know about her. I guess I listed them together because they are the two most significant stressors for me right now. Tal is just questioning everything, which I know is normal, but I have no obvious course of action. As you know, he's extremely smart and capable. He's bored to death in his condition-ing, so I set an appointment to discuss options with his team, but I'm not holding my breath. The last time we talked, they assured me they could provide options, and obviously it hasn't happened. I'm hoping they will allow me to take over some of his conditioning personally."

"That's a good option. Is there any precedence for that?" Matt asks.

"I honestly have no idea. I did also talk with Tal, trying to drive home the fact that conditioning isn't just a personal thing. It's a collaborative effort. He needs to become comfortable with leadership, but right now, he doesn't see how that would be helpful. He actually even said that he felt like the Tier system is outdated," I say, incredulous.

"Huh. He really is questioning everything."

"Yep," I agree, using my feet to sweep pieces of mulch back into the planting beds. "I have no idea how to deal with it. I haven't ever questioned like that, but he's beginning to make me think."

"What about?" Matt asks.

"Well, could he have a point? Could there be a better system? Nobody has even approached me about trying to qualify Tal for Tier 1 initial testing. His scores are through the roof. His instructors have told me that his behavior and attitude stems from losing his mom at such a young age, but I am starting to disagree. He doesn't act out at home, only when he isn't utilizing his potential in conditioning. Shouldn't that tell us something? I don't feel like he has an advocate. Well, besides me, but I'm obviously doing a terrible job."

Matt is silent for a moment. "Maybe I could put in a word," he says. "And Eric, you might not remember questioning as a kid, but I remember you going through a very similar stage. Not as intense, definitely, but it's not like you always accepted things blindly."

I nod. That's good to know. It makes me feel slightly better about myself, knowing that I wasn't always completely spineless.

"Is this it?" I ask softly. "Is this the whole purpose of my life? Help my son and help people eat?" I say bleakly, and even I hear the futility in my tone. Staring at the grass, I let that settle in for a moment.

"Eric. Tell me about this woman," Matt requests, snapping me back.

"Why? There isn't anything to tell."

"Just tell me about her."

"Okay. Her name is Val, she works with the Committee—she's over food production—so I run into her at the storage facility sometimes. She has been—*is* interested in getting to know me better, I guess."

"You guess?"

"She asked to run our numbers awhile ago. I told her I wasn't at a point where I could even consider pairing."

"Eric, it's been nine years," Matt says, attempting to meet my eyes, but I look away.

"It still feels like it was only yesterday that I lost her," I admit, almost to myself.

"You talk about being frustrated with life and I would postulate that it's because you aren't really living one. You go through the motions, you excel in everything you do, which is maddening because you aren't even trying. You have so much more to give. Have you considered therapy?"

"You mean reversal?" I ask, jerking back.

"That, or just talking with someone regularly," he continues calmly.

"That's why I have you, right?"

"I'm not a therapist, Eric. I love talking with you, but I don't know how to help. I just know that I care about you. I want you to live fully and for Tal to have a mother—"

"He has a mother," I mutter, interrupting him.

"Does he? He didn't even know her! He has no models for relationships, no opportunity to understand women—" he stops, taking a breath, and lowering his voice. "You talk about Tier 1 initial testing, but he will never qualify as it currently stands. Yes, he is smart, but he isn't in a position to be successful and you know it."

I sigh. I do.

"I'm not saying you should pair with this Val, but I think you need to get yourself into a position where you could have a relationship —even just a physical connection."

Anxiety is already building in my chest. Gripping the bench, I count internally. It doesn't dissipate, but it doesn't intensify either, so I sit quietly until I can manage.

"How would I go about starting therapy?" I ask, having a difficult time getting the words out.

"That I can help with," Matt says, clapping his arm around my shoulder. Despite my best efforts, the physical contact loosens something within me, and I begin to sob.

"Hey, Nick, Mom, can you help me with my assignment?" Bentley asks. The girls are down for the night and we are relaxing in the backyard, enjoying the evening. It's been raining all week and the air feels cool, despite the sunshine. Our trees and shrubs are lush and vibrant, as if showing their gratitude for all of the moisture.

"Sure, Bent," I say, gathering the blanket around my shoulders. "Want to bring it here by me?"

"Could you come over here?"

"I could, but I'm kind of comfortable on this chair. And there's room for two," I suggest, hoping he will take the bait. He picks up his tablet and cuddles in beside me. It is immediately noticeable how big he has gotten. There was a lot more room in this chair for the both of us a year ago.

"What's up?" I ask as Nick drops into the seat next to us.

"I am supposed to ask you guys about what it was like when you were kids," he explains. I stiffen involuntarily, and Nick jumps in, recognizing the situation.

"Can I start?" he asks.

"Sure," Bentley agrees.

"Is there a specific category or topic you are interested in? Or should I just start talking?"

"Just start talking."

"Okay, hmmm. Well, it wasn't all that different for me then, but I didn't necessarily have a traditional life. I was like you, Bent. I accelerated through a lot of my conditioning and that took up a lot of my time. I do remember, though, that the cars weren't as available when I was young. Kate, do you remember we used to have to share one car with the entire neighborhood?"

I laugh. "I remember not even having access to a car, so count yourself lucky!"

"That's true, I guess I shouldn't complain."

"Did you work with Tier 3? Were they the same?" Bentley asks.

"I really didn't," Nick says. "I actually told your mom that I had never seen a Tier 3 individual before and she thought I was crazy."

I look at him puzzled. "I don't remember that," I say.

The strangest expression flickers across his face, and when he laughs, it feels somewhat forced.

"How do you not remember that?" he asks. "Maybe it only made an impact on me because I felt so lacking compared to you, with your vast experience," he says and I grin, but worry laces my thoughts.

This has happened a few times lately, where Nick recalls a conversation that I don't. Am I losing mental acuity? Or maybe his memory is simply better than mine? He has heard my complaints about aging, as well as my frustration with my lack of memories from my childhood, too many times to count. At times like these, I would love to have experiences that I could share with my kids. I do, of course, remember some things. Just not as much as I would like. Am I losing more recent memories now, too?

"You have experience with Tier 3, right Mom?" Bentley asks, pulling me back into the conversation.

"It's been a long time, but yes. My mom—your grandma—used to serve there and I loved listening to her stories. I don't know if that really counts as experience—"

"What was it like?" Bentley interrupts.

"They were suffering then, I remember that. I know it's a lot better now. At the time, they didn't get nearly the variety or quantity of food that we did, and very few of them qualified for work assignments. My mom loved them, but there was always an underlying current of caution present when she was planning to make a visit. I assume that was because there was more crime and violence in Tier 3. People there didn't have the skills needed to avoid those behaviors completely. It sounds awful, but I remember being intrigued and slightly put off by their outward appearance. They had different teeth and markings on their body. Some of them weren't very clean," I say, trying to explain in terms that won't be disturbing.

"What about Tier 2?" he asks.

"I can add something there," Nick says. "I started working with Tier 2 years ago and have been really impressed with them. Kind, simple people who just want to live their lives. Some struggle, but an overwhelming majority are working hard to improve society, just like we are."

"Do they look different, too?" Bent asks.

"Not really," I say. "You can tell they aren't Tier 1, though. They just don't look quite as healthy." I don't know how else to describe it. "In conditioning, have they told you anything about Tier 2 and Tier 3 in their current forms? Is it different than how we are describing it?"

"No, it sounds the same. And that confirms my suspicions," he says, snapping his book closed and hopping down from the chair.

"What suspicions?" I ask, amused.

"That Tier 3 doesn't exist," Bentley says nonchalantly.

"What?" I ask, completely taken off guard. I look at Nick and he seems equally baffled. "Why would you say that, Bentley?"

"Think about it, Mom. The Committee has been talking about the decrease in Tier 3 births for years. Lifespan there is half of ours. I played with some numbers while they were talking about it in conditioning today and even with the most *generous* estimates, there should only be a few hundred people left."

Nick laughs heartily. "Bent, that is awesome. I am so impressed that you spent the time to try to figure this out. I think you may have forgotten about a few things, though."

"What?" Bentley asks, not amused.

"You can't just take into account Tier 3 birthrates, you also have to calculate the Tier 2 births that result in Tier 3 individuals. It's surprisingly high. And there are some people that end up in Tier 3 as teens or adults based on life experience or a failure to improve with therapy," he explains.

Bentley's eyes narrow. "But don't you think, even taking those numbers into account, that something would have changed over the years? With more opportunities to work and condition, more food and resources? How is it *exactly* the same?"

It's a good question. "I doubt it is exactly the same," I say. "Maybe your instructors are giving you the quick version. Glossed over. Most of them probably haven't been there personally, and I'm sure they didn't anticipate someone so young taking such an interest," I suggest.

This seems to connect with him. "Do you have recent numbers?" he asks Nick.

"I don't, but I'll see if I can pull up some reports when I am at the lab," he says. Seemingly mollified, he walks toward the house.

"Was all of that really for a conditioning assignment?" I call after him.

"No," he says simply, opening the door.

When it shuts, Nick and I burst into laughter.

13 / NICK

I LAUGH with Kate until I am breathless. Watching Bent so serious about his research somehow released the tension I have felt about my own trials. I hope he didn't see us laugh. His intensity is inspiring and I would never want to embarrass him.

Kate goes back inside shortly after him, cleaning up dinner and getting him tucked into bed. I pull some weeds in the flower garden and sweep the debris off of the walkway from all the precipitation. The ground is spongy and my feet sink slightly every time I leave the paving stones. As the sun begins to set, the entire backyard seems to glow with intensity. The greens somehow more green than they were before. Of course, I understand the physics of the transformation, but it's still beautiful to witness. I find myself waiting until the colors begin to fade.

Inside, I find Kate typing into her display. Probably prepping for her assignment tomorrow. Not only is she back serving, but we also have our community volunteer assignment to complete.

Tomorrow will be a busy day for all of us. I give her hip a pat as I walk by and see her smile in response. My heart leaps.

"I think I'm going to head to bed early," I say. "I can wake up before I go to the lab and at least get the mowing done at the park. Then we will only need to work in the garden tomorrow evening."

"Sounds great. That's the kids' favorite part anyway," she says. "Goodnight."

I wake to my sensor at around 5:30am, the early morning light barely creeping in the windows. Putting on my work clothes, I sneak out of the house and walk down the street. My sensor activates the keypad on the storage shed, and I pull out the electric mower. It's been charging all night, thankfully. Forgot to check that.

Virtually noiseless, the mower expertly cuts through the grass, taking very little effort on my part. I take pleasure in watching the clean pattern emerge as I make my way around the field.

An hour later, I am covered in grass from the knees down, and the park looks fresh and pristine. Wiping down the machine, I secure it back in its dock and head home. The birds are out this morning, enjoying the sunshine as much as I am. Their songs bring a smile to my lips, and I practically bounce into the house. Carefully, I remove my pants and place them in the sink by the washing machine. I will need to treat those later. Kate is in the shower, and not hearing any children yet, I quickly hop in with her. She jumps in surprise.

"You scared me!" she accuses, slapping my chest with a soapy hand.

"I can see that," I say.

"The girls are going to be up any minute, I have to hurry," she rushes.

"Let me get your back, then," I offer. She hands me the soap, and I massage her shoulders and neck.

"Thank you," she says, turning so the water rinses off the suds. "As much as I would love to stay—"

"I know, it's okay," I assure her. "See you in a minute."

She hops out and I quickly wash myself. The cool water is perfection.

Patients greet me upon entering the lab. Tier 1 individuals are prompt, directly contrasting with my experience last week in Tier 2. I quickly prep the machine and turn on my display, then instruct my assistant, Tamara, to begin patient briefing. The whole trial is fairly simple. My goal is to find a way to minimize these echoes so we can use reversal therapy without the negative after effects. I sigh. It seems to be a simple objective, but finding those echoes is proving difficult. I haven't made much progress in the last few weeks. Initially I tried stimulating different parts of the brain while administering the therapy. While I haven't received any official dream reports, the headaches were reported almost immediately for these repeat patients. Typically, patients experience them within the first week after treatment. We always assure them that it is a natural symptom that should dissipate with time. Most people don't experience them chronically, though in extreme cases —like Kate—it can become debilitating. She is doing incredibly well, considering.

Back to the drawing board, but this time around, I am going with my gut. It occurred to me that we don't know enough about the brain to determine where precisely these subconscious echoes are hiding, but they *must* be present in the dream state, since this is when they manifest to the patient. If I can simulate a dream-state and *then* do reversal, I have a hunch that I might be able to eliminate the echoes. Or at least significantly reduce them. Of course, there is a good chance that I could be completely wrong. And, the difficult part is simulating the dream state in the first place.

From the first batch sent from the Director, I have narrowed the subjects down to those who have specifically reported headaches and dreams, and are also looking to have reversal therapy again. This way, I can provide them with their desired treatment while also testing my hypothesis, instead of trying to correct prior damage. If it works, then I can attempt to deal with that mess.

While the patient list is available to my staff, I do have to keep the rubric private. Not only because it would affect the study, but because the general public is unaware that reversal therapy—in large doses—can have side effects. The general public is actually unaware that we use it to inflict such sweeping change in the first place. It's better that way, but makes confidentiality doubly important.

These patients, as far as I can tell, haven't recognized that their current symptoms are still connected with their reversal treatments. The headaches and dreams are so few and far between that it isn't causing them significant stress. The Committee wants to keep it that way.

This group of patients today was required to attend one evening of sleep monitoring before showing up today. I check, and sure enough, I have REM sleep scans of each patient on the docket. Bless Tier 1 individuals and their compliance. Tamara will be placing a tap and monitoring patients while I anesthetize them and create a similar brain pattern, inducing their personal dream-state. Tamara is well trained, but this is new to me and the possibility that we could cause harm weighs heavily on me. My hands shake slightly as I realize what we are about to do.

Before I can work myself up further, Tamara enters with our first patient. The tap is placed beautifully.

"Good morning, Sarah," I say, attempting to appear at ease. If I am nervous, I am sure Sarah is, too. I remind myself that this has been approved, then utilize my own emotions to empathize with her.

"Hi," she responds, clutching the sleeves of her shirt.

"Today should be completely relaxing. I know you have had reversal before. This time, we will actually be stimulating the brain in a different way, so you won't be able to remain awake during the procedure. Did Tamara explain all of that?"

"Yes," she nods.

Tamara smiles and helps her get strapped in while I connect her port. Once she is comfortable, I twist the nozzle and begin the drip. She closes her eyes and is out within seconds. I initiate the scanner and adjust the drip, adding the orexin blocker. As opposed to traditional reversal, this will transition the patient to REM sleep and I should be able to adjust the dose until I see a brain map that matches with her initial scan.

Within minutes, Sarah's brain is lighting up. I adjust the amount slightly until I am satisfied with the image. Keeping the blocker constant, I place the reversal electrodes and begin the therapy. Sarah would like to remove an upsetting event that occurred with her father a few months ago. I don't love knowing the details, so I simply follow the brain map I've been given. Carefully, I treat each synaptic cluster, moving methodically through the targets. Barely getting into a rhythm, I finish the last section. Quick and easy. Stopping the drip, I wait.

As the patient begins to wake, Tamara soothes her and helps her move to a rolling, reclining chair. She will need to remain here for at least an hour before she can be cleared to go home. We have a recovery room assigned and a nurse should be arriving to help with transport, giving me ten minutes to prep for the next patient.

Dabbing rubbing alcohol on a cotton pad, I wipe the equipment down, prepping new ports and disposing of the old ones. Surprisingly, nobody has opened the door yet, so I figure I will try to find the Tier 3 numbers I promised Bentley. Typing my login into the main database, I search. Immediately, I am met with a plethora of charts. I scroll through each one, looking for recent data. After a few minutes, I am flummoxed. Each chart is listed as being from a distinct year, but the numbers, as Bentley noticed, look almost identical. Even the Tier 2 numbers don't change much when compared over a ten year period. I am well aware that random variations are out of our control, but with programs that have been instituted to decrease unauthorized Tier 2 pregnancies, those numbers absolutely should be going down. Am I somehow missing a variable that needs to be accounted for?

My next patient is escorted in, interrupting my thoughts. We begin the process over again, inducing the dream state. Though I am more comfortable, this one takes slightly longer—her reversal request stems from a childhood event, so I have to be much more investigative with my localization. To stay on-time, I help prep the next patient and Tamara and I work side-by-side for much of the day, not giving any extra time to continue my Tier 3 research.

Eventually, we finish with our last patient. I am exhausted, and I know Tamara must feel the same way. Thanking her, I encourage her to head home, offering to take care of the cleaning myself.

Halfway through sanitizing my last piece of equipment, the door opens and a woman I don't recognize pokes her head in.

"Can I help you?" I ask.

"Oh, no. I was just looking for Tamara," she says, exiting hastily. I drop my cloth and move quickly to the door, swinging it open.

"Tamara actually left for the day," I call after her. She stops, turning back toward me, looking anxious. "Is everything okay?" I ask.

"Well...I don't want to bother you," she shakes her head, waving me off.

"I insist," I say. "No bother, how can I help."

"We used more of the orexin blocker than we anticipated today. I submitted the request for more, but it won't be delivered in time for our trials tomorrow. I was hoping Tamara would be available to go to the medical facility to retrieve the bottles, but...it's ok, I can do it," she concludes, turning to go.

"I would be happy to get them if it would help," I offer and she turns, surprised.

"You've been here all day—are you sure?" she asks doubtfully.

"It's no problem. I assume it's the one down south? If so, I can take a short nap on the way."

"That would be fantastic," she says gratefully. "I was really hoping to be home for dinner tonight. I will forward you the order information. Thanks again."

"Happy to help," I assure her, smiling. Having been home so frequently lately, I know Kate won't mind if I am late. I quickly send her a message before returning to finish the sanitization. My sensor notifies me of the order and address right as I am returning the cleaning supplies to their cabinet. Luckily, I have a car today.

After a brief nap, I stretch, feeling much more normal, and pull a snack bar out of my bag. This should hold me until I get home for dinner. Kate mentioned that she is making chicken and roasted vegetables tonight. I sit up straight, realization dawning on me. Tonight. It's the night of our gardening assignment. I check my sensor—nothing from her yet. I sigh, feeling deflated. This was definitely not the best night to be late. Nothing I can do about it now.

I check the navigation and it shows another ten minutes to go. Making it home before bedtime will not be a realistic option. Something on the map catches my eye, and I glance back.

'Tier 3 distribution center' is marked, sitting just west of my destination. I inhale deeply, resting my back against the seat. If I'm late anyway, would an extra twenty minutes really hurt anything?

As soon as I buzz in at the medical facility, I find our package sitting there waiting for me, ready to go. This errand has humbled me slightly. I didn't realize how much the staff was doing behind the scenes to ensure the success of these trials. I know it's their service assignment, but somehow it feels personal, and I need to be better about showing appreciation for their efforts.

Returning to the car, my heart starts to race. Am I really going to do this? I don't break rules. Is this breaking a rule? Am I *not* supposed to randomly visit a distribution center? At night? I laugh. Pretty sure that would be way beyond protocol for someone—especially from Tier 1—to show up unannounced. I wrack my brain, trying to think of a logical reason I could stop in. They all seem flimsy, but it really doesn't matter. I know what I need to do, and I feel compelled to do it. I tap on the facility and set the destination.

The ride isn't long, only a small detour off of the main road. Since the sun hasn't set yet, this stop is thankfully less creepy than it could have been. The car pulls to a stop and I glance around, not noticing any signs of life. No cars, no bikes, nobody. This in and of itself isn't concerning...but the broken window is.

I slowly approach the dark building. The back door hangs open, twisted on its hinges. The hair on the back of my neck stands up and I breathe slowly, trying to calm my nerves. Turning my sensor flashlight on, I peer into the blackness.

There's nothing. It's completely bare, every surface covered with a thick layer of dirt. There are vines growing along the floor and draping along the walls. This building hasn't been used in some time. I hastily exit, turning off my light, and quickly get back into the car.

14 / NICK

It's dark when I get home—later than I anticipated—after dropping the meds back at the lab. Kate didn't ever message me back, so I don't know exactly what I'm walking into. Everything is quiet inside the house, and I am a little jumpy, my nerves still heightened from earlier. There are two place settings at the table and a ceramic dish on the stove. Not finding Kate, I walk to the bedroom to change my clothes, realizing I still need to treat my pants from this morning as I pass the sink. I add 'start a load of laundry' to my to-do list before opening the door.

Kate is sprawled on the bed, reading, and she smiles at me as I walk in.

"Hey," she says, reaching for me. Pulling my dirty shirt off, I go to her.

"I missed you tonight," she says softly.

"I am so sorry I scheduled over our garden appointment," I apologize. "I volunteered to help with something else before I remembered about our assignment."

"It's okay," she murmurs. "We had a great time. The girls loved everything about the garden. I am committed to giving them time outside every day. It's ridiculous how much they light up in nature." Her eyes dance with enthusiasm and I can't help but absorb some of it.

"That's great," I respond, grinning.

"Are you hungry?" she asks.

"Starving," I laugh.

"Well good, because I have a full meal waiting out there. The kids hardly ate anything."

"You didn't eat?"

"I snacked. I wanted to wait for you."

Though I am grateful, my smile fades slightly as I quickly change my clothes. My mind is still troubled, trying to process what I saw earlier. There's no way that Tier 3 is completely gone, right? But Bent's prediction niggles at me. No, it can't be. If that were true, why the service assignments? And why falsify that information? I have personally seen shipments of resources heading for Tier 3. I can't wrap my brain around it. I force myself to let it go—I can process and analyze later. There has to be a logical explanation, probably including information that I am not privy to at the moment. Right now, all I want is to enjoy a delicious dinner with Kate.

. . .

My sensor dings, waking me earlier than expected. Adrenaline courses through me as I read the message that appears on the display.

"Kate," I whisper, "Kate, get up."

She moves away from me, stubbornly ignoring my attempts to wake her.

"Kate, my dad is coming to visit," I say, slightly louder. This time, she rolls over, her eyes wide.

"What?" she asks, her eyebrows drawn together in confusion. Her hair is disheveled and, frankly, she looks adorable. I smile and reach out, wrapping my hand around her waist.

"I just got the message. I guess he was able to break away from his research project to stop in for a couple of days."

"That's quite unexpected," she asserts.

"Yes," I acknowledge. "And wonderful?"

She sighs. "Yes, and wonderful," she agrees, flopping back onto her pillow. "Sorry, I am now mentally adjusting our schedule over the next few days. It feels a bit overwhelming, but I'm sure that's my morning brain talking. I really am excited to see him."

"I know," I assure her, jumping out of bed. "He should be here this afternoon. Is it okay if I head into the lab early so that I can be here when he arrives?"

She nods, and that's all I need.

. . .

"Nick!" my dad says affectionately as he greets me on the step. "Thanks for having me on such short notice." We embrace, his broad shoulders dwarfing my own as his arms wrap around me.

"Glad you could come," I say. "How were you able to get time off? I know your project has been really demanding this last year." This is our own personal code. As a kid, I made the choice to keep him as my only mentor. There wasn't really a better option genetically, and we have always had a close relationship. I tell him everything, which means he knows the reason for my move to another territory. He was the one I called when Kate rejected me that morning at the Celebration. He has sacrificed more than I have to make this happen, now living territories away from his only grandchildren. Since it is impossible to justify extra travel to Kate—or explain the true reason for his distance—we settle for digital communication most of the time. The goal was to have him here with us eventually, after his research concluded next year and Kate and I had solidified our bonding. Now, I am regretting the decision to wait.

"Hey, Sam," Kate says, warmly embracing him.

Bentley runs out to greet his grandpa, hearing the commotion from his bedroom. The girls kick excitedly on the floor, aware that the energy in the house just shifted dramatically.

"Bent, my boy, look at you! You've grown at least a couple of inches since I saw you last," Dad says, lifting him up to get a better look. Bentley wriggles out of his arms, laughing.

Taking large strides into the living room, he drops down to the floor and begins playing games with Beth and Leah. They coo with delight.

"Sam, can I get you a drink?"

"I'm good, Kate, thanks. Maybe in a minute," he replies. I take a seat next to him on the floor and watch him interact with the girls, wondering if this was how he talked to me when I was their age. Kate joins us, settling comfortably on the couch.

"How have you been?" she asks. "Nick gives me updates, but I would love to hear it from you."

"I'm good. My health is declining, which is only expected at my age, but I'm grateful to still have time left," he replies, avoiding the details. Kate and I have discussed his diagnosis at length recently. Though it is a relatively slow growing cancer, our treatments still haven't been consistently effective in eradicating it in older patients. It isn't typically a cancer that we have access to in older patients—only because sarcomas and glioblastomas have typically already taken their toll by then. Sam is lucky to have evaded those at this age. But, since Berg hasn't had many patients to study, we don't necessarily know exactly what to expect.

We spend the rest of the afternoon allowing him to be with the kids, knowing that was his primary reason for making the trip. Our meeting with Shari, Grace, and the Director is tonight and, considering the circumstances, I don't feel comfortable canceling. They thought it would be a good idea to meet mid-month to allow Kate's involvement sooner rather than later. With the excitement of having a visitor, we both wait until the last minute to get ready.

She is nervous and excited. It's really quite cute. I find myself teasing her and force myself to stop, getting a warning look from my dad, and realizing that it's patronizing. Her input would be just as valid as mine in any normal situation. The problem is, I keep forgetting that *she* doesn't know we aren't normal. Another pang of guilt hits me. And then I remember what I need to do tonight, which floods my already convoluted system with cortisol, creating a veritable cesspool of stress hormones. Splashing water on my face takes a little of the nausea away, but I still don't feel like eating.

Since Shari obviously wasn't available to watch the kids, Kate had arranged for a neighbor to come over, but Sam's presence made that unnecessary. It was actually quite convenient that he arrived when he did.

I hesitate slightly to leave him with all three kids when he is no longer used to being around children at all, but push any doubts away. This is the man that raised me, and Bentley is a fantastic helper. Plus, the girls are fed and shouldn't cause much trouble, especially since we will only be gone for an hour or so.

"Nick, do you want any of this?" Kate calls from the kitchen.

"No, I will eat when we get home if that's alright," I answer.

"Sure, I'll pack it up for you."

As we prepare to walk out the door, there is a flurry of goodbyes, kisses, and instructions. Finally, we step outside and hop on our bikes. Doing something physical to release all of my energy is a relief.

"Are you okay?" Kate asks.

"Me?"

"Yes, you. You seem uptight," she laughs.

"I think I'm just tired. The trials require me to be constantly 'on', if that makes sense. And, while I love having my dad here, it still somehow requires more energy to have someone—anyone—in our home."

"Sorry you weren't able to relax after getting home today. I should have just had you stay on campus. Maybe you could have rested in a storage closet or something," she teases. "You could have visited with your dad after the meeting."

"They do have actual rooms for that, you know," I say, feigning offense.

She laughs. "That's better."

I smile, in spite of my nerves.

Kate and I settle in a few minutes early. Shari is the next to arrive.

"Hey, Kate," she says, embracing her. "Nick, you look a little tired," she comments.

"Charming, as always," I say, tipping my proverbial hat. The women laugh and start chatting. I quickly log in to see how many patients I have lined up tomorrow. It's our last day of initial trials. By Monday, we should know if we have any reason to hope for success. At that point, we can determine whether to continue with full trials next week. That's when I intend to bring Kate in.

The Director and Grace walk in together, putting an end to the friendly conversation.

"Thanks for coming," the Director says, greeting us warmly. "Kate, so glad you could join us. I apologize for not including you sooner. I hope you understand it was done out of consideration."

Kate nods. "Glad to be here, thanks."

"We will first ask a few questions about your pairing, and if you have any concerns, feel free to voice them. Then we will meet with Nick separately to discuss some classified information pertaining to his research," Grace explains. Kate nods again, expecting this.

"Kate, why don't you tell us how you feel about your pairing and your family in general?" Shari suggests. Kate reaches under the table and her fingers intertwine with mine.

"I love it. I had my reservations before accepting the pairing. I'm sure you remember—I don't need to rehash that part. I don't feel like my age has been a problem. Maybe Nick can speak to that," she looks at me, winking, "but I think we are equal partners."

"I agree," I say, smiling and squeezing her hand.

"The girls are doing well and the pregnancy was simple, considering. I think—well, we are considering getting pregnant again," she says hesitantly.

The Director is beaming. "So good to hear," he congratulates.

"I would love to know—how are the other pairings doing?" Kate asks.

Grace repeats the numbers she reported at our last meeting and Kate's eyes are bright.

"This program is making a huge impact," Grace concludes. "We are so glad you are a part of it."

Kate nods with a smile stretching from ear to ear.

"Kate, do you feel that there were any drawbacks to Berg initiating your pairing with Nick? Now that you have had some time to bond?" the Director asks. Kate seems to ponder this for a moment.

"No, I really don't. There wasn't as much initial suspense, which could be a positive or a negative, I guess, but for me, I think it was exactly what I needed."

Receiving a few blank stares, she elaborates. "I just mean that, as a kid, you hear about people finding pairings. They tell stories of their first meeting, or the first time they ran their numbers. So, I had kind of built that up in mind. Meeting this way took out any of that excitement and suspense, you know? We still had some, especially because we had the opportunity to accept or decline, but it was different than I had always seen it in my head. Again, not necessarily a negative, just...different."

"Thanks for your input. We will consider it and see if we can better align our processes with cultural norms in the future," the Director muses. "I look forward to seeing you next time. I don't ever want you to feel obligated to come, but know that you are always invited," he says sincerely. Kate thanks him, moving toward the door.

"I will wait for you in the courtyard," she whispers to me as she passes.

"Oh, Kate, before you go, I wanted to let you know that I am sending over some options for potential service assignments," the Director adds. "Nick put forth your request, and while I can't guarantee your preferred situation, I hope that something will stick out to you." Kate nods happily and steps out into the hall.

The door closes, and adrenaline immediately rushes through my veins.

"How have the trials gone this week?" Shari asks.

"Good, so far," I say, too quickly. "We have two days under our belts. I hope to know more about the results early next week."

"We have high hopes," the Director says.

I take a deep breath. "The other day, I was researching in the database and came across a chart showing statistics for Tier 3," I blurt out. I might be making it up, but I am almost positive Shari stiffens in that moment. "I was perplexed because these numbers seem to have been static for years. I wondered if more current research is needed?"

The Director begins to speak calmly, "I think those numbers are correct. There are plenty of—"

"I was also very interested in your response to Kate's request to serve with Tier 3, sir, and I looked up the current statistics on Tier 3 service assignments. It took some searching, because those numbers aren't all available in one location. Piecing it together, I found a massive discrepancy between the number of actual Tier 3 individuals and the number of Tier 1 and Tier 2 individuals assigned to serve there."

The room is silent now. I am not planning to tell them about my stop at the Tier 3 distribution center unless I have to.

"Based on those numbers—if they are, in fact, correct, as you say— there are only two possible ways to interpret the data: either we are severely mistreating the people of Tier 3—in which case it would be ideal for Kate to serve there—or there aren't many people to mistreat." Nobody speaks. Then the Director clears his throat.

"I think you should leave for now, Nick."

"But—"

"We will discuss this at a later date, thank you." His mouth is pinched into a thin line and he doesn't meet my eyes.

Not knowing what else to do, I hastily pack up my display and step out of the room. For the first time, as I rush down the hall—feeling the air against my skin—I notice my body is damp with sweat. How long was I talking? Maybe thirty seconds?

Though I am still humming from the conflict, my body slightly relaxes from simply being further away from the room. Hearing sudden footsteps behind me, I spin in surprise. It takes me a moment in the dim light, but I recognize Shari moving briskly toward me.

"Nick, stop pushing this!" she hisses, gripping my bicep and moving me quickly along the hallway. "I promise you will get your answers, but leave it alone for now." She stares at me, pleading. "Trust me," she begs, then turns on her heel and marches back the way she came.

NICK ENTERS the courtyard and looks like he just ran for miles. I take him in, his hairline wet with sweat, shirt rumpled.

"What did they do to you?" I ask, laughing initially, but quickly noticing that Nick is somber. "Are you ok?" I question, my mood quickly shifting to concern.

"Yes, I know. I look terrible. It was warm in there and I got really nervous talking about some new information. Also...I might be in trouble and I am so sorry if I caused problems for us," he says hurriedly, pulling me toward our bikes. I yank my arm away, forcing him to stop.

"Nick, what is going on?" I ask, seriously worried at this point.

"Nothing," he says, placing his hands on my shoulders. "I'm sorry, I didn't mean to upset you. I—don't know if I pushed too hard on something that I am not meant to be a part of. I felt like it was right, but...I may have upset the Director," he sighs, gulping in a breath of air. "I am sure it will be fine, I just want to go home and eat."

I hold his hand, attempting to ground him. "I trust you, Nick. I'm sure if you felt like it was important, you did the right thing."

By the time we arrive home, I am also covered in sweat, so Sam doesn't think twice about Nick's physical state. That hill to our house is brutal. We listen to him recount the evening while we eat, then begin the process of putting the kids to bed. Once they are tucked away, we shower and head to bed ourselves, seeing that Sam had fallen asleep on the cot in the living room.

I am extremely curious about what happened in the meeting room tonight, but Nick isn't inclined to discuss it at the moment, and I don't want to push. We undress in silence. When we are comfortable on our pillows, Nick reaches over and runs his hand along my arm. My skin tingles.

"Thanks for supporting me today," he mumbles softly.

"Always," I say, and watch him close his eyes.

"Mom?" I scream, reaching for her, somehow moving in the opposite direction. I try desperately to make forward progress. She is wrestling with something, being pulled through the door frame against her will.

She screams my name, over and over. I can't get to her! I run and scramble across the earth, never getting closer.

"Mom?" I hear a small voice next to me and I stop, whipping my head toward the sound, my mother's voice fading on the wind.

"Bentley?" I ask. He's so much smaller, but it's him.

"Hi Mom, are you ready to come home now?" he asks.

"Yes, that sounds wonderful," I say, holding his hand and following him through the trees. There is a small clearing and I look up to see Eric standing in the doorway, leaning against the wooden frame and staring at me, smiling brilliantly.

"Hey, Mom!" Tal calls from garden, waving and showing me his pile of weeds.

I gasp awake, and tears streak my cheeks, my chest burying sobs. Nick wakes and pulls me to him, as he always does. I cry into his shoulder while he strokes my hair until, eventually, I drift back into sleep.

When I open my eyes, morning light is streaming in and my breasts feel like rocks. How did I sleep so long? I groan, rolling gently to the side, hoping to avoid pressing on them. Stepping down to the floor, I pull on pants and practically run to the girls' room, but they aren't there. Hearing noises in the kitchen, I rush toward them, realizing too late that Sam might be out there. And I am not dressed.

"Hey, Mom!" Bentley says, and the night before comes crashing back into my mind. The girls start whimpering as soon as they see me.

"I'm never as good as Mom, huh girls," Nick states, feigning disappointment. Not seeing Sam, I rush to them. He hands Beth to me first, then Leah, while I position myself to feed them. I sigh, feeling instant relief as soon as they begin to drink.

"A little full?" Nick laughs.

"Just a tad," I grimace. "What time is it? Where is your dad?"

"It's 8:30, sorry. I wanted to let you sleep. Dad is up at the soil research center. He needed to meet with someone there before heading home tomorrow."

"Don't you have to be at the lab?" I ask worriedly.

"I do, but I rearranged my first hour. After what happened last night...I figured you could use a little extra help this morning." He grins and I smile gratefully. Seems like he is less concerned about his situation this morning. Hopefully it isn't as big of an issue as he initially thought?

"Thank you, that was really sweet. I might feel almost normal," I laugh, looking down at my swollen breasts.

"They didn't eat much from me, so they should be hungry, at least," Nick chuckles. He is already dressed and ready to go. I breathe a silent sigh of relief seeing him so chipper.

"I will take Bent to conditioning on my way, we missed drop-off," he says.

"You're the best."

He swoops over and kisses me, then walks out the door with Bentley, leaving me alone with the girls.

My headache is as bad as it's ever been. Throbbing pain is emanating from the base of my skull and fingers of pressure stab the back of my eyes. I blame it on my horrible night and the fact that I probably tried to accomplish too much today. I quickly swallow a naproxen sodium tablet, hoping to find some relief. Bentley is entertaining the girls, but I know I need to get them all into bed soon. Because of Nick's later start this morning, I don't expect him to be home anytime soon. Closing my eyes, I attempt to salvage some strength for the bedtime routine. Sam still hasn't returned home, and for the moment, I am grateful. I don't want him to see me like this.

When the girls are successfully in bed, Bentley and I retreat to his room for stories.

"Bent, do you think you could read to me tonight?" I ask, holding my fingers over my eyes.

"Sure, Mom. Are you ok?"

"My headache is really bad and the light is aggravating it. It's hard for me to open my eyes right now."

He selects a book, then pauses, noticing something tucked behind the main stack of reading material.

"Hey Mom, it's 'In the Meadow'," he says. "You used to read that to me all the time. Can we read it?"

I don't respond immediately. Something inside me clenches and I see stars behind my eyelids.

"I don't know, I guess it's only for babies," he mumbles, interpreting my lack of response as a judgement.

"No, Bent, not at all. Let's read it. Sorry, my head is getting worse and I was distracted." I lie down on his bed and motion for him to join me.

"Kate?" I hear, my shoulder shaking gently. I open my eyes, disoriented, and see Nick.

"Hey," I say, taking in my surroundings. Why am I in Bentley's room?

"Looks like you fell asleep in here. I thought you might want to sleep in your own bed," he says smiling. The pounding in my head has retreated a bit, but it's still alive under the surface.

"Is Bent ok?" I ask.

"Shhhh, he's right next to you, c'mon," he says quietly, lifting my elbow. I follow him, stumbling slightly.

"Are you ok?" he asks, his amusement sliding into concern when he sees me in the light of the hall.

"It was just a weird day," I mumble. "My headache was awful. I tried to do too much."

Nick turns to me, pressing his hands to the sides of my face. "Tell me about it. What does it feel like?" His sudden intensity sobers me.

"It's better now...I don't know how to describe it. It...got progressively worse during the day. It felt like it wrapped from the base of my skull to my eyes in an arc, if that makes sense?"

"Mmm-hmm," he says, pressing gently along the back of my neck, finding the cranial pressure points behind my ears. He holds his thumbs there, gradually increasing his force. My head throbs and I hold my breath, but I can feel a slow release.

"Thank you," I say as his hands slide away.

"Kate, I think you should come in for a scan. I really want to see if I can help."

"Are you sure you won't get in trouble?"

"No, but I will deal with that if I need to. I'm worried about you," he says, his voice thick with concern.

"I could go in and get a work-up," I offer.

"You have done that already and it didn't help. Let's try something else."

I nod. "Just let me know when and I'll be there," I say.

He leads me to bed and the darkness of our room is pure bliss. I allow myself to drop back into the relief of sleep.

Movement catches my eye and I glance up, watching the door open. Kate has been resting peacefully for a few minutes now, but seeing my dad enter the room makes me grateful that I waited instead of joining her immediately.

"Long day?" I ask, noticing the circles under his eyes.

He nods. "Lots to cover. Sorry I missed so much time with the kids today," he says, disappointed.

"Kate wasn't feeling great, so I think it was actually fortuitous."

He shrugs the bag from his shoulder, his eyebrows furrowing. "Is she doing alright?"

"She's resting now. Can I get you something to eat?" I ask, and he nods gratefully. With his arrival, we were given a few extra portions to cover another adult in the house for a few days. I heat up the stew that Kate set aside for him earlier this evening. He sighs at the aroma, shoveling it into his mouth as soon as I serve it.

"How are you two doing?" he asks mid-bite.

"Great," I say, not entirely knowing where to go from there.

"Great?" he asks.

"I—yes. Really good. You know, Dad. I still feel insecure in this whole thing, but every week seems to bond us a little more. Having the girls obviously continues to pull us together and Bent and I are as close as we've ever been. We are on the right path."

He nods.

"Do you miss Mom?" I ask, knowing that he has been with another woman regularly for the last few months.

"Every day," he says.

"But what about—"

"Nick, nobody can ever replace the bond we shared. You know that. I'm not lonely, if that's what you're asking. But yes, I miss her."

"Do you—well, considering your health and everything involved with that, do you feel happy with your life?" Heat rises to my face as I realize I just alluded to his death.

"It's okay," he says, noticing my concern. "I know my journey is nearly at its end. And yes, I am happy with it. All of it. Watching you grow and learn, being willing to sacrifice and make immense contributions to our growing society—what could be more gratifying than that?"

"Sometimes I question my contributions, Dad. With everything I have working in my favor, it seems like I should be doing more," I admit.

"You will," he assures me. "One step at a time. Trust yourself, Nick. You're not meant to follow the systems we already have in place. With the growth and change we have experienced—even solely during my lifetime—we need sustainable innovation more than ever. Being a pioneer is never easy, but I am convinced that you are just that."

I swallow, allowing his words to sink deeply into me. He might be convinced, but the internal struggle for me remains. What if I never find that opportunity? What if my brain and body are primed for progress, but the right moment never comes? As if reading my thoughts, my dad grips my shoulder.

"Don't think so much, son. You'll know it when you see it."

The results from the lab are posted by the morning, waiting for me when I open my display. Tamara has completed the one week post-treatment interviews with our patients. Hovering over the file, my finger hesitates, momentarily overwhelmed by how much I want this to have made a difference. If it didn't, I don't know what's next. Taking a deep breath, I open it and scroll. My eyes frantically scan for the results. When I find them, my heart leaps. I read it again to be sure I understood correctly. No new headaches. Nobody reported headaches. It's too soon to tell if dreaming will be an issue, but this is significant progress.

A wave of goosebumps crosses my skin. I can't believe it. This might have actually worked. If these results hold with the rest of our patients, I may be able to start trials with those who have had more extensive symptoms from prior treatments. Questions and implications flood my mind. Could this possibly be restorative for past damage? Or is it only effective for new treatments? Maybe with a mixture of spinal adjustment and REM induction, we could release previous echoes and eliminate them? My excitement builds, relief replacing tension I didn't even recognize I was holding. My mind is solely focused on helping Kate. I want to be the one to solve this. I *need* to solve this for her sake. And mine.

After my dad leaves, I spend the next week plugging through trials and, in my spare time, finding ways to hack into Kate's file. My research hasn't given me any solid leads on Tier 3, so I have completely immersed myself in her well-being to avoid the cognitive dissonance that exists there. I know she is wondering why I haven't asked her to come in, but I may only get a few shots at this before someone notices Kate being used as a subject. I have to know as much as I can. There might also be a small part of me avoiding it out of fear, which I hate admitting to myself. I haven't heard anything from the Director since our last meeting, and I can't imagine that is a good thing. Honestly, though, that should give me more reason to break the rules, not less.

Getting into her recent file wasn't hard, especially since Shari inadvertently gave me the password a few months ago when the Director had accidentally logged in under a different user. Accessing her scans pre-Eric is proving difficult, though. I can see the file exists within Kate's profile, but it's restricted. This will be my project once trials are done for the afternoon. Solely considering the images I currently have access to, I am flabbergasted that her headaches are so infrequent. In her most recent session alone, her neurons and pathways were significantly altered—more drastically than any scans I have seen—in a matter of days. The before and after scans are shocking. I need to get to her childhood history. If they are anything like this...I may be out of my depth.

As my patients disperse, I retreat to the office to 'finalize trial files'. Since I have already tried hacking into Kate's restricted file with no luck, I have determined that I need to go another route. Our lab coordinator has a higher level of access than I do when it comes to Tier 1 patients. I'm not completely sure if that means he will have clearance for this particular file, but it's the easiest and least risky option I have available. Besides directly asking Grace. Given the fact that the Committee hasn't been overly excited to give me access to Tier 1 files for legitimate research, I don't anticipate that going over well, especially considering the current situation.

Last month, I had issues with my profile. I had used a scheduling app that was developed as a prototype to assist with shift coordination in the lab, but it somehow crashed my login. I was kicked out and, upon trying to get back into the system, was locked on dark screen. A Systems tech had to reset my profile. Berg has since improved the program, changing the app, and it no longer crashes, but the original version is still present on my profile. A fact I plan to exploit. Tapping on it, I am hopeful that it will wreak the same havoc it did last time.

Initially, nothing happens and my heart drops. Then, my display flicks to the login screen. When I type in my credentials, the screen goes dark. Success. I tap my sensor, messaging the lab coordinator.

Hey, I am so sorry, but I accidentally tapped on the wrong version of PlanIt and it crashed. I don't know why that version is still active on my profile!? I need to complete these patient profiles and it will take hours for Systems to reset my info. Would it be possible for you to log me in to your profile for an hour or so? Tamara only has access to basic patient information and I was hoping to edit scan info before I head home. Thanks. Again, sorry for the dolt move.

I press send. Then I wait. There is a good chance that he will tell me I need to come in early tomorrow when my profile is reset. I purposely don't say anything to Tamara in case she decides to be helpful by finding another analyst to log me into their profile. They have the same clearance as I do. Not helpful. That is another option that the coordinator could propose, but I cross my fingers, hoping he won't think of it. I busy myself with sanitizing the lab equipment, my heart pounding. A few minutes later, I still haven't received a reply, fear and doubt beginning to creep into my thoughts. As I am working on the last electrode, however, the door to the lab opens.

"Nick, looks good in here," Bey states.

"Thanks, just cleaning up for tomorrow," I smile sheepishly. "I am so sorry to make you come all the way down here."

"I was actually in this wing helping with a technical issue—one of the reversal machines is struggling this afternoon. I'm hoping the problem is just a bum electrode, but I'm having a technician take a look in the morning."

"Frustrating," I comment, trying to look concerned, yet at ease.

"So what is this about PlanIt?" he asks.

I sigh. "Did you ever use the previous version of the software?" He shakes his head. "It has a glitch that crashes profiles. It happened to me last month when it was first released, and somehow that version of the app is still available. I accidentally tried to open it, intending to access the current version. Anyway, my profile is locked and I hoped you could help me out so I can finish up. If not, I can just message Systems and wait until morning." I pause, hooking my fingers in my back pockets. "Tomorrow is our family rec time, so I was just hoping to avoid cutting into that," I say, again, trying not to look like I care. Breathing purposefully slow, I hope he can't tell that I am now sweating profusely. I resume my task, wiping the electrode and placing it gently into the tray along the reversal machine.

"I can do that," Bey says, "but access has changed so that profiles can only be active on one display at a time. I still have to set up that appointment with our technician and meet with inventory about a discrepancy before I head back to my office. I would think that should buy you about 45 minutes. After that, I'll have to kick you off," he says, walking to the display and typing in his information.

"Thanks Bey, that should be plenty of time," I say gratefully, relief swelling within me.

"Next time you could probably walk up to the next compartment and get Chris to log you in," he suggests.

"Huh, good idea. I hadn't seen her today, so she didn't come to mind," I lie. I saw her this morning, walking past the windows. This is the second time I've been dishonest with him and the guilt is emotionally draining. I thank Bey again as he leaves, pushing away my self-disappointment as quickly as it came, and eagerly move to the display.

"I THINK IT GOES HERE, MOM," Bent says, showing me where the puzzle piece should fit. Feelings of inadequacy sit heavily in my mind as I attempt to help him work through this assignment.

"Bent, why exactly do you want my help?" I ask. "You find the variations much faster than I can."

"I know, but it's still fun to have someone to watch me," he answers, grinning.

I laugh. "I am just an audience? Thanks a lot," I tease and his grin widens. He places the wooden pieces in silence for a few moments, focusing.

"Mom, why do you think you have had headaches more often the last few months?" he asks unexpectedly.

"I—I don't know," I stammer. "I usually connect it with stress—"

"I don't think that's it," he says. "I think there's something else. That doesn't make sense because our lives are built around low tension and stress. Why would it happen to you more than anyone else if it were just that? And, I don't think you have a genetic link, so it has to be an external factor."

"How would you know if I have a genetic link?" I ask, impressed and taken off guard by his analysis.

"Well, I don't for sure. I just assumed. Maybe I got lucky, but that variation is dominant and I don't have it. Do you?"

"No, I don't," I answer slowly, watching his face take on a very satisfied expression. "I do think it's time for bed, though." He slumps his shoulders in complaint.

"Can I finish this first?" he petitions.

"Let's finish in the morning. I'll give you more 'help' then," I say, and we both laugh. He embraces me, his now not-so-tiny arms wrapping around my neck, then runs to the bathroom and I notice that, for the first time, his pants didn't fall down. My heart aches a little, mourning that goofy little boy with no hips.

I wait for Nick. He is late and I am starting to get anxious. Tapping my sensor, I still don't see a message from him. Trying to take my mind off of it, I wipe down door handles and dust the shelves. My breath catches when I finally hear the front door open, feeling suddenly absurd that I was worried in the first place. Setting my cloth on the counter, I walk toward the hallway and meet him halfway.

"Hey," I say, reaching for him, and he crushes me in his embrace.

He is surprisingly emotional; intensity exudes from his every movement.

"What's going on?" I ask, pulling away to look at his face.

"Nothing," he sighs.

"Is it something to do with the meeting the other night?" I ask, hoping to drag it out of him.

"No, just a long day at the lab." I can almost visibly see him closing off, putting on a face.

"Nick, stop," I say, sharper than I had intended. "I know something is going on. You have been cycling between emotional highs and lows for a while now. I can almost physically feel the turbulence inside of you. I love you. Please talk to me. I am not afraid of most things, but this. This terrifies me. Not being able to help, knowing you are shouldering something alone. Please, Nick," I practically beg. The panic I feel at him shutting me out is irrational, and yet like I have felt it before. Emotionally, this is impossibly familiar and that realization pushes my confusion further. Nick doesn't answer, looking conflicted.

"What is going on?" I demand, watching Nick's expression turn to hurt and surprise. Dread settles on my chest and I start to hyperventilate. "Something is going on with me, Nick!" I blurt, tears filling my eyes. "I'm so sorry," I sob, and he immediately pulls me close. "This isn't about you, it's me. I'm scared because I don't understand why I am dreaming, why my head hurts, why my child is so concerned about me that he's trying to figure out a solution," I blubber nonsensically. "Things have always made sense and you always thought they made sense." I pause, breathing. "Do they make sense, Nick?" I plead.

"Whoa, Kate. Slow down. What is—"

"There's something wrong with me, Nick!" I practically shriek. He stares at me then, unblinking, his arms pressed on top of my shoulders. He stares at me and we stand unmoving, the air thick between us.

"Kate, I think you had reversal therapy," he says quietly—gently—but he may as well have slapped me.

"What? I have never had reversal," I respond, my voice hard.

"When you were a kid. I think that's why you are having bad dreams. That's what I pushed in the meeting, when I came out stressed and upset. I wanted to use you as a patient and see what is going on. I want to help you, Kate. I didn't want to say anything until I was sure, but—I'm certain at this point. As far as I am concerned, that is what is causing your trauma. I assume it was something about your mother, which is why your dreams are centered around her," he explains, pausing to evaluate my reaction.

A peace falls over me as he clarifies, my initial shock and offense melting away, and I immediately know in my heart that what he is saying is right. I don't understand how or why, but this makes sense of everything. Sighing in relief, I close my eyes and lean against his chest.

"Is there anything we can do?" I ask. "Do you know why it

happened? Or how to fix it?" So many questions race through my mind, I can't keep up.

"I don't know why, but yes, I think I can fix it. At least, I hope I can. Based on the results of my most recent trials—"

"When?"

"Whenever you're ready."

"Now?"

He laughs. "I wish. Let me get things set up and we can do it later this week. Will that work?"

I nod, every cell in my body begging for rest.

"Kate...there's a good chance that I have no idea what I'm doing. I don't want—"

"I trust you, Nick."

I enjoy a night of euphoric, uninterrupted sleep. Waking, I mentally prepare for a completely normal, busy day in the life of Kate, but it already feels completely different. There's something I don't know about myself. About my history. If my parents felt that it was necessary to do reversal, I am sure they had a good reason for it. But why wouldn't they tell me? They likely didn't understand that there would be any reason for me to know. How could they have predicted that it would cause this kind of trauma? Especially when Berg didn't even know. Yet, despite all of this rationalization, I don't know if I can let it go. Even if Nick knows how to heal my symptoms, do I want him to erase my knowing? Is it even possible to elim-inate these residual pieces of memory, considering that my most recent scan was *last year* and this is such a miniscule piece of infor-mation, probably lost in the abyss of my childhood? I can't see how it would be easy to locate without also affecting other information.

Something else tickles at my subconscious, though I fight it, not ready to give it full attention. My dreams aren't always about my mom. I haven't told Nick about the last few, but they have all included Eric, Bentley—and Tal. A child that doesn't exist. If my dreams with my mom are legitimately linked to an event...I shud-der, forcing that thought out. There is no way that I have a child who I have forgotten. It isn't possible. And Eric has been dead for years! I *watched* him die. Tears fill my eyes, the weight of remem-bering nearly bowling me over. Perhaps those dreams are connected to the same event, just manifesting in different ways. When the pathways are repaired, maybe they will disappear, too. I can only hope.

A cry from the girls' room snaps me back. Throwing my legs off the side of the bed and wiping away my tears, I stand up and force myself to move forward. I can do this. Just a normal day.

Sitting across from Shari, Grace, and the Director, I nervously clasp and unclasp my hands under the table. The Director is pulling up his display, while Grace actively avoids meeting my eyes. Shari shoots me a wink and my shoulders relax a little.

"Nick, thanks for coming in at an unorthodox time. First. Let me apologize for my reaction last time we met."

This is not the introduction I was expecting, but I am grateful for it.

"I hadn't anticipated your questions, they were completely out of context, and I didn't process them well," he continues. "I would like to give you a proper answer now, but first, I need you to understand something." He leans on the table, eyes searing into me. "This is classified information that we—the three of us here and the entire Committee—have determined to share with you. We do not take this lightly, and neither should you," he says, and his tone almost carries a hint of a threat. So much for relaxed shoulders. For a moment, I question whether I should walk away. Are the answers I seek worth whatever burden they will obviously carry? Knowing this is impossible, I nod my acceptance. The display lights up as the door behind me opens.

People begin filing into the room, one after another. I don't recognize any faces, but the Director is listing off names, introducing them quickly.

"...Nasser, Faye, Cameron, Polly..." he prattles on. There is no way I will remember all of them. I try to focus on one or two names, to at least gather something from the exercise. Eventually, everyone is seated, filling all forty seats around the table.

"Nick, we have invited our territorial Committee to join us today. Have you met any of our members—besides the three of us—before?" the Director asks.

I didn't realize that Shari was officially on the Committee. Glancing over at her, I catch an almost amused look on her face. Looking away, I shake my head.

The Director continues, "Nick, I am pleased to announce that today we would like to offer you a seat on the Committee." The table erupts with applause before I have time to process this. Did I hear that right? What is even happening right now? Confusion at this offer is met with a realization that I have no idea what most people on the Committee even do.

"I—I'm sorry, this is literally the last thing I could have anticipated today and I don't think I am understanding. Could you flesh this out a little?" I stammer over the din, flushing. The applause slowly dissipates.

"What details are you interested in?" the Director asks.

"Ummm...pretty much everything," I answer. "A few moments ago, you alluded to some answers that would be given. Regarding the questions I asked during our last meeting. Now you are offering me a seat." I scan the table, taking in all of the smiling faces. Is this how it happened for them? "I would love to know why you have invited me to join and what you would expect me to do. So, yes, lots of details. About everything," I finish, my eyes darting around the table again. Nobody seems obviously taken aback.

The Director chuckles. "Luckily, my answer to your initial petition should clarify all of that, so let me start." He motions to the display. "You were concerned about numbers in Tier 3, correct?" he clarifies. I nod. A chart that I don't recognize appears. The numbers are completely different from those that I pulled up when researching for Bentley. In this image, Tier 3 population numbers drop drastically—not stable at all.

"These numbers were recorded in our territory. As you can see, the Tier 3 population has significantly decreased over time, reaching a record low five years ago. With such a low number, it was impractical and inefficient to continue providing resources for them. We integrated those we could into Tier 2 and the others were released— "

"Released?" I interject. "I'm sorry to interrupt, but I don't understand what that means. They were left to fend for themselves?"

"They were no longer needed in society, so they were released from their responsibility," he answers kindly.

"So that's a yes?" I fish, refusing to accept a vague answer.

"They were released from their physical burdens. As you know, people in Tier 3 had significant challenges. Their lives were difficult and complex. Because we have always valued life, Berg has consistently felt that they were to be preserved and provided for as long as it was possible *to* provide. It was no longer possible. Our resources were being essentially wasted on the few. Few who were not capable of serving or providing necessary benefits in return. Those that we could not integrate were *released*," he responds with finality. I nod, my throat clenching. Their lives were taken, in some form or another. Tier 3 doesn't exist because we killed the last of them in an effort to be efficient. I take a deep breath, reminding myself not to jump to conclusions. That I know none of the details. Yet the pit in my stomach remains.

"This pattern has been followed—or will soon be followed—in every territory. We are all at similar points, give or take. I will remind you that this is what Berg expected and planned for. The goal of the Tier system was always to use resources efficiently in creating a safe, thriving society, ripe for improvement and evolution. We have arrived at what we are calling Phase Two. With reproduction rates, it is an eventual certainty that we will see Tier 2 follow a similar pattern, leaving only Tier 1 individuals in Phase Three. At that point, Berg has a plan in place for categories of division—creating three new Tiers based on evolution at that point in time."

We are eliminating Tier 3 and Tier 2 only to create new Tiers?

This answers questions that I have had since childhood. Evolution-arily, it's brilliant. Always surround top candidates with the best, allowing them to be fed daily by those of similar capability. Exposing them through service to those who struggle, creating intense responsibility and accountability, all while allowing them the freedom and flexibility to innovate and explore possibilities in whatever area suits them best. Bentley would be thrilled to hear this. The potential for continual progress is—well, it's exciting.

The Director smiles, as if interpreting my thoughts. "Obviously, this process will extend far beyond our lifetime, but currently we are faced with a dilemma. During this interim period where fixed Tiers are being phased out, awaiting the transplant of new, higher Tier divisions, we are left with resources that exceed our needs. Not only physical resources, but the time and talents of those in Tier 1, desperate to be utilized. How would you solve this prob-lem, Nick?" he asks, his eyes almost dancing.

I ponder this for a moment. "Well..." I begin. "We could slow our physical resource production, or use extra resources to focus solely on industries in need. Advanced technology comes to mind," I postulate.

"That is exactly what we initially thought—" the Director starts.

"But," I interrupt, "we can't necessarily use all of our human resources toward tech. Tier 2 and even many Tier 1 individuals are not directly suited for innovation in that field. They would need to still be utilized in some way, but," my mind spins, "if we are trying to slow production, how could we use them to their full potential and allow them to progress individually if we have no need for their end result?"

"Yes, Nick. Yes. You see the problem." Another image appears on the display. "This is our current population in our territory. You can see the percentage that we have allocated for technology service and innovation—much higher than in the past. Here you see the allocation for the remaining population. This equates to production that is far beyond what we need or could possibly use. Some excess is sent to other territories that can use it, but most are in the same situation."

"Current research still demands a Tier system?" I ask.

"Yes," Grace answers. "Berg is still sure that this is the most reliable way to achieve peace and progress simultaneously."

"Nick, with everything continuing to move forward with few—if any—undesirable effects for society as a whole, it would be impossible to argue a change of trajectory. Why would we give this up for an unknown? For a system that could fail when we have one that is succeeding?" Shari contributes. I see multiple heads nodding around me and reluctantly agree. Too many unknowns with any other options at this point.

"Given this situation, five years ago, a council was held with all Berg territorial committees and an agreement was reached. We, as committee members in all territories, are to serve as keepers of these extra resources. We are to allow ourselves to be served by those who need to serve, which enables us to better problem solve and give back. We have to use physical resources that would be wasted otherwise, utilizing the excess so that we may provide better administration, organization, and leadership to those we have stewardship over. We feel like you have the insight and skills needed for this incredibly important assignment and would like to invite you to join us." The Director sits and his display goes dark.

I hesitate, not sure whether I should speak.

When the room remains silent, I ask, "What exactly does that look like?"

"Travel, Nick," Shari says, smiling. "We travel. In order to preventatively care for our territories, we have to understand the issues that could potentially be introduced. Seeing diversity first hand allows us better perspective in our leadership."

"Service provided to our families gives us time and energy to create stronger bonds. With life expectancy higher than ever, we can dedicate ourselves to the mentoring of our children and grandchildren, potentially creating the first long-term family groups in the Tier system," a man contributes.

"Complete access to anything we want or need, along with absolute freedom to explore. I can invent without fear of failure or waste and I don't need approval for any of it. We are trusted to use resources wisely, but aren't limited as we have been in the past. Think of the good you could do without any limits on your research!" another woman speaks out.

Complete access. Flexibility. One hundred percent of my time spent with Kate and the kids, or pursuing the hundreds of research projects that are on my mental docket. And my dad, we could see him regularly. No more research check-ins or limitations, no more community responsibilities, no more stress. Only meaningful contribution. There are at least five projects I can think of right now that I know have been shut down because of a lack of available resources. Projects that I believe have the potential to break research on the brain wide open. And those are only the few I can list off-hand. How many more exist—perhaps with some data already collected?

"Is family included?" I ask softly, dazed by the thought of this. "I mean—"

"It's a package deal, Nick," the Director answers. "Your pair would be extended the same responsibility if you accept. Children will obviously need to remain unaware, for consistent conditioning experiences, but we have protocols in place for that. I would hope that you and Kate would move forward with another round of fertility, fulfilling your commitment to the current project. This assignment will be a transition, and we have a procedure that will need to be followed where your pair is concerned, but—"

"I accept," I say. How could I not? The applause resumes and I am greeted by handshakes and embraces all around, voices telling me that my new assignment will begin immediately and, eventually, we will need to make arrangements for relocation. It is only then that I realize I probably should have asked for time to discuss this with Kate. Maybe at least a night to process. Overwhelmed, I excuse myself, reminding everyone that I have young children at home who need me.

I step into the silence of the hall and tears fill my eyes. Out of relief? Yes. Out of excitement for a life of utter freedom to do good? Yes. A million times yes. My life has been on an upward trajectory with so much potential, and yet no obvious space for me to break through to something big. This is it. The opportunity I have always hoped for.

Are my tears also out of worry that I have upended our lives with no input from my partner? Out of sadness for Tier 3? I didn't even get the chance to know them...

Yes. All of it. Something inside of me dreads telling Kate, knowing —at least in part—what her reaction will be. And this? This is what hurts the most. She can't know how Tier 3 was dealt with. It would crush her. I cry out of frustration that I don't measure up to her goodness. To her compassion. That deep down, I know I am a substitute. A second best, despite all that I do to prove otherwise. Even this incredible opportunity can't make me forget that *she loves someone else.* I weep. Pressing my hands against the rough brick, forcing myself to remain upright. I heave in anguish and euphoria both, releasing everything that I have held wound up within me for the last year. Then, gathering myself, I walk home, thoroughly spent.

"THAT'S WHY I'M HERE," I say. "The people who love me, and even those who just know me, have recommended that I take some steps to move forward. I don't know what that will look like but, for Tal, I'm willing to try," I say, falling back gently against the chair.

"I think that's admirable of you, Eric," Dr. Houser states. She mirrors my behavior, leaning back as well, and it isn't lost on me. It works despite my recognition. I feel slightly more at ease. "What does 'moving forward' look like to you?" she asks.

"I—I honestly don't know? Practically, I think others would like to see me re-pair, but the thought of it," I pause. "Well, the thought of it makes me nauseous, frankly." I laugh nervously.

"Do you wish you could consider re-pairing? I mean, if we were able to get to a point where your physical feelings surrounding it changed, is it ideally something you would want?"

I think for a moment. "Is it possible that I don't know what I want? Or want to want?" I don't even remember the last time I thought about what *I* wanted. "I love my son. I love watching things grow, and I love the sun on my face. That's about as far as I've gotten," I answer.

"That's okay, Eric. We can work with that. How about we take pairing out of the equation. What relationships do you have in your life?"

My mind scans through the people I interact with and am immediately disappointed in myself. "I don't have many," I mumble, clearing my throat.

"There's no judgement here, Eric."

I nod. "The only relationship that I put any effort into is with Tal."

"Let's start there, then," she says kindly.

I arrive home to find Tal working at the kitchen counter. I've only been gone an hour, but it seems he is almost finished with his project.

"Hey, Dad," he says, not looking up.

"Hey," I say, ruffling his hair.

"How did therapy go?" he asks.

"It was good, I think. I set some goals. I am going to try a few things to help me build new relationships," I say hesitantly. Complete openness is my goal with Tal, but already I can tell it's going to be uncomfortable.

"You do need some friends," he teases, grinning.

"You don't like being my only friend?"

"It's flattering, but no," he laughs, pausing in his task. "Dad, I want you to be happy. Stop worrying about me, just—well, yeah. Build some new relationships."

"Apparently I should come to you for therapy, no need to leave the house," I joke, moving closer to him and catching his gaze. "I will, Tal," I add seriously. "I'm going to work on this, and I'm sorry I've used you as a crutch."

He nods slightly, then returns to his work.

I smile in spite of myself, watching Val walk toward the table. Standing to greet her, we awkwardly shake hands, not knowing whether to embrace, and she sits across from me. I haven't seen her outside of work, and she looks stunning.

"Hey," she says. "So. What prompted this?"

I take a deep breath. Openness, I remind myself. Vulnerability. "I have set some goals to build new friendships. Turns out, I haven't put forth much effort in that area, and when I thought of who I would like to get to know better...you were at the top of the list," I say, noticing her blush.

"I'd like to get to know you better, too," she says.

We order our food and ask each other questions. I find that easier than coming up with topics at the moment, and she is more than happy to play along.

"What were your parents like?" I ask.

"They were hard workers," she answers. "They weren't concerned with pushing for Tier 1 or improving their status, they only wanted to do what was best for us kids and give us as many opportunities as possible. They were incredibly annoying when it came to nutrition," she answers and I chuckle. "It's true! My mom used to practically stuff vegetables down our throats!"

"Well at least they cared, and you lived to tell the tale," I tease.

She daintily takes a bite of the popcorn that sits on the table as an appetizer. "What about you?" she asks.

My mind goes blank for a moment. I haven't thought about *my* life in ages. Thinking of my childhood and parents feels somehow separate. A different me, or a long-forgotten character in a book I loved. Nostalgia and warmth envelope me and I smile.

"What?" she asks.

"Sorry, I haven't thought about it in a while. A long while. Remembering makes me happy."

"Well that's the best endorsement of a family I've ever heard," she says, grinning.

"They were wonderful," I agree. "Both of them were always supporting and pushing us to accomplish anything we wanted. To 'find our path', my mom used to say."

Val's smile fades slightly and I notice a quizzical look on her face.

"Are you ok?" I ask, concerned.

"Yeah, it's just—I find it fascinating that your parents had that mentality. That seems to be more of a Tier 1 mindset. If I would have heard that I could do anything when I was growing up, I wonder if that would have shifted any of my decisions. Despite my parents' contentment, I was focused on doing everything right. Checking every box. Making sure that I maximized my potential to qualify for Tier 1. Then, when it didn't happen...well, I wish I would have embraced my Tier 2 life sooner," she determines, looking down at her lap. "Did you feel lied to when you did everything you could and still didn't get a shot?"

"Huh," I say. "I guess I haven't ever thought about it that way. I don't clearly recall ever being worried about qualifying for Tier 1, I was only focused on finding a way that I could make an impact. I don't know if I've succeeded," I chuckle introspectively.

"I think you have," she says encouragingly.

Our food is brought to the table and I am grateful for the break in conversation. Why didn't I ever want to qualify for Tier 1 testing? I understand why it's not possible now, but could it have been before—before Kate? Why can't I remember? Puzzled, I take a few bites of my potatoes. Was I really that complacent?

"This is really nice, Eric. Thanks for inviting me. It's rare that I use credits for a night out and I needed a break," she says gratefully, wiping her mouth with the corner of her cloth napkin.

"I think I have enough credits to go out every night for a year," I laugh.

"Really?" she exclaims. "How? Don't you use them for time off or specialty food? That's where all of mine go."

"No, Tal and I are pretty simple." And there it is. Tal. I don't remember if we have talked about him before. I hesitate, wondering what she is thinking.

"How old is Tal again?" she asks, not missing a beat.

"He is eleven," I say. "Acts like he's older, but only eleven."

"How is he doing with conditioning?"

I chew slowly, mulling this question over. "He struggles, to be honest. He, like you mentioned, really wants to qualify for Tier 1, but I don't think that will be a possibility. We've been through too much. I don't know that his brain will respond the way they want it to, even if we did more rounds of reversal." I sigh. "I wish I could have the attitude my parents had, but I'm too practical, I guess."

She nods. "I think it's a good thing. Not to get his hopes up. Speaking from personal experience," she jests, but her face belies the hurt and disappointment she spoke of earlier.

We enjoy the rest of our meal and walk for a block or two before our paths separate. At the corner, she looks tenderly up at me.

"Thanks for letting me be a friend, Eric. I really enjoyed talking with you."

"Thanks for being patient with me, I'm sorry—"

Her hands shoot up between us. "No apologies. We all move at our own pace. I'm glad that you are making progress and happy to be a part of it," she says, dropping her arms to her sides.

Not thinking for once, I reach out and pull her close. Her head rests beneath my chin and her hair smells of warm honey. My body hums at the connection. After a few moments, I reluctantly let go. With a warm flush in her cheeks, she waves and we go our separate ways.

UPON RETURNING HOME, I feel desperate for Kate. My emotions are volatile and I know she can sense it. Since I don't trust myself to talk—nor do I understand what I am able to discuss with her yet —I kiss her deeply before she can ask me anything. Feeling her body respond to mine sends tingles across my skin. I will never take for granted that I get this. That I get her.

Lying beside her, I feel silent tears slide down my cheeks. Kate is unaware, her head buried between my shoulder and neck, and my hand errantly traces her shoulder blade, her hair falling softly around my fingers. My emotions war within me, the decisions I have made weighing heavily on my heart. If everything I have done is right, consistent with my priorities, why don't I feel at peace? Even now, when all seems to be perfectly falling into place? Reason and logic have led me here, yet I feel I am slogging along blindly. The small deceptions and secrets have seemingly created a house of cards—one that could come crashing down around me at any moment. Nothing feels solid, though logically I know that it is. Even if it did come crashing down, reversal could fix it, yet...I fear loss so much. I realize it must be different to be with someone who hasn't been manipulated to love you.

The initial relief I felt at the meeting is quickly dissolving into worry and doubt. The Director's explanations initially made perfect sense, but I shrink at the idea of telling Kate what I've agreed to. *But think of all the good I can do.* We can do, together. Shouldn't she be excited at this opportunity? Is she holding us back? Is my bond with her preventing me from fulfilling my potential? Has *she* become what I am loyal to? I regret these thoughts as soon as they materialize. Why am I deciding her feelings for her? Once I explain everything, how could she not understand? Kate is the best of us. Being with her should do nothing but ensure my ability to contribute. Resting there, holding her, I eventually slip into fitful sleep.

After having a few weeks to ponder all that has happened—along with continued success in trials—my excitement for these changes has been rekindled. Along with my new assignment, I have requested to continue on with my current research. Despite my intense desire to begin new projects, my focus is still on reversal. I won't be able to move forward until I have closure on this, especially where Kate is concerned. With the added benefit of having full access to any resources I deem useful, and no longer having to attain approval, I am compelled to see this through. Instead of trying to constantly mentally justify my reasoning for the trials, I give myself permission to accept the fact that curiosity and concern for Kate supercede anything else at this point. Since she is purely a microcosm of the Tier 1 individuals I could potentially heal, this priority is justifiably placed.

With every passing day, I become more and more convinced that this new procedure is the solution we have been hoping for. With the success of our treatments with patients seeking new reversals, the Director has sent over new batches that need to be treated for echoes alone. Our results thus far have been equally as successful. I work long hours, becoming borderline obsessed—rationalizing that I wouldn't be able to begin moving on with new experiences with Kate anyway, before the transition period is complete. Having received the protocol for families days ago, I have yet to initiate the first steps. While I can tell Kate that I have been given a new assignment on the Committee, I am not free to expose many details. Slowly, over the course of months, I will introduce new responsibilities and benefits. We can have more children during that period and hopefully wrap up results of my trials. The timing literally couldn't be better.

Though it is later than we had initially planned, tonight is the night. Kate tiptoes to the door of my workspace after lab hours, and I usher her in. Tamara has left for the day, so I don't anticipate us being interrupted. Theoretically, I shouldn't have to hide this from the Committee, but I'm not sure that research subjects are considered 'resources' at my disposal. Kate understands that we need to move quickly and immediately prepares herself for a scan. As soon as she is settled, I hit the button. My heart drops as the image takes form on my display. After pouring over her prior annual scans for weeks, I practically have them memorized and immediately recognize the areas that have been repeatedly treated. It's a literal mess. I had previously determined to work on her childhood reversal, since her dreams have consistently stemmed from that, but now I am not so sure.

"Kate, you can sit up now," I say, moving toward her. "How would you feel about doing a repair session?" I ask, acting more confident than I feel.

"Like, now?" she asks, surprised.

I nod.

"What would it entail?"

I explain the process of inducing REM sleep, the treatment, and the results we have seen thus far.

"But, full disclosure: I haven't ever tried repairing reversal treatments that have occurred this far in the past," I admit. "I have only been working with new or more recent procedures. I can't see why it would be any different, though. If anything, it may just not work, but I don't anticipate any negative results. It's experimental, and I understand if you don't want to try it." I nervously pat my leg with my left hand. "The only reason I suggest it is...it may be awhile before we move into new trials and I—I have an extremely difficult time watching you in pain."

She smiles at me then, trusting, and puts her hand on my cheek.

"Let's do it," she says.

Obediently, I place the port and gently strap her to the reversal table. She flinches when I tighten the restraints.

"Is it too tight?" I ask and she shakes her head, remaining silent. Not for the first time, I find myself wishing I could get inside her head.

I begin the drip, explaining to her that she will only be asleep for a short period. As her eyelids droop, I move to the display to make adjustments as needed.

Her brain lights up and, at first, it's difficult to locate the specific area I am looking for. When I do, I slowly begin treatment, acting much more conservatively than I normally would.

What am I doing? What if it is possible to add damage to her already fractured neural pathways? I shake as my fingers clumsily continue on. Eventually, I slip into routine, forgetting for the moment that this is anything beyond a normal trial. When finished, I slow her chemical load, remove the port, and allow her to wake naturally, as I do with every patient. Having nothing else to do, I sit next to her and hold her hand.

Back home, a soft knock on the door surprises me, and I rush to open it, hoping whoever is there won't make more noise and wake the kids or Kate.

"Shari?" I say, surprised, as the door swings open. She motions for me to step outside.

"What are you thinking, Nick?" she hisses.

"What do you—"

"You know what I mean. Why would you do this?"

My thoughts are reeling. How did she find out so quickly? Why is she so angry and here so late? My tired state contributes to send my typically slight paranoia shooting through the roof.

"How did—"

"Nick, your searches in the records system are logged! Did you think we wouldn't be checking up on you after trusting you with such sensitive information? Eric is none of your concern!"

Relief and fear collide at once in my system. She isn't talking about Kate. She doesn't necessarily know about her treatment earlier tonight. This particular search she is referencing was days ago.

"I was just curious, Shari. I've made a lot of difficult decisions lately and I felt like—well, if I knew he was flourishing, it would help."

"Eric is fine, Nick. I'm sure you saw that in your search. You are just lucky that I am the one who found it. I deleted it. You're welcome," she spits angrily. I swallow my pride and place my hand on her shoulder. Huffing, she shrugs it off.

"I'm sorry, Shari. It won't happen again."

"Nick, I went out on a limb for you. I recommended you for the Committee. There were plenty of other options considered, and I gave you a chance. Please stop questioning. Accept this amazing opportunity in life and give back as much as you can to make up for anything that doesn't sit right with you. That's what we all do and it has worked out pretty well for us. Please," she practically begs. I have never witnessed Shari so vulnerable.

"Thank you," I say. "Sincerely, thank you...for recommending me. I *am* grateful and I will do my best." She stares at me, then stomps down the steps and into the car that is waiting at our curb. Should I have said something else? As I watch her car drive away, I commit to at least being more careful when accessing the database.

21 / KATE

WAKING UP, I can feel it. Something has shifted. My body somehow feels...lighter. Had I not known what was happening, I probably would have simply gone on with my day. But I do know, and I am convinced that a part of me is now permanently gone. I don't even understand fully what that memory was. I allowed it to be eliminated without even considering that it may have been something worthwhile. The grief overwhelms me, whether out of exhaustion or legitimate sadness, I can't tell.

Nick walks in, carrying a breakfast plate and a glass of water. When he sees me, he immediately sets them down and pulls me onto his lap.

"It's completely normal to be emotional, your body went through a lot last night," he soothes.

Catching my breath, I refrain from speaking until I am able to bring my emotions to a manageable level. Nick simply holds me.

"The good news is that I know your treatment works," I finally manage to get out.

"How?" he asks, sitting back to look at me.

"I just know. I don't think I'll ever dream about her again," I say, the tears starting to flow. Nick looks confused.

"Why is that making you upset? That's what we wanted right?"

"I didn't like the dreams, they were horrifying. But they have been my constant companion for as long as I can remember. Somehow it tethered me to her, a mystery that kept her alive. Now, what if there's nothing?" I pause. The reality sinking deep within me. "Or what if I *needed* to know whatever she was trying to tell me. I am grieving the loss of a memory I didn't even have," I explain, sniffing.

Recognizing the hurt on his face, I backpedal. "This all sounds very ungrateful, and I need to say thank you." I sit up straight, wiping my tears. "Thank you, Nick, for putting in so much time and effort into finding something that will undoubtedly change the way we use reversal therapy. Thank you for taking a chance to help me. I love you," I say, pressing my lips against his.

He doesn't sink into the kiss as I had anticipated, rather pulls back and speaks abruptly. His voice is so quiet, I can barely hear him.

"I got a new assignment."

"What?" I gasp, my voice matching his. "An assignment?"

He nods.

"Will it—will you still be doing trials?"

"Yes, I will be able to finish my current research, definitely," he answers, pausing. "I was invited to serve on the Committee," he says hesitantly, gauging my reaction.

My head jerks back as if hit by an invisible blow. "Wow," I exhale. "That is...I think I need a minute. A moment ago I was thinking about my mom, and I can't switch gears that quickly.

"It's alright, let's just sit here for a moment."

He settles in next to me, and I focus on my breath. That memory is gone. I can think more on it later, but this is something I have to think about now.

"What does a seat on the Committee even mean?" I ask, my voice at a more normal level.

He looks at the floor. "I don't know exactly what my responsibilities will be yet, but it will be a transition. I'll give you more info as soon as I get it."

"They must really trust you, Nick," I say, surprised and suddenly proud. I honestly don't know what members of the Committee do, beyond the few small tasks I have witnessed through my service assignment, but I know they are important.

"I will do my best," he says modestly. "Hey, I also made an appointment for us. I can cancel it if you want, but I am feeling a push to start fertility. With all of these potential changes, I want to be available for you during those first few months, since I know they are the hardest."

My mind spins again. New assignment, new baby...

"Nick, this is a lot for one morning."

"I know, I'm sorry. I've been holding all of this in, and it seems that I am no longer able to. I didn't intend to dump this on you all at once."

"It's okay, it's just...a lot. As far as the fertility goes, I've been feeling the same way, but mostly because I am getting older by the day," I needle him, hoping to assure him that I'm not upset.

"Better by the day," he responds and I feel a pang of regret, my mind returning to the reversal. Lesser. I feel lesser.

"We could practice, you know, for when the fertility takes effect," Nick flirts.

I laugh. "Nick, the kids have got to be getting up any moment and I need to get Bentley off."

Nick looks at me strangely and bursts out laughing.

"What?" I ask, confused.

"What time do you think it is?" he asks through his guffaws.

"I—I just woke up, I thought it was maybe seven?" I stammer, suddenly questioning myself.

"Kate, it's nearly lunchtime," he says, laughing harder

I press my hands to my breasts. "How am I not leaking every-where?" I ask, horrified.

"You were under anesthesia, you won't be able to feed the girls for another couple of hours and that first amount will need to be discarded anyway," he says, calming himself. "You will likely have to supplement for a day or two—the stress caused by the procedure will have lowered your production."

"But...where are the kids?" I ask, still not wrapping my brain around the morning.

"Bentley is at conditioning, and I dropped the girls at the childcare center. They were thrilled," he says, grinning, obviously proud of himself.

"They took bottles?" I ask, warily.

"Like champs," he answers. "So. Practicing?" he repeats, leaning toward me.

"Pass me that breakfast first!" I exclaim, sneaking out from under him. His hands grasp my waist and I land gently back on the bed, laughing, the quilt covering my face. I can always eat later.

"Where are you?" I shout into the trees. "Tal! Bentley?" I hear giggles and move toward them. "I wonder where they could be," I say, feigning ignorance. Pulling the branches away, I expose their hiding place. "Gotcha!" I proclaim, throwing myself toward them.

"That took forever, Mom!" Bentley laughs.

"Well, stop finding such tricky spots and I will find you faster!" I laugh. "I still haven't found Dad."

"I think I know where he went," Tal says. "Follow me."

Tal leads us through the trees to a small clearing and Eric is standing there, beaming.

"It's like you aren't even trying, Dad," Tal sighs.

I run to him, kicking off my sandals and pressing my feet into the soft, spring grass. Suddenly, I see movement behind him. Shari? And Grace? They flank Eric, each holding one of his arms. Eric doesn't flinch, just continues to smile at me.

"It's ok, Kate. It's for the best," he says, allowing them to pull him back into the trees.

"Eric, wait!" I call, trying to follow after them. My feet are moving, but I am not gaining any ground. He is disappearing! I run faster, then faster. Pumping my legs as hard as I can. Tears streak my cheeks.

"Eric!"

"Kate!" I hear distantly. "Kate!"

"Kate! Kate! It's a dream, it's ok. I'm right here," he murmurs. I wrap my arms around his back, clinging to him. When my breathing slows, he tilts my face toward him.

I wake, pressed against Nick's chest, his strong arms enveloping me as they have countless times before. My breathing is shallow.

"So much for not dreaming about your mom, hey?" he asks, concern evident in his tone.

"It—it wasn't about my mom, Nick," I say, my voice barely audible. His eyebrows crease with worry. I don't need to say it. He knows.

"This will allow for simultaneous entry across systems..." the presenter drones on. I focus on my template, tweaking the formulas and watching the results, hoping to master the new system before leaving tonight. This is a constant strategy I employ every time we have new tech to play with at training. With three kids at home, I can't guarantee that I will have additional time to practice, and I don't want to be left behind. Tonight I am struggling more than usual. Nothing seems to be sticking. I keep slipping back into portions of my dream last night. It was particularly vivid and disturbing, and I want to hash it out—but with who? It will hurt Nick's feelings, regardless of whether he insists that he wants me to be open with him. And Shari—I don't know. I still hesitate to open up to her, despite the guilt that accompanies my inaction.

"Why am I still having these dreams?" I practically scream inside my head. The force of the thought takes my breath away, and I stare at my display, unmoving. Alright. You won't let me focus?

Let's hash this out then. I place my fingers on my sensor, attempting to appear engaged while I begin what is sure to be an intense mental conversation with myself.

"Yes, I am still dreaming about Eric, Bentley, and a child that YOU have made up," I assert. "I know that this is due to damage in my brain. Nick is working on it and already I have seen improvements. That's it! You will heal, I promise!" I suppress a hysterical laugh at the absurdity of this internal dialogue.

"Will I? Why are you dreaming of *them*? Your reversal damage was from when you were a kid," I shoot back.

"Memories are stored in multiple locations in the brain—did you consider that memories could overlap? That certain memories could randomly link, meaning that damage in that area could have affected another traumatizing moment in my life? Or, or! That reversal has gotten significantly more precise over the years? Maybe they screwed up!"

"Or, or? We're really saying that now?"

"Whatever."

"You're mad, Kate. You're mad and terrified, pushing those feelings so far down that they are gnawing at your subconscious so persistently that you are talking to yourself. Trying to explain it away. You can't! You know there is something else going on here and until you face it, you will continue to dream. You will continue to panic. You will—"

"STOP!" I shout, my hand nearly knocking my sensor to the

ground. The person next to me glances over and I straighten up, feigning interest in the speaker.

"Stop," I whimper internally. "I can't do this. I don't know what you are talking about. There's nothing else! Am I going crazy? Did having twins catalyze a mental break? I am doing all that I can!" I cry, tears welling up in my eyes. Blinking, I quickly wipe them from my cheeks.

"Why do you think you don't want to talk to Shari? Why do you think you still dream—"

"Stop!" I silently plead again. "I don't know, I don't—"

Emptiness swallows me then, from the pit of my stomach, rising toward my throat. Heat throbs through my arms and a cold sweat breaks out on my forehead.

"Hey, are you okay?" my neighbor asks, reaching out to touch my arm. I recoil instinctively, standing and knocking my chair to the ground with a clatter. Not even noticing the turn of heads in my direction, I bolt to the washroom. Bile is rising in my throat and I barely make it through the door before vomiting violently into the sink. Coughing and sputtering, I empty the contents of my stomach, moaning softly. Tears stream down my cheeks and, when I am sure it is safe, I slowly gather myself and rinse my mouth. The water swishes through my teeth, taking the accumulated acrid substance with it. Spitting, I reach for a compostable towel and fiercely wipe it across my lips, blowing my nose as an afterthought. My legs collapse and I sink to the cold tile in a heap.

Moments later, I force myself to rise, rinsing my mouth again and stare at the chunks of half-digested food stuck in the drain. Grabbing another towel, I scoop it out and wipe the porcelain clean with a soapy hand. Satisfied, I stumble out into the hallway. With each step, my resolve intensifies, and soon I am practically jogging toward my destination. Turning the corner, I see him.

"Nick!" I call desperately, my voice hoarse. He turns, seeing my pale face and stringy hair, and rushes toward me.

"Kate? Are you ok?" he questions, cringing as the scent of vomit registers. "What is going on?" It is only then that I notice the other committee members gathered behind him, moving toward us. Oddly recognizing the faces of two people standing behind him stops me in my tracks. Where would I have seen them before? I shake my head. That will have to wait. I need to say this now.

"Nick, I don't think the reversal therapy I had was a one-time thing," I blurt out. "What if it happened more than once? Wouldn't that explain the intensity of the dreams? The headaches? And, if my previous reversal surrounded my mom, the next one must have been about—"

"Stop!" Nick shouts forcefully, his face pinched into an expression I have never witnessed on him before. Reeling as if slapped, I step back.

"Nick, I'm trying to tell you—"

"No, Kate. You don't understand. I have personally seen your scans and there is no other evidence of reversal. I know this is frustrating and you are under an incredible amount of stress with the girls—"

"That's not it, Nick," I say, pursing my lips and shaking my head.

"This is the first time that I have felt solid. That I potentially have understanding and answers for the uneasiness I have felt for months."

"You have felt uneasy for months?" he asks, a pained expression on his face. "And here I thought we were doing well," he mutters, not meeting my eyes.

"No, I don't mean uneasy with us, I mean—"

"Seems like it would be the same thing," he concludes. My heart starts to pound and tears burn at the corner of my eyes. Something moves in my peripheral vision, and I realize that the Committee members are all still standing there, watching our interaction. Heat rises to my cheeks.

"I'm sorry, Nick. I am really emotional and I should have waited until we got home. Everyone, I'm so sorry to interrupt," I say, addressing them, then swiftly turn on my heel, moving as quickly as possible toward the exit. Remembering that my sensor and display are still in the training room, I change direction and run directly into something. Falling sideways, an arm reaches out to steady me. I look up to see Nick, searching my face. This. We have done this before. I freeze, absorbed by the odd deja vu of the moment.

"Let me help you, Kate," he says. Concern and something else I can't quite place in his expression.

"I forgot my things—" I whisper.

"I'll get them," he assures me, "sit," and lowers me to a bench along the wall, disappearing into the auditorium.

FINDING KATE'S sensor and water bottle quite easily, I reenter the hallway and realize that I also left something behind in all the chaos. My tablet is still in the Committee room, so I hurriedly make my way that direction, not wanting to leave Kate alone for long.

Walking briskly along the hall, I stop short, hearing hushed voices ahead of me. I slow my pace, walking softly toward the door, so as to not interrupt. As I approach, recognition makes me stop dead in my tracks.

"It seems to have worked effectively," I hear Grace say softly.

"How is her pair reacting?" the Director asks.

"It's been difficult, but he is adjusting nicely," she replies, still hushed. "Ellen is still experiencing some confusion with the shift."

Ellen? I treated an Ellen last week. Could they be referring to the same person? I'm being ridiculous. There are likely plenty of women named Ellen in Tier 1...yet I inch closer to the door, my heart hammering in my chest.

"That's to be expected," he replies. "At least, with this new procedure Nick has developed, we can be assured that the information is safe."

My breath catches in my throat. Information? Though I didn't pay close attention to the reason for her treatment, I think I would have noticed if it was linked to Committee information. Not hearing a reply, I back up silently, then walk quickly and loudly toward the room.

Grace and the Director startle as I enter.

"Hey," I say, "I forgot my tablet, and yep, there it is," I announce triumphantly, picking it up and adding it to my bag. "Sorry to interrupt," I add, hastily waving and retreating back to the hallway.

After dropping Kate off at home, I take the car back into the lab. The hallways are dark, and my fingers search the wall for the emergency lights. Flicking them on, I am momentarily blinded. As my eyes adjust, I make my way to the dock and log in, pulling up Ellen's file. Scanning, I find the intake information and am validated in my initial thoughts.

Reason for trial: Self reported headaches

Reason for initial treatment: Injury to child on 7/16, anxiety

. . .

No reference to 'information'. What does that even mean? And why would it need to be protected? I quickly review the initial scans I received, indicating the location in the brain that was to be treated. Frontal cortex and hippocampus. Predictable, but—wait. I scroll back through, leaning closer and double-checking. Why no amygdala? If it was an emotional, traumatic event—and I assume an injury to a child would be both—that would absolutely be affected. My heart begins to pound and a weight seems to settle on my chest. I open three more patient files from the same treatment batch and, after closely analyzing the prescribed reversal areas, it becomes obvious that there are more discrepancies. My cheeks flush, dread building in my stomach, as the realization sinks in. These patients. They weren't coming in voluntarily. Well, that's not completely true. They obviously walked in of their own accord, but they were lied to about the purpose for their visit. Opening file after file, I continue to absorb the inevitable truth. Could there be an explanation for this? How did I not notice this previously? I trusted the information I was given and didn't question, so intently focused on Kate and my own internal struggles. Selfish—and reckless—yet again. Running my hands through my hair, I log out and exit the lab, nearly slamming the door behind me.

I CAN'T SERVE them both. Kate, in her dramatic—very public—monologue, mentioned having answers for the first time and though I cringed when she said it, I resonate deeply with the sentiment now. Fear and embarrassment propelled my reaction in that moment. I couldn't allow Kate to continue and possibly harm my rapport with the Committee, or get herself in trouble. My harsh response was an attempt to protect her, though she likely won't see it that way. But all of that has shifted now. Understanding and peace flood my mind for the first time in what seems like forever. Finally. I know. It is as if the chaos that has been building within me for months has suddenly snapped into order.

I can't serve them both. The goals are not compatible, and I now realize that this is what I have been preparing for my whole life. The constant conditioning, service, leadership opportunities, all of it. Culminating in what some may perceive as a piddly conclusion, yet for me, life-changing. Everything within me is more full, more alive.

Walking into the meeting room tonight, I practically bounce on the balls of my feet. Shari is already seated when I enter and she looks at me, a quizzical expression on her face.

"That...is not how I expected to see you arrive tonight," she comments.

"What do you mean?"

"You look like you just made a world-altering discovery or something, and after last night—wait, *did* you make a discovery?" she suddenly asks, her eyes widening.

I laugh freely. "No, I wish," I say. "I don't know, I feel fantastic and I guess it shows?"

She shrugs, rolling her eyes at my apparent naivety.

The Director walks in, flanked by Grace who closes the door as she enters.

"I promise," I say, breaking the silence, "this meeting will not be long. I appreciate you coming and hope that what I have to say will relieve you of any concerns you may have after last night's...occurrences."

Their expressions are hard and it makes me almost giddy. I continue.

"As you know, I have been running trials on patients who are both receiving new therapy, as well as those who are suffering from side-effects of previous involuntary reversal treatments."

At this, their heads all snap to attention and I chuckle.

"Nick, that was never—" the Director starts.

"As a Committee member, I took my position seriously and did my homework, sir," I say pointedly, and his eyes dart to Grace. Good. Let him be uncomfortable.

"These trials have been extremely successful and I am positive that I will have a complete report with a full plan of action for reversal treatments moving forward within a couple of weeks. These," I say, pulling up a chart on my display and magnifying it, "are the results we already have."

Their eyes scan the data in unison, eyes widening. The Director clears his throat.

"Nick, this is impressive. How did you do it? What is the treatment?"

"I will outline everything in the report," I say.

"Surely you could—"

"I'm sorry, sir, but nothing can be implemented until I have the final trial honed and the results reported. Once I do, you three will be the first to know."

"I have to tell the Committees in other territories now, Nick. If we have something that could eliminate these negative effects—I mean, this will absolutely revolutionize the technology."

"I would be happy for you to share these results," I say.

"When will your report be ready?" he asks, practically salivating.

"I could call a regional Council meeting and we could share it all in person."

"If that's what you would prefer, I can give you a specific date by the middle of next week, once we have treated our last group of subjects." He nods in agreement.

"Nick," Grace interjects, "don't take this personally, but it seems like you are in the midst of a personal crisis. Kate looked terrible last night—"

"I know," I acknowledge, "but that's the beauty of it. Kate is struggling with adverse strain on her frontal cortex due to her extensive round of recent reversal therapy—administered in a matter of days, I might add."

All three of them look down.

"Kate will be one of my first subjects this week and I fully expect that her symptoms will disappear. Obviously, all of these patients will need to be monitored over time to ensure no symptoms crop up in the months and years to come, but we at least have a solid base to go on," I conclude, my body humming. This has unfolded exactly as I anticipated.

"Impressive, Nick. I have to admit, I was...quite concerned after last night's display."

"I know, that's exactly why I felt this meeting was necessary. One last thing I wanted to mention. I won't be following the transition guidelines with my family. With Kate undergoing more therapy, it will be better to keep her apprised."

"I don't think—" the Director begins, but I cut him off.

"With all due respect, sir, I have determined that this is the best course of action given the situation. I wasn't asking for permission. I know this is probably not typical of a new Committee member, but I hope you trust me enough to know that I wouldn't be altering protocol if it wasn't medically necessary."

The Director nods, his lips pursed.

"Thank you, Nick," Shari says, and I take that as my cue to exit.

On the way home, I send a message to Kate, asking if Bentley is available for some one-on-one time. I've been so wrapped up in trials, I haven't had the chance to connect with him. I haven't even talked with him about his Tier 3 questions, not that I can really say much at this point anyway.

I have to tell Kate first. My hands practically vibrate in anticipation of that moment. Days ago, the unknowns of her response kept me up at night, but now—I nearly laugh out loud at my recent former self. Why was I so unwilling to be honest with myself? Why did I continue to force an outcome that so obviously wasn't possible? Freedom isn't a byproduct of perfect outcomes. It is gained through the acceptance of *any* outcome that is a direct result of integral action. Today, I am finally a free man.

Bentley hops down the steps, trying to hide his enthusiasm. He adjusts his lips every few steps, but a shy smile continues to pull up the corners of his mouth. I step out into the golden evening light, arms stretched out to embrace him.

"Hey," I say through my smile, "thanks for hanging out with me."

"What are we going to do?" he asks.

"I thought we could go play some baseball—we haven't done that in a while. But if you have something you would rather do, I'm flexible," I add, searching his face for a reaction.

"Baseball sounds good," he says, still jumping from one foot to the next, kicking at small pebbles on the sidewalk.

"Baseball it is," I conclude, walking to the back of my car to take the gloves out of the storage compartment.

"How come you always have sports equipment back there now?" he asks.

"It's a perk of the job," I say, "these are ours to keep." His eyes light up.

"Really? How?"

"I'll explain another time," I say, handing him a glove. He immediately loses a ball in the neighbor's yard, trying to toss it to himself. I motion for him to follow me down the path toward the park.

Water droplets from afternoon rain still shimmer on the foliage that lines the walkway. Bentley taps the branches of trees and bushes as we pass, sending microcosmic rain showers to the ground below. When I notice a few mosquitos whining near my face, I regret not grabbing skin protectant. Hopefully someone else will be at the park and we can borrow some. Walking back home at this point would be quite anticlimactic.

"So Bent," I ask, "what's new with you these days? Are you

researching anything new?" He purses his lips, tapping another bush.

"I don't know, I'm taking a break right now."

"You are?"

"I still don't have enough information for my last study. Did you find the charts?"

"I did."

"Was I missing something?" he asks, pausing and cocking his head to the side.

"No, you definitely weren't. I think the information isn't up to date," I say. "I put in a request with the Committee, citing the inconsistencies you noticed." That part is actually true, I just can't give him the full truth. Yet.

"You did?" he asks, moseying along again.

"I did."

"When are they going to update it?"

"I'm not sure, but I think I will have more information for you soon. In the meantime, what else are you interested in?" I ask, noticing a small mushroom growing at the edge of the path and stopping to inspect it.

"Growing," Bentley answers, squatting down next to me. "I want to fix the soil so we can grow things everywhere again."

"That," I say, ruffling his hair, "is a worthy goal."

"Hey! I just brushed that!" he says, standing up and frantically straightening the strands.

"You say you just brushed it?" I tease, reaching toward his head with a dramatically outstretched hand. He laughs and runs further up the path.

"I won't mess it up, again," I chuckle, calling after him. "C'mon, don't get too far ahead!"

"Race you!" he shouts, his short legs kicking up rocks as he takes off. I laugh out loud as he passes, his right fingers gripping the waistband of his pants out of habit as he runs, taunting me, and disappearing between the trees.

25 / ERIC

VAL'S LONG, blond hair hangs down her back, obscuring the back of the bench she is leaning against. As I approach, her head turns and she lights up. Standing, she greets me with a warm embrace. This has felt natural to me for a while now. I'm not sure exactly when it shifted, but I'm glad it did.

Returning herself to the bench, Val shifts, allowing me space to sit next to her.

"How was your day?" I ask, a smile slightly lifting the corner of my mouth. I try to tone it down, not wanting to come across too strong, but I can't help it.

"Just a normal day," she says, laughing breathily. "What about you?"

"We prepped the legumes—they should be thoroughly soaked by tomorrow for planting. That took up more time than I had anticipated, but I was able to get to that fertilizer spill, you'll be glad to know."

"Ugh, finally!" she goads. "Will we actually have a date where you don't smell like fish?"

My mouth drops in mock disgust. "Val, here I am telling you about my deep, loyal servitude and you are criticizing my scent?"

She laughs, throwing her head back the way she does, brushing her hand against my arm. The sun glints off her hair, almost creating a halo effect around her face.

"So...this is a date?" I ask softly.

"Oh, I didn't mean—"

"No, it's okay, I'm just giving you a hard time," I say lightly. My hand, nearly of its own accord, reaches out and my thumb caresses her jaw line. Her laughter stops abruptly, her eyes not leaving mine. I move closer to her, feeling her arm slip around my waist. Suddenly, my sensor buzzes—then pings—breaking the spell.

I smile apologetically and check my messages. What could possibly be this urgent?

Tal in nurse's office, in pain. Please come quickly.

My lips draw into a frown as I hastily scrawl a response.

"Is everything alright?" Val asks hesitantly.

"I'm not sure," I say. "It's Tal."

"Do you want me to come with you?"

"Of course I do," I say, "but I'm not sure what I will be walking into. Given—well, I think it may be best for me to go alone," I conclude. She nods.

"Totally. Call me when you know? We could still take our walk a bit later," she suggests and I nod.

"Thanks for understanding," I say apologetically, turning and beginning to run the three blocks to Tal's location.

Entering the office and finally able to stand still, sweat drips down my back and I gasp for breath. It's been awhile since I full-out sprinted anywhere.

"Hi Eric," the nurse greets me, hurriedly whisking me to the back room. My heart sinks when I see Tal, his face covered in blood, holding a rag to his nose. Lacerations pepper his cheeks, and his eyes are lolling back in his head.

"What happened," I whisper, tears stinging my eyes. At the sound of my voice, Tal focuses and gives a wan smile. He attempts to answer me, but the nurse shushes him.

"I'll fill him in, you just hold still so I can continue treating these wounds, okay?" she instructs, taking a seat near his head. I am mesmerized watching her fingers deftly manipulate the sealing tape in a delicate line, pulling both edges of his clean wound into their original position.

"I don't anticipate any scarring," she comments, reading my thoughts. I release my breath, not even realizing I had been holding it.

"It was a lab accident," she says. "Tal added the solution to his beaker and it exploded almost immediately. Thankfully, the solution itself had mostly neutralized during the reaction. He only has a few small chemical burns on his arms, but those are mild and should heal completely within a few days. The main damage was caused by the flying shards of glass."

I shudder, imagining shards of glass penetrating his eyes, the vitreous oozing—

"I was wearing eye protection, Dad," Tal says, his voice muffled. Am I that obvious?

"And it's a good thing you were," the nurse comments. Looking at the pattern of cuts, closest together around his nose, fanning out toward his scalp, I can't help but agree.

"Thank you," I say, "for calling me. I am so sorry this happened, Tal." Reaching over his midsection, I hold his free hand.

"How did the solution explode, exactly?" I question. The nurse looks at me pointedly.

"That...is under investigation currently," she huffs, her eyes flashing. "According to Dr. Jesmer, there is no possible way any substrates in the lab today could have reacted that violently. We think—well, there's a possibility that this was someone's idea of a practical joke."

"What?" I ask, incredulous. "Seriously?"

Tal meets my eyes. "It happens, Dad."

"Since when?" I ask, my voice rising in volume.

"Don't worry, we will be thorough in our report," the nurse soothes. "Tal's right, though, every once in awhile, we have a student suffering more than most. They don't always act appropriately and we have to intervene," she prattles on, moving swiftly from one cut to the next.

"Okay, Tal, time for the worst of it," she announces, removing the rag from his nose. She soaks a large pad of gauze in cleansing solution and begins to gently dab the area. Tal begins to almost look like himself again, just slightly...puffier. He winces as she presses over a section of raw skin above his lip.

"Do you need more pain meds?" she asks.

"No," he answers bravely, clenching his teeth.

Tal sleeps on my shoulder the entire ride home. They were considerate enough to call a car for us, and my legs practically hum with gratitude.

Suddenly remembering, I tap my sensor to send a message to Val. I didn't realize it was already so late, and I hope she understands. Tonight could have been definitive for us. My shoulders slump, wishing things would have played out differently. Tal moans and I immediately react, shifting my body to accommodate a more comfortable position for him.

He wakes enough upon our arrival to walk into the house, but he isn't completely lucid. I repress a laugh at his mumbled responses. He likely won't remember anything from tonight, but with my luck, he *would* recall his Dad laughing at him in his time of need. In his bedroom, I am barely able to administer his next dose of medication before he completely crashes.

With Tal sleeping peacefully in his bed, the weight of the evening settles on me and I lie on the living room floor, not even taking the time to put the used vial in the sink.

I am awakened hours later by the haunting sound of someone wailing. Blinking, my eyes dart around the room, taking in my surroundings. The sound is coming from the bedroom, and the previous evening clicks into my memory.

"Tal," I think, jumping to my feet.

"Tal?" I call out tentatively, slowly opening the door and creeping toward the bed. Even in the dim light, I can tell that his wounds are still beautifully sealed, which is impressive, considering the intensity of his thrashing.

"Tal," I say gently, shaking his shoulder as I avoid his flailing arms. When he doesn't wake immediately, I apply more pressure. His eyes shoot open, wild and frenzied.

"Tal," I repeat, "it's alright, you are having a bad dream. It's alright," I soothe. He blinks, staring intently at me.

"Where's Mom? And Bent?" he blurts out.

"Tal, you are on some pretty intense medication," I say. "You had a bad dream."

"No Dad, I feel fine," he assures me, lifting himself up to a sitting position. Beads of sweat lace his forehead. "It was real. I remember. We were sitting in a room, maybe in a medical office? I don't know, it was really bare bones. Bent and I were sitting on chairs, watching you hold Mom. She was crying, and then you both laughed, then Bentley and I hugged you—something bad was happening. I was so sad," he says, stumbling through with misty eyes. "Dad, I have had dreams before, but this was different."

My heart aches, listening to him imagine a life where Kate and I were together. Where he had grown up with her, possibly having a brother.

"Tal, I—"

"It wasn't a dream, Dad," he asserts.

"Okay," I say, capitulating. Driving the freshly opened tide of anguish down, I swallow hard. "Okay, not a dream. I will see what I can find out." He nods, sinking back down to his pillow.

"How is your face feeling?" I ask, hastily changing the subject before I break.

"Pretty good, I think."

"Would you like more medication?"

"I'm okay," he says yawning.

"Well, let me know if you change your mind," I reply, giving his shoulder a pat. Closing the door, I walk across the hall and drop my clothes to the floor, collapsing into bed, my chest tight. I give in to the tears then and eventually fall into a fitful sleep, my pillow damp.

I CAN'T LOOK at him. We still haven't discussed what happened the other night, but the memory of it burns within me. All those people, looking at me like that—Nick not even listening to what I had to say.

We sit here, side by side, feeding the girls and yet I feel like a chasm has opened up between us. He coos while he feeds Leah, and I literally want to punch him in the face.

"I think she's finished, Kate," he says cheerily.

I nod, continuing to fill the tiny spoon for Beth.

Nick leans on the counter, watching me.

"Kate, c'mon. How long are we going to do this?"

I focus on Beth, my hand suddenly shaky.

"I am so sorry for how I acted. It was slightly stressful, if you remember. And I have seen your scans, I—" Sighing, he shakes his head and begins rinsing out Leah's bowl.

"It's not that, Nick," I murmur and his head snaps hopefully toward me. They are the first words I have spoken to him. "I had something really important to tell you. It felt so intense and you were the one person I thought would understand. I don't care if I was right or wrong, I needed someone to listen and you...humiliated me," I finish, tears beginning to overflow with the physical release of these words I have been holding so tightly. I look away, wiping them on my sleeve.

Beth spits out her last bite. Wiping the food off her lips, I pull her out of her seat, moving her to the living room to play. Leah complains, seeing her sister's newfound freedom. Nick lifts her out so she can join her.

"I am truly sorry, Kate. I don't know what else to say," he says softly. Reluctantly, I go to him then, allowing him to hold me. I think of all the times he has comforted me, waited patiently while I struggled, and my ears burn with the realization that I have been punishing him for a singular, isolated mistake.

"I'm sorry," I say. "You are so supportive normally, I shouldn't have made such a big deal out of it."

He kisses the top of my head, his breath hot against my skin. I raise my eyes to his, reaching around the back of his neck and pulling him toward me. Our kiss is tender, searching. I begin to kiss him more intently and he pulls back.

"Nick—"

"The girls—" he says.

"They'll be fine," I argue. "They haven't figured out how to stand yet, the play boundary will keep them safe."

"I—"

"Please, Nick," I whisper, watching his face for any sign of why he is resisting. Finding nothing, I lower my eyes and drop my arms to my side. I take a step back, only to be pulled fiercely into his embrace. His lips crush against mine and my heart races. I pull at his clothes, wrapping my legs around his waist as he picks me up and carries me to the bedroom.

Hours later, after going through the motions for the remainder of the day, I lie between the sheets, staring blankly at the dark ceiling. It didn't help. Though this afternoon was a wonderful distraction, the knowledge within me still resides, as solid as it existed that day at training. I know something is missing. I *know* those dreams are telling me something. But what? What is the truth? And why won't Nick even consider the possibility? I know he has seen my scans, but how does he know that he's seen everything? Normally, he is open—eager, even—to exploring my ideas. Why is this different?

"Are you still up?" Nick whispers.

"Yes," I say, unmoving.

"What are you thinking about?" he asks, flipping over onto his back. He doesn't reach out, just lays beside me, our arms gently touching.

"So much, Nick. So. Much," I answer, exhaling loudly.

"I need to tell you something," he says.

"I'm listening."

"This new position...it's given me access to information not readily accessible by the general population of Tier 1. When Bentley talked about Tier 3 the other day—"

"I thought you forgot about that."

"I didn't forget, Kate," he says, propping himself up on one elbow, looking down at my face, my eyes still fixed directly into the blackness above me. "I searched everything I could find and came up empty. Do you remember that night after our meeting? When I was a complete mess?"

I nod. "I thought you already explained that moment to me—"

"Only part of it," he interjects. "I brought those questions up with them. I didn't know what to think after the Director asked me to leave, but I was terrified."

"Then you were offered the position," I say, finally meeting his eyes.

"Right," he sighs, dropping back to the pillow. "I know they still aren't giving me every scrap of information, but I do have some. Tier 3. It was phased out years ago."

I sit up straight, holding the sheets to my chest.

"What?" I demand.

"I know, it sounds impossible, but it's true. Think about it. Even Bentley noticed the inconsistencies in the numbers."

"But what about the service assignments? The resources that we prepare? How—"

"I had the same questions, and I asked them. Our society works because everyone has a purpose. Everyone is required to sacrifice, and that necessitates someone to sacrifice for—"

"Hold on, Nick. This makes no sense," I say, pinching the bridge of my nose between my forefinger and my thumb. "My mom worked with Tier 3. She was responsible for distribution, we have talked about this! How could—"

"Kate, will you please let me finish?" Nick says softly. "I don't know what your mom was working on, but it wasn't Tier 3 distribution. It's possible she was working on reintegration. I can look into it, but I doubt there's much to go on," he says, pausing. When I don't answer, he continues. "Back to your previous questions, with Tier 3 petering out, the Committee had to adjust things to continue on with our current model. Could you imagine? People sitting around, useless?"

"But we have plenty of resources. Why would Tier 3 need to be eliminated if we have plenty?"

"It's not a matter of having enough, it's an issue of progress. Efficiency."

"If we have resources available, why couldn't we at least improve the quality of life for Tier 2? For Tier 1, even? Couldn't we open that up to everyone?"

"Play that out, Kate," Nick says patiently.

The Tier system would truly be obsolete in that situation, so what would replace it? I can't come up with anything that doesn't resemble a past government that ultimately failed.

"I don't—I don't know what it would look like," I admit.

"We would be taking a chance on something that has absolutely no history of success, risking the possibility that it could become something that *does* have a history of failure."

"Couldn't we put our best thinkers together?"

"That's literally what the Committee did," he argues, putting his arms behind his head. I glance over, my eyes lingering on his chest before reaching their intended destination.

"What did they decide?" I ask, my face inches from his.

"That it's better to continue with what we know. Safer," he says.

"How?"

"The Committee is absorbing the extra resources," he answers, pausing for my reaction. Any words I conjure seem to die in my throat. What does that even mean?

"We will be responsible for pushing society forward, and those resources will allow us the flexibility to do that. How can we have the creativity to think outside the box when we haven't experienced anything *but the box*. We can travel, study whatever is important to us, there aren't any limits. Only unlimited growth," he explains and my mind grows wild with possibility. Travel? No limits? It's literally every fantasy I have had since I was a child.

Then, the realization that I would be taking more than my share—using resources for my personal benefit—hits. I couldn't. I couldn't do that. How is this justifiable?

"All of these people. Nick, all of these people are contributing. And for what? For personal growth? It seems like there has to be a better way to accomplish that," I argue, turning to him.

"I think they will continue to get plenty in return," he says. "Think of how much better our society could be if we had enough resources for all of my research projects alone. I have no doubt that each of those will shed light on significant issues. And Bentley? Unlimited access to technological research. He just told me the other day that he wants to clean the soil, Kate. Everyone will benefit from that progress."

"In Tier 1, but what about Tier 2? How will this benefit them? Will they just be an afterthought like Tier 3? They still suffer, there's still violence..." I counter.

He nods. "To such a lesser extent than in the past, though, you have to at least recognize that."

"Definitely, I know. I'm not trying to say that we haven't made progress, but—I guess it just seems like this would be a natural time to evolve—to take the risk—and assimilate. Try something better." I pause, something clicking in my subconscious from earlier in the conversation. "Wait, Nick, what happened to those left in Tier—"

Nick shifts positions and sighs. "Someday, I would love to see assimilation, too. It's just not going to happen now. So we have the choice: either jump in and help design the future, or let it pass us by. I'm not good at being a bystander, Kate, and this is an incredible opportunity to make a contribution as a family."

As a family. I am sick. I can't go on living like this. I—

"Your appointment is tomorrow," Nick says.

"My appointment?" I ask, drawing a blank.

"The follow up treatment, I thought I told you about that?" he questions, lifting himself to his elbows.

"I must have forgotten," I mumble. "Nick, I'm worried about my milk supply. It hasn't been fully restored after the last procedure. If I go in tomorrow—"

"The girls will be fine, Kate. They are taking bottles regularly now, and we have plenty of milk in the freezer. You may...well, depending on how this visit goes, you can determine if you would like to continue going in for boosters. I don't know if they will make a difference. We could consider treating another area to—"

"No," I say. "I am sure the other dreams will fade in time. Like you said, I don't have any other history of reversal."

"I'm sorry, Kate. I wish I had more answers for you," he offers, but his eyes are guarded. My chest squeezes, perceiving that Nick can't be my ally in this search for truth. He has made it clear that my opinions on this topic aren't open for discussion anymore, yet I know I need answers. I am on my own.

NICK PLACES the electrodes gently on my skin. My arms tense involuntarily, a frustrating, irrational response. There is nothing to fear, but I can't convince my body of that reality. The port has already been placed and, as Nick connects it, I am mesmerized by the consistent drops, slowly entering my system. Eyelids heavy, I rest my head...

The door opens and my eyes search the room, finding Eric, Tal, and Bentley seated along the wall. I rush to them, dropping to my knees and wrapping my arms around them. Bent's hair tickles my face, Tal is taller than I remembered. It's been only a day, but I swear they look older. We cry together, emotion draining out of us into a collective whole. Eventually, my eyes hunt for Eric. Rubbing their backs, I release them and go to him.

I am immediately home. His strong arms seem, to me, a barrier, and my fears dissipate with every rise and fall of his chest. I laugh through my tears when I feel Bentley worm between us, creating space for his body to join the embrace. I hate this. All of it.

We pile into a heap on the benches, none of us wanting to miss a moment with each other.

"What happened yesterday?" I ask.

"I shouldn't have told you to go," Eric blurts out. "I was trying to be considerate of Nick, which I still think was the right thing to do. But I had no idea the Committee was aware of what we had in mind. I thought we would have more time to figure something out. That we could go to them with a plan." He looks down. "I was completely naive."

"What is happening?" Bentley whimpers.

I breathe. "I don't really know," I say. "Dad's research has made it so we need to make some adjustments, but Dad and I don't want to be apart. Somehow we haven't been able to make the choice that is best for the most people." I don't really know how to explain this. "We are stuck. Berg is trying to help us. I know it's really hard, guys."

"I don't want to be split up!" Tal shouts. "This is crazy!"

He obviously understands more than I thought.

"I don't want that either. But do you remember when we used that machine on the tour? How good it felt? They are going to use that to help us all get through it," I assure him.

"But why? I don't understand *why* this is happening," Tal says. I look at Eric. It won't hurt to tell them the whole story. It will be gone from their brains after today, anyway.

"My research...well, it created a new rubric for pairing. We needed to find people who matched with these particular markers and we weren't having much success. Long story short...your mom was a match with Nick. There are so many complexities that we can't get into right now, but I made the commitment to—" he chokes, unable to breathe. The boys stare at him, eyes wide. He composes himself and continues.

"I made the commitment to step away so Mom could be placed into this new pairing, but I couldn't do it guys. I came back for the ceremony—" The tears freely roll down his cheeks, and his lips are agonizingly curled, barely allowing him to speak. I jump in.

"Dad came home because he was having a really hard time being away from us. He thought he would never get to be with us again. We talked, and he told me what was going on. It was so helpful for me to have more information."

We continue to discuss, answering their questions to the best of our ability, though neither of us knows exactly how this will all play out. Bentley breaks the silence.

"So what do we do now?"

"We just enjoy these last few moments together. Enjoy being who we are now. We had a pretty great run, didn't we?" Eric says.

My throat constricts. Eric looks at me and smiles. He rises and moves toward me, his motions so familiar. I laugh when he reaches down to pull up Bentley's pants. After hugging the boys, Eric asks them if he can talk with me privately for a moment. They sit down obediently and pretend like they aren't waiting to absorb every word.

"Hi," he murmurs, looping his arms around my waist. He pulls me close.

"Hi," I say. "Not quite the day I had planned for us."

"What did you have planned?" he asks.

"Lots of entertainment for the boys," I whisper conspiratorially.

"Seems like that would leave us on our own," he says, softly kissing my cheek.

"Huh," I say, heat rising to my face. "Pretty sure they are watching us in here."

"Does it look like I care?" Eric says, moving his hands under the back of my shirt. It's so familiar. I am losing all of this. All of this knowing. A wave of emotion swells up from my gut and I suppress a sob. His fingertips press into my back as he crushes me to his chest. His breathing becomes shallow and I bury my face in his neck, tears streaming down my cheeks, soaking his shirt collar. We stay frozen like this for what seems like hours—yet not nearly long enough.

"I love you, Kate," he whispers. His voice is coarse and shaky. "I don't care if that makes me weak or hinders me from doing my societal duty. I believe in my research. I know it will make the world a better place. And even then, I can't force myself to leave you. I made myself physically ill trying."

I push back and look up at him, trying to gain some semblance of clarity.

"You do look terrible," I choke out, and he laughs heartily, coughing at the unexpectedness of it.

"Thanks for validating my self-diagnosis," he says when he can breathe again.

"Sorry, for some reason I feel a bit hysterical!" I say, patting his face. The contact with his stubbled chin immediately sobers me. "I don't want to do this, Eric. And I am so sorry that I moved forward with everything...with Nick. I was trying to do what I thought— "

Eric puts his fingers on my lips. "No, it's ok. You are amazing. I was so grateful that you were willing to be strong. I am sorry I couldn't be."

Our connection is broken when the door opens. It's Shari.

Blinking awake, I take in my surroundings. Nick hovers over me, and his hand is steadily grasping mine. My heart pounds so loudly that I can't hear anything over the sound of rushing blood. For a moment, Nick seems as if he is about to cry. My eyebrows draw together and I squint, trying to clear my vision. When his face comes into view, his lips are drawn into a concerned smile, but his expression looks unimpeded by emotion.

"I told you it would be quick," he jokes, knowing that I have absolutely zero reference point for time. "How do you feel?"

I try to speak, but the words won't form. I stare intently into his eyes, searching for some indication that he knows the monumental shift that just occurred in my brain.

"I'll give you a moment," he says, patting my hands. "The goal with the boosters is to solidify the first treatment—release any other potential echoes. Basically ensure that you won't have any chronic issues. In a week or so, we'll scan and compare your current image with the one we saved previously. We should be able to tell if everything took."

He begins sanitizing the equipment and I finally regain control of my breathing.

"Nick, would getting more boosters be equivalent to what I just experienced?" I ask, my voice a hoarse whisper. He nods.

"They are almost identical," he says. "See how you feel in a few hours, then we could potentially do a few more if you think there's a benefit," he shrugs. "I figure it can't hurt and I'd rather have more solidity before we do your final scan. I have to report that to the Committee in a few weeks. Selfishly, I want my work to look good," he laughs. "But your brain always looks good, so no worries there."

I smile, trying to react normally. He has to report these scans to the Committee? That was a memory—it *happened*—I can feel it in my bones. This definitely cannot be the booster that Nick intended to give, and the fear of being discovered jumps in my chest. I can't tell him because I selfishly yearn for more. Is it possible that somehow, other memories will be restored? The idea that I could receive actual answers to the questions that plague me daily sends me into a fit of near desperation. My fingers grip the sterile bench as I turn away from Nick's view.

If the memories do continue to be restored, what will my scans look like? Will the Committee be able to tell the difference? Of course they will. Wait. Nick took a scan of me after my first treatment and it would have to be in my file. What if—what if I could receive the boosters and somehow save that initial scan as my *final* scan instead? My heart is pounding when Nick comes into view, reaching out a hand to help me up. *Is this possible?*

"Sleep," Nick says, and my head snaps up, eyes flashing. He pulls me close, laughing under his breath. "Trust me," he whispers, "you need sleep."

"BETTER," I nod. "A lot better."

Dr. Houser smiles. "What do you think made the difference?"

"I don't actually know? I've thought about that this week, and it's probably a couple of things. Meeting with you that first time was kind of an eye-opener. I thought I was doing just fine, but having to physically admit how few people I interacted with...that definitely brought things into perspective. And, I think, somewhere deep down I wouldn't allow myself to let go of her."

"Of Kate?" she asks gently.

"If I'm honest, I still don't want to. I can convince myself that, if I think about her all the time—really fiercely hold her in my heart throughout the day—she will somehow exist again. I can keep her with me."

"Does it work?"

"I mean, you already know the answer to that. It obviously was not working for me. And it didn't keep her alive. It only tethered me to her—kept me dead, in a way. Don't get me wrong, I will always love and treasure her memory, but, I don't want it to anchor me anymore. I need to float. To move on in my own journey. I can come back and visit it whenever I want. If I need to."

Dr. Houser smiles knowingly, raising her glasses to sit atop her head. "It sounds like you are well on your way. How is Val?"

My cheeks flush. "It has been extremely beneficial getting to know her. She's a really good person."

"I'm glad. Eric, while I would be happy to continue meeting with you, I don't know that you need it. Now that you have opened yourself up to new and healthy relationships, I suspect that will be all the support you need."

I nod, sitting straight in my chair. "Thank you—" I start, my voice choking up.

She moves from behind her desk and I stand to embrace her.

"You're a good man, Eric. It's been my pleasure."

The walk home feels lonelier somehow. Is it appropriate to grieve a relationship that was never intended to mean this much to me? The depth of my sadness at parting with Dr. Houser serves to highlight the obvious lack of intimacy in my life. I know she's right. I can move forward now on my own. But it still isn't easy.

"Thanks for helping me with this," I say appreciatively, handing

Val another seed box. "Normally this takes me all day, but I think we may be done in another hour."

"Happy to help," she smiles, scanning the box and categorizing it in the appropriate transport cart.

"I could be keeping up with this all year, but somehow it seems more efficient to just get it all out of the way one time instead of having to sort and rotate every week. Is that poor logic on my part?"

"We may need to have a clinical trial to properly assess that opinion," she says with a laugh. As she reaches over to retrieve another box, my eyes are drawn to the smooth, lean muscles on her arms. How did I not notice her strength before? I look away, not wanting her to notice my lingering eyes. Is it possible, without explanation, to show my attraction while expressing a true depth of emotion? I want Val to know that I am attracted to her, but not only physically. To her positivity, selflessness, attention to detail, strength, all of it. Somehow, getting caught staring at her arms doesn't seem like the right way to send that message.

"Are you ok?" she asks. "You seem distracted."

I clear my throat. "Tell me more about your assignment. You know the ins and outs of mine," I tease, pulling another crate down.

She smiles. "It's really not that exciting. You know most of it,"

"I know the basics, but what does an actual day look like?"

"When I am out visiting sites or at headquarters?"

"Headquarters, unless site visits are different than this?"

She pauses in her task, breathing deeply. "Well, I typically only visit any given site once in a calendar year, so it's quick and dirty. Get in, interview coordinators, and take notes on any obvious issues. Everything else can be submitted over the network."

"Wait, only once a calendar year? You've been here at least three times this year, and this visit has lasted, by my count, much longer than a day," I accuse in good humor, leaning against the shelf.

Val blushes, looking down, a box still in her hands.

"Are we doing something wrong here?" I ask, suddenly concerned. "Val, if I'm not fulfilling my assignment, I hope you would be honest with me—"

"Eric, are you really that oblivious?" she blurts, throwing the box into the nearest cart. "This center is run immaculately! Everything is organized, the production is better than almost any other site I visit, the soil is in better condition—"

"Wait, those are all good things, right? Are you mad at me?" I ask, backing up at her sudden intensity.

"I'm not mad, I'm—I'm frustrated!" she stammers, exasperation in her tone. "How do you not see this? I come here more frequently because of *you*. I enjoy being around you—I am ridiculously attracted to you, Eric, and I respect your work ethic, your dedication to your son, all of it. Do I really have to spell it out?"

I stare at her, my body still. That's how you do it, I guess. Everything I wanted to express, she just said out loud. And it wasn't awkward, at least not for me. She looks a little worked up. Before I grin, or laugh, and get myself in trouble, I close the gap between us and pull her to me. With her face cupped in my hands, I kiss her. Her arms slowly weave around my back, making every nerve ending come alive. How have I been living without this in my life? I kiss her slowly, softly, desperately hoping that this moment will last forever.

DAY AFTER DAY I ask for boosters. Day after day, my memories are returned. I've lived them over again—each instance feeling as real today as the moment in time when they originally occurred. The soul-crushing loss of my parents, the ache of losing that pregnancy, the exhilaration of watching the boys take their first steps, the giddiness of feeling Eric close to me for the first time. Every fiber of my being thirsts for them, and it is all I can do to walk through my routine each day as if nothing has changed. When Nick and Bentley are absent, I hold the girls and silently weep. Though I blame physical fatigue, it's mostly due to emotional closure that Nick no longer comes home early. There are some things I just can't fake.

Today is my last session and it can't come fast enough. I frantically prepare bottles for the girls. My hands shake, and milk spills on the counter—drops of liquid gold going to waste. I mutter under my breath, hastily wiping it up and securing the nipples to the bottle lids. My milk hasn't ever come back and, with the extra procedures I am doing, I don't anticipate that it will. The girls still tug at my shirt when I hold them, adding to the guilt I already feel daily at being distracted and emotionally absent. As I lay them down to nap, I embrace them fiercely, their soft hands tangling in my hair and exploring my ears. I laugh, despite my inability to find humor in anything these days. As tears spring to my eyes and roll down my cheeks, the girls graze them gently with their fingertips, seeming to connect in a way that no adult could with the emotions warring inside of me.

Walking into the lab is routine at this point. I navigate the empty halls, never seeing a soul, passing the familiar doors until I find the one I know. Opening the door today, I stop in my tracks. Tamara is sitting behind the display, her hair pulled up in a tight bun, working furiously.

"Kate?" she acknowledges, looking up.

"Hey, I wondered if Nick was here?" I say hesitantly.

"No, he was called into an unexpected meeting. I had to stay late to finish the trials." She stands upright and her hand settles on her hip. "Not exactly what I had planned for today," she laughs.

"No kidding," I say.

"Can I help you with something?" she asks.

"No, that's alright," I respond, turning back toward the door. Turning my head as an afterthought, I ask, "How have patients been doing with their boosters?"

Her face pinches together. "Boosters?" she asks quizzically.

"I guess that's what I call them, maybe that's not their actual name," I laugh. "I meant their additional sessions to solidify the original treatment."

Tamara doesn't respond immediately. "I think you might be confused. We don't ever do additional treatments, that would be redundant," she says slowly, eyebrows drawn together.

"I must have misunderstood something Nick said," I say hastily. "Please don't say anything to him. That would be embarrassing," I joke.

"Hey, there is so much going on here, it's easy to mix things up," she says knowingly. "Have a great evening, Kate."

I nod and step through the door frame back into the hall. Pausing, I close my eyes and breathe deeply, pressing my back against the door. The wood feels smooth against my fingertips and its solidity grounds me. I tap my sensor, wondering if I somehow missed a message from Nick in my rush to leave the house. Nothing. Utterly confused, I begin the long walk to the exit, only to stop halfway.

This might be my only chance. I need to access those images and see what I am working with. While I don't have a recent scan to compare, I could at least gather the information they already have on me. I turn and walk back toward the lab.

Opening the door, Tamara again looks up from her desk.

"Hey, I am so sorry to bother you, but when I messaged Nick, he asked me to transfer a spreadsheet for him. Something the

Director is asking for that he doesn't have saved on his shareable file. He said you might have a data traveler here for me to use?"

Tamara rummages through a small drawer in the corner of the table and retrieves a sleek metal oval, about the size of my thumb.

"How large is the file?" she asks, and I shrug my shoulders.

"If it's a spreadsheet, this should do it," she says, passing it to me.

"Can I find it on your dock?" I ask.

"No, private patient and trial information is only stored on Nick's personal dock for security purposes. Did he give you his login information?"

"I—"

"That's a trick question," she laughs. "It would be against protocol if he did."

I sigh in relief, thankful not to have to come up with a false excuse for my lack of information.

"Though I don't have the same level of clearance, you should be able to access any non-restricted trial information with my login on that dock," she says, pausing, her eyebrows suddenly drawing together. "Why didn't Nick just ask me to securely transfer the information via superwire?"

I laugh. "He probably just wanted me to feel useful."

A smile crosses her lips and she rolls her eyes. "Sounds like him."

After typing in her credentials, she leaves me to it. I am overwhelmed with the sheer expanse of information before my eyes as the dock boots up to the main screen. Does he not know how to organize information? There is hardly any blank space on the display, and seemingly no pattern to the placement of the files. Then, something catches my eye. A small image of a columbine with a 'K' next to it sits near the bottom of the screen, standing out from the bland labels surrounding it. I press on it and find a grid of images, all labeled by date. I breathe a sigh of relief.

Minimizing the display below the edge of the standing desk, I open the one closest to my estimate of when Eric and I were separated. Next to it, I pull up the one labeled one week later. The difference is striking. Though I'm no expert in interpreting brain scans, I can see large areas—specifically in the amygdala and hippocampus—where neural activity is significantly altered between the two. Checking the other images, I don't find any that match the circumstances as well as these two. Then, I see my most recent scan. The one taken right after my initial treatment. Opening it, I see yet another transformation. The cluttered areas from the previous scan are softened, almost smoothed out. I transfer the images to the traveler, slipping it into my pocket. Studying these images should allow me to recognize patterns in my final scan. To know whether all has been restored, or to recognize other areas that have been erased without my knowledge.

"Are you finding everything okay?" Tamara asks, sending a jolt through my spine.

"Yep," I answer. "His display is a mess, but I finally found what he needed."

Tamara snorts. "At least I'm not the only one who struggles."

Logging out, I shut down the dock and retreat for a second time back into the dimly lit hall. My shoulders finally relax and, though I want to collapse, I force myself to make it to the car.

THE SOUND of a car door closing outside the house later that evening sends adrenaline shooting through my veins. Kate's home, and I know she will have questions. I didn't intend to miss her tonight, but when the ball was rolling, I certainly didn't try to stop it. Though I want to keep her in the dark, there is also a small part of me that hopes to get caught.

When she still hasn't entered the house a few minutes later, I stand and walk toward the window. A knock on the door startles me and, without pausing, I close my fingers around the knob and swing it wide.

"Shari?" I say, trying to process a reason for her to be standing on my step.

"Hey Nick, is Kate home yet?" she asks briskly.

"Honestly, I thought you were Kate. She should be home any minute," I say, glancing behind her at the slowly setting sun.

"Kids are all in bed?"

I nod, inviting her in. "What can I help you with? Or did Kate set something up that I'm not aware of?"

"No, nothing like that. Let's wait until she arrives and I can explain. I don't want to have to repeat myself." She slips off her shoes and finds a seat, demurely crossing her ankles and placing her hands atop her tablet on her lap.

"I thought you were headed home after our meeting," I comment. "Did something happen after I left?"

She shakes her head, giving a small smile, reminding me to be patient. She is apparently serious about not talking to me about it before Kate is present. I try changing the subject.

"So, what travel destinations are on your list for the next year?" I ask, running a few inches of water into the sink to wash the dinner dishes.

"I have a trip planned to the southern territories in a few months, but other options are up in the air until we find out whether we will officially be expanding into South American territories or not."

I nod. This had taken up much of our last Committee meeting. "Do you think it's a good idea?"

"I don't know," she sighs. "Logistically it makes things so much more complicated. But, I guess if they are able to start small and become self-sustaining, it could be a great opportunity to expand."

"I'm not convinced we are at the point that we need to focus on expansion. But what do I know. I've only attended a few meetings."

"Is that why you never say anything?" Shari teases.

"I will. When it's right," I say, smiling. As I wash the last bowl, the front door opens and Kate walks in. Her face is pale, and at first she doesn't respond to seeing Shari in the living room. She just stares.

"Kate?" I ask, jolting her from her frozen state.

"Hey, sorry, I wasn't expecting company," she responds stiffly.

"Shari wanted to wait until you got here to discuss something with us. Do you need anything to eat?"

She shakes her head, her hand reaching into her right pocket. "No, I don't feel well at the moment."

I nod, and we both move to the sofa.

"As you know," Shari begins, "Nick has been doing some incredible work with his reversal research. I think you have witnessed the effects at this point, right Kate?"

Kate nods, glancing down at the floor, then lifting her head again with a smile.

"We are all excited to hear more about the process and the Director has actually called for a special meeting in two weeks so that Nick can present his findings to the region,"

Kate inhales sharply, and Shari pauses. "Are you ok?" she asks.

"Sorry, that just took me by surprise. I had no idea your results were going to be published so widely," she explains.

"Nick, have you not told her how groundbreaking this research is?" Shari asks, seemingly incredulous.

"I have been so busy with the trials, and Kate has been undergoing procedures herself—I guess we haven't really had a chance to sit down and discuss ramifications," I hedge.

"Kate, what has your experience been?" Shari asks.

31 / KATE

My hands go numb, my right hand still pressing the traveler into my thigh, and my throat is thick. Keeping my face even, my mind races wildly, attempting to sort through possible, appropriate responses. It's difficult to focus amidst the seething rage that pounds against my skull at seeing Shari again. As my memories have been restored, any minor hesitancy I felt in our relationship has given way to full anger and betrayal. How could she do this to me? How could she split up my family and strip me of my most meaningful relationships?

I close my eyes and breathe, reminding myself that she seemed to legitimately think that this was best. I had convinced myself of the same thing at one point, so how can I blame her? Knowing now the position she holds—along with the prior secrecy—makes that reasoning a little difficult to swallow. Because of the discrepancies in the story she has chosen to share with me, everything in my previous life with Shari is questionable. I don't know what to believe.

"After my first treatment, I felt a noticeable difference," I say calmly. "It was like a weight I had been carrying was suddenly lifted."

Shari nods, giving me a measured look. "How many treatments have you had?" she asks.

"Only three," Nick interjects. "Though the last one was quite intense and she is still in recovery."

Why is he lying? I have had upwards of fifteen procedures at this point. And why haven't boosters been administered to other patients? Or was Tamara lying? I still know nothing about his experience after that day with the balloons. What happened to him? Does he remember everything that happened to me, or was he simply trying to treat the echoes and somehow it backfired? *Does Nick know that my memories are back?* He can't possibly. And I can't possibly give any indication that something is off. My mind is overwhelmed with questions and anxiety surrounding the lack of information, nearly incapacitating me mentally. Somehow, as my head begins to pound, a realization clicks. Despite the fact that I know next to nothing, I now have another piece to work with: the Committee doesn't know about these extra treatments. And Nick doesn't want them to.

"Well I will just cut right to the chase," she says, leaning back in her chair, seemingly relaxed, when her expression is anything but. "The Director doesn't feel comfortable going into this meeting with zero tangible data, so I am here to collect a handful of patients' before and after scans for review. Since Kate has specifically had such fantastic results, we would love to include her in the first batch."

My blood runs cold. I need more time. I thought I would have days, at least, to figure out a plan for altering my scan files. Surely, I could find an excuse to see my final scan. Plead curiosity after this conversation and somehow distract Nick while he is logged in.

"I would be happy to send them to you when I am back at the lab in the morning," he says. "As you know, those files aren't publicly held; they are only accessible from my dock there."

"The timeline is actually a lot less flexible," Shari explains. "We need them tonight. I'm sorry to cause inconvenience, but I would love for us to head down there now. I have a secured travel dock available for transferring the information, for privacy and informational safety."

I force myself to relax my fingers, the tension in my arms becoming unbearable.

"We actually haven't completed a final scan for Kate yet," Nick admits. "I was waiting for complete recovery before compiling that information. I do have final scans for quite a few other patients—"

"But none with such intense symptoms." Shari cuts him off.

"True."

"The Director isn't going to budge on this," she says apologetically. "We will need to do the scan tonight, as well."

"Couldn't we postpone the meeting? Nick could give his report a few weeks later?" I propose and Shari laughs lightly.

"If only it were that easy," she sighs. "Do you want to come in my car or drive separately?"

They are going to see it. Tonight, Nick and Shari are going to see that my memories have been restored, if not in their entirety, at least to an unacceptable extent. Not only will it ruin Nick's ability to present his research, but—before I can finish my thought, nausea threatens to envelop me. I grit my teeth and breathe down the panic. I can't lose those memories. Especially now that I know they can be erased forever. *I can't forget them.* Not now. Not ever again.

"Let's go together," I say sweetly, steeling myself. "No sense wasting resources when we don't have to."

Nick looks at me in surprise, then nods his agreement.

"I do need to use the washroom first, if that's alright," I say, not waiting for Shari's response.

A FIRE BURNS in me as we enter the lab. Tamara is, thankfully, long gone. I wouldn't want to have to explain a third appearance here in one night. I have absolutely zero idea as to how I am going to alter the files, but whether it's adrenaline or a sheer mental break, nothing but confidence exists in me. I will figure it out, because I have to. It's as simple as that.

Nick logs into his dock and turns on the equipment. Peeking over his shoulder, I ask to see my initial scans. My voice seems to startle him and I notice that he is deleting images within my folder.

"What are those?" I ask innocently.

"I accidentally saved images from a few other patients in your file," he says. "I already copied them to their correct locations, but forgot to delete them here." I nod, watching until there are only two images left. Again, the dishonesty. I saw those images and they were mine. What is he hiding? My eye catches movement and I glance down. Something about his finger motions seemed slightly different on that one. Looking back at the display, only one image is visible.

Nick brings up my initial scan, and the colors appear in front of us.

"It's beautiful," I say.

Shari crosses to our side of the room and takes it in. "It's...chaotic," she sighs, almost in awe.

Nick nods. "Based on her reports, I assume this next image will be much more streamlined. But you can see why we needed multiple sessions to repair this," he jokes.

"Standing right here," I tease, trying to keep the mood light. Where did my second scan disappear to? I pat the traveler in my pocket, thankful that I accessed the images when I did.

Moving down the row next to Kip, I slice the cabbage heads off one by one. As I hit my rhythm, I push myself to move slightly faster to get ahead of him. It's not a competition, but I get some strange satisfaction from finishing the row first. Our entire crew is out today harvesting. We've been at it all week, and my whole body is feeling it.

"I hope they appreciate this," Kip mumbles under his breath.

"Huh?" I ask, not hearing him fully.

"I hope they appreciate this," he repeats gruffly, bending and slicing.

"They?"

"Yes they. People in Tier 1 who never have to lift a finger, but benefit from our sweat and tears. *They*," he sneers.

"Do you seriously believe that, Kip?" I ask, standing in my row for a quick stretch, then bending again, not wanting to get behind.

"Don't you?"

"Tier 1 individuals don't just sit around doing nothing. They have extreme responsibility and work hard."

"How do you know?" he asks, smirking.

"I mean—everyone knows that. It's how society works."

"So you know because that's what Berg told you?" he quips, both of us now facing each other.

I nod. "How would we have so much innovation, such equality in resources if it wasn't true?" I ask honestly.

Kip laughs out loud, bending as if needing to prevent a total collapse into hilarity. "Seriously, Eric? How do you know the resources are equal? How do you *know* that innovation doesn't come from Tier 2, from all of us working day in and day out to fulfill *our* responsibilities?"

I stare blankly, a compelling answer escaping me.

"You need to wake up, man. Everyone here works to support an upper-class that doesn't give anything back to us, as far as I'm concerned," he says, bending again in his row. Quietly he adds, "If you want to learn more, you can meet at Taylor's tomorrow night."

I stand in stunned silence, sweat dripping along my temples. Kip is at least four plants ahead of me, but I can't seem to make myself move. Is this really how my peers think? Have I missed a cultural shift in my isolation? Slowly, I bend and continue on, filling my bag with ripe heads. Maybe it's just Kip; he's always been a little surly. My mind continues to chew on this information as I lag behind, finishing my row.

Standing outside of Taylor's home, I hesitate, having absolutely zero desire to hear more of the negativity I absorbed in the field. At the same time, I have a responsibility to be aware in my community. And possibly more importantly in this instance, to share my opinions and conclusions. Moseying up the path, the door opens before I can knock.

"You came," Kip announces, impressed.

"I did," I say, smiling slowly. "I'm mostly here to observe. Hopefully that's okay."

He ushers me into the living room, and I take a seat on an open bench. Two other men filter in while I wait, then Taylor stands and calls our unofficial meeting to order. His hair is still wet, slightly curling behind his ears, and he is dressed in a clean shirt and slacks. There are only ten of us, but the energy in the room is palpable. I attempt to conceal my discomfort by relaxing my hands onto the bench next to me.

"Thanks for coming everyone," Taylor greets us, taking his place at the front of the room. "For you newcomers, we have been getting together for a few months to discuss community and governance policies that we feel are important and need to be adjusted. I assume, by your presence, that you also have concerns. While meeting together isn't necessarily frowned upon by Berg, some of our topics might be, so we ask that you keep this discussion to yourselves. We want this to be a safe space for self-expression," he explains.

That's fair. While I likely won't agree with much of what's said, I am all for freedom of speech and opinion.

"Kip, why don't you fill the new guys in," he says, moving to the side and perching on a stool next to the doorframe.

"Sure, no problem," he replies, standing and pulling his sagging belt up to his waist. "I think we can all agree that after the Crisis, something had to be done. Whether it was right or wrong isn't up for discussion. It happened, people did the best they could, and even if they didn't, we can't really do anything about it anyway." A few people chuckle lightly. "What we can do something about is society right now. Things have changed a lot since then. Heck, even in my lifetime I've seen dramatic changes. But this isn't about me. Let me show you some stats."

Kip pulls out a display and opens a window in front of us. A chart appears, showing resource levels for Tier 2.

"Look at this pretty curve," he drawls, bringing more chuckles from our small group. "Our physical resource levels have been exponentially increasing for years. We are literally maxed out, and yet somehow, we still have to use credits for extra food or entertainment." He swipes to another image. "This shows our population. I have my doubts that this is current, but it has been steadily decreasing. This is likely the reason for our increased resource levels per capita, only solidifying our opinion that it is time for resources to be freely accessed." Closing the display, he takes a seat and motions for Taylor to continue.

Before he can speak, I raise my hand. "What would that look like?" I ask. So much for observation only.

"What do you—wait, do I know you?" Taylor asks when he sees my face.

"Eric. Sorry, I should have introduced myself. I work with Kip"

He nods. "Eric, what do you mean?"

"If resources were freely accessible, what would that look like?" I repeat. "Would we adopt similar policies to Tier 1? Adjust our service assignments? Lose the credit system?"

The men glance around the room at each other and there is an accompanying low hum of voices.

"We're thinking bigger than that, man," Kip says, smiling. "It's time for freedom from everything. The whole system."

"I have a hard time wrapping my brain around that," I admit. "People tried that in the past, and it always—I repeat, *always*—led to a lack of freedom eventually. Without someone to structure our conditioning—I mean, if future generations were left to their own devices, what would prevent another Crisis? More power hungry leaders? More conflict?"

Kip smiles and looks toward Taylor. "That's exactly what we're trying to prevent now, Eric," he says softly. "Who do you think has all the power?"

"We all do," I say, without missing a beat. "We all work together for our communal progression."

"Who's progressing here?" Kip says. "Are you progressing? I'm certainly not," he spits. "Tier 1 might be progressing, but it seems to me like we are serving without much benefit."

"Their progression benefits us all—" I start, but am cut off by chatter within the group. Realizing I am definitely in the minority, I close my mouth and sit still.

The anger that Kip spoke with is something I had never experienced before. Everyone around me seems to agree with him to varying degrees and this knowledge rocks me. This can't possibly be the general feeling within our Tier. Could it? How could they have forgotten the standard of life our predecessors suffered before the Crisis? Their arrogance at professing to know a better way is appalling. And simply irresponsible. As my frustration rises, hearing the arguments around me, I stand and thank them for the information, moving toward the door.

"Eric," Kip calls behind me, "think about it. This movement is alive and well, whether you agree with it or not." I nod and walk out into the hot evening air.

KATE LIES STILL as the sleek, metal halo glides around her head, the soft whirring of the machine breaking the silence. A cold sweat makes the palms of my hands slippery, and I surreptitiously wipe them on my slacks. Though I am trying desperately not to show it, the frustration within me fights to rise to the surface. The Director has some nerve interrupting our evening to force a scan. Did my assertiveness the other night somehow set him off? Any effective leader should be thrilled when an apprentice takes the initiative to begin a project and then is successful. His reaction—and Shari's immediate obedience—serves to solidify my understanding of the situation. He doesn't want equals on the Committee, he wants minions; people who will do his bidding without question. Though that may have been me a month ago, that agreeableness has died within me now.

I adjust Kate's head position and run the machine again, only one more position to go. Shari sits in the corner, legs crossed, fingers tapping on the chair. Though I have only known her for the last two years or so, my respect for her has continued to decrease exponentially. Based on her comments to me that night in the hall, she is aware of the Director's need to be in control, yet she has done nothing to raise a warning to our regional leaders. I have to assume that not every member of leadership is corrupt. We couldn't possibly be that far gone.

Tier 1 has been built upon principles of service, selflessness, and the communal good. Witnessing this lack of integrity—along with the secrecy and manipulation—in the Committee's actions sends me back to history conditioning. Over and over we studied societies following the same pattern. In every case, societal decline occurred after one small shift. Someone with less than worthy goals asserted dominance. And nobody stopped it. Of course, it's much easier to diagnose in hindsight and incredibly difficult to assess in the present.

How can we determine whether someone's goals are worthy? As humans, we rely on social cues and we trust those who seem trustworthy. Especially in Tier 1 where we have supposedly eliminated those characteristics that lead to selfish conflict. Our society isn't set apart by a better system, it's successful because of our collective unwillingness to regress to something lesser.

The scanner beeps definitively, and I reach out to help Kate sit. Her hands are ice cold; I rub them between my hands, smiling, though she doesn't look up. She stands abruptly, moving toward my dock.

"The image hasn't processed yet," I say.

"I know, I just wanted to be ready," she answers. Shari beats her there, taking her place at the computer.

"Where will the image appear, Nick?" Shari asks assertively, guarding the dock with her body. I raise my eyebrows, staring in her direction.

"I love the excitement here, but I am going to need access to the display for the image to be processed," I answer nonchalantly, forcing my anxiety about the situation to take a backseat. Shari huffs and moves out of the way. What fire has been lit under her to inspire this level of intensity? I move between the two women and calmly open the imaging companion software.

Movement catches my eye at the bottom of the display. A data traveler is attempting to connect. My eyes narrow. It's Tamara's. I clear it from the dock, shutting down any potential uploads. Kate grips my arm, unsteady, and as I turn, her eyes roll into her head before she falls.

"KATE?"

I hear Nick's voice above me and blink, attempting to focus.

"Hey, there you are. Do you see me?"

I nod. Nothing hurts. Nick must have caught me when I went down.

"I should have had you stay seated for a few minutes after the scan."

Reaching up, looping my hands around his neck, I make an instantaneous decision. "Nick, that scan will destroy both of us," I frantically whisper into his ear. "The booster—"

"It's okay, Kate. I know you're probably out of sorts," he replies gently. "Just lie down and I will take care of it."

"No! Nick!" I hiss fiercely. I should have told him about this earlier, I think, panic building in my chest. All of my previous confidence has dissipated, virtually sucked out by Shari's refusal to give me any space to work. I had hoped that the image from the traveler would upload and open on the display. Even facing a terrible outcome, I know I couldn't have told Nick earlier. He would have taken my memories away again, gone forever. Do all roads lead to me losing my family for the second time? I close my eyes, lying back on the bench, and silently weep.

"Is she okay?" I hear Shari ask.

"It's normal to be emotional after a loss of blood pressure like that," Nick says. "Here, looks like the image is ready."

This is it. I force myself to breathe, apologizing desperately to Tal and Eric. I didn't even get a chance to find out where they are or how they are doing. My brain still hasn't fully processed all of this and now it's over. For good this time.

"Wow," Shari exhales. "That's really impressive work, Nick."

"It's amazing, right?" he agrees.

What is happening? Taking a deep breath, I lift myself to a sitting position and allow my equilibrium to settle.

"Can I see?" I ask meekly. Shari, still staring intently at the image, moves to the side, allowing me space to move in beside her.

As the image comes into focus, I inhale sharply. That's the right image. The image I was trying to upload. Did it somehow get there despite Nick's intervention?

"Do you want to see the side-by-side?" Nick asks, more for Shari's benefit than mine. She nods and he places the images next to each other, the colors swirling madly on the first.

"I'm sorry to pull you here this evening," Shari says apologetically. "I don't know why—" she stops short, inhaling deeply. "Just put these images on here and I'll get them to the Director," she says, handing her data traveler to Nick, frustration and exhaustion evident in her tone.

After finishing the download, Shari places the drive in her pocket and hastily exits the lab. I breathe a silent sigh of relief as Nick begins to tidy up the space and move to walk out to the office, when his voice stops me in my tracks.

"Would you be willing to give Tamara's traveler back?" he asks softly. I stand stock still, every muscle tensed.

"It's okay, Kate. It was a good idea, but I never would have thought that your uploaded file was the new image," he says with a wan smile.

"How did you—"

"I moved your earlier scan into the recent imaging folder. I didn't actually scan you tonight. Just moved the machine around a lot. I'm sorry I didn't say anything earlier, but I didn't know how—" My head whips around toward him at the sudden silence, and find his face twisted in anguish, a hand over his mouth. What is happening? He moved my image...and didn't scan me? Does he—

"Nick," I sigh, walking quickly to his side and pulling him close. I hold him then, glad for the opportunity to give comfort when he has done it for me so many times before. His shoulders shake silently, his head hunched over my shoulder. I rub his back and wait. The silence stretches on, but slowly, he begins to breathe normally.

"Kate, I have so much I want to say to you. Something shifted in me weeks ago, but I couldn't allow myself to sink into it. And it wasn't safe—well, honestly, it still isn't, but...I still don't think I can handle fleshing out the ramifications of the actions I have taken. As long as it remains surface level, I can deal with it. I know I'm on the right track, I just—"

"Nick, it's okay. Let's go home and talk there," I soothe, "I'm going to be honest, I have a lot of questions—"

"I know, and we *need* to get everything out in the open. But there's something I have to do first. Can you give me a second?" he says, moving toward the dock.

THE SUNSET over the lake is stunning tonight. Since I had too much nervous energy to simply head home after the meeting, I ended up taking a walk around Washington Park. This place has always felt somewhat nostalgic to me, though I haven't actually spent much time here. Perhaps it's merely the fact that it is tied to a previous society, a past culture. Watching Tier 1 and Tier 2 individuals meet here during the day to collaborate also represents the best part of our current society. All of that melded together leaves me feeling almost reverent as I walk the quiet paths.

Finding a bench, I sit for a moment as the colors diffuse across the sky. There's no room for anger here. I struggle to reconcile the things I heard tonight—the attitudes that I was previously oblivious to. How have we all come through the same conditioning and yet, somehow, arrived at such opposite conclusions?

A message appears on my sensor, and my heart jumps at the thought that it might be from Val. We still haven't had a chance to get together after our interruption the other night. She was sent out of territory for a project, and any free time I have had has been taken up with monitoring Tal. He returned to conditioning yesterday, but it took a lot out of him. A part of me wonders if he is struggling with emotional trauma more than physical.

Tapping the message, I'm disappointed that it's not from her. Though I don't recognize the sender, I open it anyway.

Eric, forgive the blunt delivery, but you need to know that Kate's alive.
I'm working on it. -a friend

My heart stops. I re-read the message three more times, my body frozen, unable to process. Is this a sick joke? Tapping on the sender, I find it blank. Untraceable, at least from here. Standing up, I begin walking briskly toward home.

Who would do something like this? My stomach swirls in discomfort, not due to any belief on my part that this message is true, but because someone out there knows I wish it were. I am nearly running by the time I reach our street, my feet pounding into the path leading to our unit. Slamming through the front door, I press my back against the cold metal and catch my breath.

"Dad?" Tal calls. "Are you ok?" he asks, rounding the corner and seeing my distress.

"Yeah, sorry. Long story," I say, rushing to the display, flicking it on. "What are you working on tonight?" I ask, attempting to sound normal.

"Just that research you asked me to complete," he answers soberly, naturally understanding that I am distracted.

"Great," I say, still not giving him my full attention. "Tal, I will definitely talk with you more about this later, but would you mind giving me some privacy? I'm trying to track something down and it's frustrating. I would really love to be alone."

"Sure, Dad," he says, patting my back and retreating to his room. The guilt at pushing him away lasts for only a moment. With my mind reeling from the meeting and then this, I don't have energy to spare for engaged parenting at the moment.

Pulling up the message on my main dashboard, I see a random string of letters and numbers listed in the 'sender' field. Using all of the tools I am aware of, I hit a series of dead ends as I endeavor to reply or track the number. All the while, the message stares me in the face. My desperation builds with each subsequent futile attempt. Tears begin to flood my eyes and, almost involuntarily, I slam my hand down on the counter, leaving my palm stinging.

Eventually giving up, I close the display and run my hands through my hair. Though this feels different from my regular panic attacks, I take a moment to breathe and count, listing off other possible solutions to the situation. The message may not be traceable under my account, but I wonder if I could trace it at headquarters? Or through a Tier 2 Committee member? Glancing at the clock, I realize it's far too late to attempt that tonight, but I could potentially stop in mid-day during my lunch break. My hands shake. An outward manifestation of my inner desire to not have to wait until tomorrow to figure this out.

Suddenly noticing how quiet Tal has been, I move down the hall and knock on his door softly. Hearing no reply, I open the door to find him asleep at his desk, his stylus still between his fingers. It's been a long time since I have carried my little boy to bed. I smile in spite of myself as I stagger to lift him from his chair and, quite ungracefully, lay him in his bed.

Since I have taken charge of a few of his conditioning responsibilities, Tal hasn't had any outbursts or behavioral issues in his group. I'd like to take credit for it, but I am almost positive that he has also begun to mentally and emotionally mature these last few weeks. His social smarts finally catching up with his academic side. I smooth his hair with my hand, remembering how his fuzzy head felt as a baby.

Tears roll freely down my cheeks. Oh, how I miss you, Kate.

Kip and I work side by side again this morning, building permaculture in one section of the planting fields. We haven't said more than two words to each other since beginning at dawn. What I really want is to understand, but my mind reacts so strongly to his opinions. It's difficult to listen without jumping in and trying to persuade him to shift his perspective. I mentally prepare myself to try again.

"Kip," I start, "I'm having a hard time understanding where you and your buddies are coming from in relation to our current structure of government. Do you mind sharing your feelings with me?"

"Eric, I don't think that's a good idea—"

"I promise I won't judge," I say, cutting him off. "You work, Kip. You show up every day and you work. I know we think differently, but I see that you are honestly trying to do your best. I'm not arrogant enough to believe that I have found the only correct world view."

Kip appraises me, leaning on his shovel. "Alright," he agrees hesitantly. "Where do you want me to start?"

"Maybe from the beginning? What was your life like growing up?"

I listen to Kip all morning. His experience seems to be fairly typical of Tier 2 individuals, though I haven't had conversations like this with more than a handful of people. While my sample size is small, I extrapolate in good faith.

"I guess, one day, I had to ask myself: what is the point?" Kip continues. "I serve, I feed people, I go home, I eat, sleep, then get up again and do it the next day."

"Are you paired, Kip?" I ask.

"I was, it didn't work out," he admits. "I wasn't approved for a child and she had better numbers. Wanted to see if she could find a healthier option." His face flushes and his shovel seems to be hitting the soil with more force.

"That's tough," I say.

"That's life," he corrects. "Again, begging that same question. Honestly, Eric, how do you stay motivated?"

I swallow, not immediately knowing how to answer. "The truth is, I haven't ever considered this, Kip. I have always felt a strong pull to contribute. Maybe it's amplified because I have Tal? Or because I feel some strange responsibility to do right by Kate? I don't know. To me, doing my part to make our world a better place is good enough."

"Is it better, though?" Kip asks.

"What do you mean? Of course it's better," I answer, out of breath from lifting another shovel of compost.

"Okay, yes. I agree, it's better than it was during the Crisis, but is it *getting better*," he clarifies. "Where do you see the Tier system in fifty, even a hundred years?"

"Ideally?"

"Realistically."

"For me they're kind of the same thing, I think," I chuckle and Kip rolls his eyes, a smile playing at the corner of his mouth. "I see cancer as a thing of the past, soil toxicity brought down to manageable levels, more opportunities for reproduction, more variety in food and fauna. Basically a better, richer quality of life for everyone."

"But why? Eric, when there's nothing to compare it to, it doesn't feel better. It just feels normal," Kip argues.

I pause, leaning on my shovel, sweat dripping down my back. "But it would be a better normal."

"Sure, theoretically, we could look back and say 'they had it worse', but nobody in Tier 2 looks back. We are only looking up. Looking at what we don't have. Regardless of how 'great' life gets here, we always know that there's something that escapes us. That we aren't whole enough to be given opportunities—"

"It's not personal," I interject. "It's simply the only way to ensure that we become our best."

"But what is our best, Eric? And who is 'we'? Don't you mean that 'they' become their best? And who determined what 'best' even means? I would argue that we have sacrificed our holistic 'best' for a narrow version of it."

He waits to continue speaking until I mix the last of our amendments into the soil. Propping our shovels into our wheelbarrows, we push them along the path toward the storage shed.

"Have you ever read anything from Alan Sears?" Kip asks. I shake my head. "He was a philosopher in the early two thousands, had some great theories on conflict. Two discussions of his have really stuck with me. First, the Tier system was never established through consensus. Again, I'm not arguing that forced participation wasn't necessary at the time, but I don't think it is justifiable anymore. Everyone—Tier 1, Tier 2, and Tier 3—should be allowed the opportunity to opt in or out. The Tier system will always serve Tier 1 as a first priority, and it isn't rational to pretend that we are all benefiting to the same extent."

My wheelbarrow bounces along the uneven ground, and I reach

out a finger to steady the handle of my shovel so it doesn't continue to clang against the side.

"Second," he continues, "human potential can't be fully realized in an oppressive state. Berg can argue all they want about how we are 'free' and 'opportunities are available to all', but here, we know that isn't true. They have fully hitched their wagons to genetics and our physical interactions in the brain as the be-all-end-all source of truth, but I don't buy it. There's power in perception. There's power in belief. All of which is intangible and, so far, quite immeasurable."

I walk in stunned silence. My own ignorant perceptions have been completely ripped apart during this conversation. Specifically, my perceptions of Kip. I have, subconsciously, always viewed him as lesser. As slightly unenlightened, but just the opposite is true. Could we have been having conversations like this every day, had I been more open? Had I been more willing to explore my own biases?

Rolling our equipment back into the covered storage area, we brush ourselves off and enter the shed to wash up for lunch. My senses are heightened when I touch my sensor. I have an hour to make it down to headquarters to figure out if they can trace where the message originated. Our prior conversation served as a nice distraction, but now, finding that information is all I can focus on. Glancing across the room, I notice Kip already rummaging through the fridge for his lunch. With nobody paying attention, I am compelled to pull it up and re-read it for the hundredth time.

I scroll, not seeing it immediately. Did it somehow get moved down the list in priority? Typing in a portion of the memorized words, I search. Nothing. My abdomen seems to hollow out, a pit opening up and threatening to swallow me whole. No. The message has to be there. I frantically turn my sensor off and then on again. Still nothing.

"Is everything ok?" Kip asks, noticing my frenzied movements.

Beads of sweat are forming on my forehead. "I—I seem to have lost a message," I say through my clenched teeth.

"Val will understand," Kip chuckles, waggling his eyebrow at me. I force a smile, then march out of the shed, forgetting my lunch on the counter.

Cuddled in blankets with warm tea in our hands, Kate and I stare up at the stars from the bench in our backyard. The sound of crickets, chirping their consistent lullabies, calms me. I relax for what may be the first time in weeks. Kate leans her head on my shoulder.

"Nick," she breathes. "Can we finally be honest with each other? No more worrying about ourselves, or the Director, or the fate of society," she says dramatically.

A sardonic laugh escapes my lips. "That's kind of all I'm good at," I admit. "I don't know how to *not* factor in all of those things."

"I know," she soothes. "But, could we try?"

"We can try. Do you want to go first?" She shifts her weight, pressing closer into my chest and I wrap my arm around her shoulder.

"Do you know about the memories?" she asks, her voice a terrified whisper.

"About you getting them back?" She nods in relief. "Yes. I took a risk—trying something that, as far as I know, has never been done before—without your knowledge. It didn't feel right, Kate. What they had done to you. Not only because you were suffering, but because...well, they basically stunted your ability to contribute. How can your mind analyze and create when half of its input has been deleted? And as much as I love having you here with me...it hasn't ever felt truly fulfilling because I know..." I sigh. "I know you wouldn't have gotten here without the Committee forcing it on you. So yes. I reinstated those memories as best I could. I am so relieved that it worked, but in my defense, I don't think I could have screwed up your pathways any more if it didn't—"

"It's okay, Nick. I'm glad you took the risk. I didn't know that you knew. I was terrified that you would find out and they would all be —" she sucks in a breath. "Do any of your patients receive boosters?"

I laugh softly. "No, that was just a cover."

"Why couldn't you tell me? All this time I—"

"It's still not safe that you know, Kate. What I'm doing—if they found out...I need the knowledge of these procedures to remain solely with me."

Kate nods, thinking. "Nick, I am so sorry," she starts, and I exhale audibly. Tension that I didn't even know I was holding escaping on that breath. "You were thrown into this messy situation and asked to shoulder massive responsibility at such a young age. You were asked to pair, asked to be an instant father, asked to hold secrets and manipulate—the list goes on. I don't think Berg has been fair to you," she concludes.

"Well, when you put it that way," I tease.

She laughs, full bodied and tragic. "I'm serious," she complains, smacking my arm lightly.

I sigh. "I know. I guess I have a hard time seeing it as 'unfair'. I have always been asked to shoulder more, to do more. It's kind of expected." Kate starts to say something and then stops. "What is it?" I prod.

"I—I feel incredible guilt even exploring this outloud, but...I am kind of disenchanted with the Committee."

"What do you mean?"

"Nick, they took my family. They lied to both of us—they have manipulated us, and who knows how many others. I know it's all in the name of progress and—I believed in that. Maybe that's what hurts the most. I was ready to do it, too. I lied to Eric. I lied to you, somehow thinking that the right outcome would justify my actions. It doesn't, Nick. It just doesn't. Don't get me wrong, I am so grateful for the girls, but that is beside the point. All of this was supposed to be for the good and...I don't feel so good right now."

I rub her shoulder. "I don't think it was supposed to be for *our* good," he says softly. "For the greater good."

"Shouldn't it be the same thing?"

"Not necessarily," I sigh.

"I don't agree," she says, her face lifted upward toward the heavens. "If we are acting in the best interest of those around us, and even those who will come after us, we should feel fulfilled and accomplished. I feel...nothing. I feel nothing, Nick."

I nod. "I know what you mean." Looking up, I take in the vast expanse of the universe. Stars prick the sky, small needlepoints of light in the deep blue. "Kate, I have never felt fully settled about pairing with you. I love you, make no mistake about that, but I have seen your scans. I have witnessed the damage that was done, and the extent that Berg had to go to in order to wipe Eric from your day-to-day. He was—and is—a part of you. When we first met, I didn't have the life experience to really understand what that meant. Even now, I probably only truly comprehend a fraction of it, but that fraction is extremely powerful. You have become a part of me. Nobody else could—" I pause, swallowing. "Nobody could replace you. I know that might sound odd, considering our current situation, but it's true. I have grown into someone different because of you. Someone better. The other night, when I reacted the way I did in front of the Committee members—I'll never forget the way you looked at me. I don't want anyone to have reason to look at me like that again."

She squeezes my hand, but doesn't speak immediately.

"Why now? What caused you to see all of this now?" she eventually asks.

"The main catalyst actually came that same night. During the trials, I had been treating Tier 1 patients—for routine things like accidents, death, the usual. I didn't look too closely, everything seemed so benign. Anyway, I went to get your sensor out of the auditorium and realized I had left my display back in our meeting room. When I got there, I overheard—well, long-story-short, I found out that my trial treatments weren't necessarily being administered knowingly."

Kate inhales sharply. "What?" she asks, her voice cold.

"Somehow, I had convinced myself that you were the only one. That ours was such a unique circumstance that extreme measures had been justified, but to find out that it was happening all the time..."

I can feel Kate shaking her head.

"I know. I was horrified, too. I still haven't had a chance to figure out if any of them were legitimately requested, or if they were all 'mistakes' that the Director needed to hide."

"Nick, this is what I'm talking about. All of this, this isn't what Tier 1 has ever been about. The Committee should be serving us—protecting us. Not *managing* us."

"I know. Seeing that flipped a switch. Well, along with our interaction. There I was, garnering that reaction from you for an ideal that I thought was worth it. It was worth it to hurt someone, to eliminate someone from *your* life, to *give my life*, for something better," I say, my voice cracking with emotion. "But, it's been twisted. Their goals are not my goals anymore. That's why I took a chance on giving you your memories back. If their ideal isn't worth fighting for, then maybe mine is."

"Can you get your life back?" she suggests.

"I don't know if that's possible at this point," I admit, and it rings true. What life? My life is society, Kate, Bent, and the girls. Regardless of whether that life came about in the right way, it came. It's here. But I now know I can't keep it. How do I move on from that?

"Maybe," I say, "I was never meant to truly have my own life. I still want to make this world a better place, Kate. I want to fix this. If the Tier system is beginning to decay, I want to find an evolution. Maybe this is truly all necessary for my growth, and nothing more."

"That's inspiring, but pretty bleak," she teases.

"Like you said, bleak is worth it if it's for something legitimately better. I can feel good about that, I think."

"Maybe this is *exactly* who we are meant to be. We have been conditioned to be *this*, Nick. Tier 1 gave us the best of everything —our genetics gave us the best chance of succeeding here. Maybe this is the next evolution. We are meant to move beyond this restrictive system, but Berg is so used to having control and knowing what to expect... This is scary for all of us. Their actions have been difficult to justify, but we are all pioneers here. There has to be a way to navigate it for the best. If our brains are pushing us in this direction, we need to embrace it instead of constantly trying to remain stagnant."

"That requires humility, Kate. The Director doesn't have it."

She sighs knowingly.

"What about you?" I ask gently.

"What about me?"

"What are you feeling?"

She interlaces her fingers with mine. "I don't want to leave you alone, Nick," she says, her voice catching. In the dim light I can see her nose wrinkle, the way it always does when she cries. Her breath comes in short bursts, her shoulders lifting gently against my chest.

How will I possibly be able to remedy this? Our lives are impossibly tangled and we still have Berg breathing down our necks. They will never let us split, let alone allow Kate to see Eric or Tal again. I've been attempting to play the hero, but I have no cards to play. Unless...I run my free hand through my hair, my mind reeling.

"Kate, you're not leaving me," I whisper, "I'm simply giving you back."

EVERY MINUTE, every mundane task, every breath is rich with meaning for me. The missing pieces of our understanding have all clicked into place. I know it, Nick knows it, and we are finally working as a team instead of working *for* a team that didn't necessarily have our best interests at heart. I still have a hard time condemning them. I can see how, in a strange, twisted way, it made sense for them to do the things they did. The fault lies in their own hubris. Or at least in the Director's. I assume everyone else was simply too attached to their newfound freedom and providence to rock the boat.

My mind continuing to process as I watch Beth and Leah attempting to pull themselves to their feet. My face lights up as they practice each new skill, and I am met with wide eyes and drooly smiles.

I am in shock, recognizing that I am personally witnessing the very first signs of societal decline. Just as in every previous society, as soon as someone with power decides that they know better—or should be more important, more worthy—than others around them and people accept it, life begins to unravel. I imagine the Director as a young man, serving and working to improve Tier 1 his entire life, then finally put in a position to make a difference, only to give in to his natural tendency to want more. To be above. Really, this is everything that Eric and I were criticized for as well—putting ourselves above the greater good. How can I judge? I empathize, remembering now how justified I felt.

Placing the girls in the buggy, we begin our daily walk to the outdoor nursery. Both girls begin to kick wildly as soon as we hit the path, already knowing where we are headed. The magnolias are in bloom and their heady scent fills the air around us, making the bird chatter and even the breeze seem romantic.

After checking them in, I head to the campus courtyard, planning to meet Bentley for lunch. I haven't said anything about my memories to him over the past few weeks, but he has been more withdrawn than usual. I worry that he has picked up on the added stress, despite my attempts to hide it.

He spots me immediately, waves, and runs my direction. Sitting down on a bench under a wide-stretching dogwood tree, I open my picnic bag.

"Hey Mom," he says, walking the last few steps, plopping down dramatically.

"Hey bud, are you already tired out?" I laugh, noticing the sweat around his hairline.

"Yeah, we were playing four square."

"So fun. Here's our lunch," I say motioning to the spread. "What are you in the mood for?" Without speaking, he appraises the food and picks out his favorite vegetables and some smoked ham.

"How was conditioning this morning?" I ask and he shrugs his shoulders. "Hey Bent, let's play a game," I propose, grasping at any idea that could open up some conversation. "I'll say a word, and then you say the first thing that comes to your mind. So, for example, I could say 'red' and you could say 'tomato'. Does that make sense?"

He nods, slipping garden peas between his lips.

"Okay, first one. Fun."

"Four square," he says, without missing a beat.

"Happy."

"Beth."

"Touché," I say, raising my eyebrows. "Okay, sad."

"Nick."

My breath catches. "Friend."

"Pace," he says smiling. One of his friends from advanced conditioning.

"Work."

"Healthy," he says, again causing my eyebrows to shoot up.

Alright, maybe I will give him something a little deeper. "Responsibility."

"Mine."

"Progress."

"Necessary."

"Family."

"Broken."

"Bent," I sigh, my heart aching for him, "we need to talk, but I don't know how to share some of the things I've learned over the last few weeks. You're obviously picking up on the fact that Nick and I have had some really rough things to work through—"

"What are they?" he asks, his eyes trained on the ants making their way toward our food.

"How good are you at keeping secrets?" I ask.

Later that night, sitting with Nick, I fill him in on my conversation with Bent.

"He really said that?" Nick asks, impressed.

"He did. I was blown away. He's so perceptive, Nick, it scares me. It's like he sees right through me."

"Seriously. So what did you tell him?"

"I—pretty much everything. Is that bad?"

"Do you think he'll say anything to anyone?"

"I wouldn't have told him if I did," I answer.

Nick nods. "How did he take it?"

"At first, he didn't make eye contact, but eventually he was absorbing every word. I think that's why I said so much. His little eyes searing into me, not speaking. I couldn't stop. When I finished, he hugged and thanked me. I told him that we are working as a team, that we will figure out what to do from here, and that it was really important not to talk about it. He just hopped up and said 'I won't', then ran back to his group."

"That's it?"

"That's it."

"He didn't say anything about it to me tonight," Nick says, his face drawn into a concerned expression.

"I know, me either. Let's talk to him tomorrow. Maybe he just needs time to process."

Nick yawns, nodding his agreement. "I'm going to head to bed," he says, standing and stretching his back as he does so.

"What are we going to do, Nick?" I ask.

He looks at the ground. "Talk to me tomorrow. Maybe I need time to process," he says, a grin pulling at the corners of his mouth.

I WAKE EARLY and find the other side of the bed empty. Pulling on a cotton sweater and pants, I start some water boiling for tea. Nick must have gone out for a walk, as I don't see his shoes by the front door. When the pot whistles, I pour the water over the mint leaves in my mug, inhaling the fresh scent, then move to the patio to watch the sun rise.

It's been a while since I have been outside this early. Waking up multiple times each night with twins kind of killed my enthusiasm for sunrise. Somehow, without even realizing it, we have transitioned to getting a full night's sleep most days. I stop mid-drink, realizing that I haven't had a headache since my memories were restored. Not one. Tears sting the corners of my eyes as I watch the horizon glow orange.

I don't know what happens from here. I can't possibly see a solution that Berg will approve, nor can I imagine a world where they would allow Eric and me to be together again, yet I am at peace. My brain is at peace. How is it possible for so much turmoil to swirl around me, and yet for there to be quiet inside my head? And, when all seemed well, for the opposite to have been true?

Pink rays stretch across the sky, flashing around wispy clouds until running out of strength above my head. Everything around me seems to absorb its energy; the flowers open their petals, colors emboldening by the second. Insects wake and follow their sleepy paths around the garden. Birds begin chirping and chattering to one another. The world is more beautiful to me this morning than ever before. The sorrow and hurt within me bring a depth of joy that can't be logically rationalized. I revel in it, not wanting to miss a thing.

"THANKS FOR ALLOWING me to come by so early," I say, entering through the open door.

"Of course," Shari responds sleepily. "To what do I owe this pleasure?" she asks, motioning for me to take a seat.

"I just needed someone to talk to, and obviously that can't be Kate right now," I answer.

Shari nods, crossing her legs, her loose cotton pants bunching between her knees. "How is she doing?"

"Good, considering," I say. "As you saw, the reversal is definitely helping, but there hasn't been much time to analyze long-term effects."

"Yeah, that's understandable."

I sigh. "Shari, do you think we're doing the right thing? I know the Director cited research and obviously understands this better than we do, but what if we've put all of our energy into one track when we should be diversifying?"

Her eyebrows furrow. "What do you mean?" she asks.

"I mean, our Committee is utilizing extra resources because we believe this system will work indefinitely. Think about it. What system can you point to that lasted indefinitely? None. Over the course of history, they all imploded. And all for the same reason."

"A reason that was out of their control," she counters. "It wasn't their system, it was the external factor—the war, the disease, the rebellion."

"No, it wasn't that. It was their inability to *adapt* to the myriad external factors—"

"But we have already proven that we can adapt. And our results have been phenomenal."

"And what happens when we are faced with something new? Our Tier is homogenous, Shari, and it will only continue to become more so. Not just homogenous genetically, but mentally as well. I haven't been on the Committee long, but it seems like the Director really doesn't appreciate people who question."

"I ask questions all the time, Nick," Shari points out.

"There are questions, and then there are *questions*," I counter. "Your queries are practical. Informational. They aren't tearing at the very fabric of what we've built this system with."

She shakes her head. "You aren't always present for my discussions with Grace and the Director. Be satisfied in knowing that I am not always so easy going."

I nod. "Good to know. But back to my original thought. Do you think this system is right?"

Shari huffs, exasperated. "I don't know what you are getting at, Nick. Of course it's right. Is it perfect? No, but we are constantly working to make it so. And I think we've accomplished some pretty incredible things on the journey—"

"I'm not denying that," I cut in, "but the Committee as a whole feels...how can I describe it properly? It feels less like a collaboration and more of a dictatorship."

Shari laughs, loud and unabashed. "Nick, I get it. At first, I had the same impression. Obviously new members are treated with caution, but give it some time. You will become an equal member in everyone's eyes in no time. Especially with this new research you are presenting. Next week right?"

I watch her, attempting to hide my disappointment. Somewhere, deep down, I really believed that Shari would be an ally. That some part of her would acknowledge the inappropriate actions of the Director. And that somehow, this would provide some shred of hope that there could be an opportunity to patiently work for change from within.

"Yep, next week. Can't wait," I say, forcing a smile. "Thanks for letting me hash this out. Everything is so new—"

"Don't think too hard about it," she says. "Take some time to relax with your family while Kate heals. You've been working really hard, Nick."

"That's not a bad idea. In fact, I was thinking about requesting resources to visit my father. What is the process for that?"

"You're still thinking too much! Just send a message to the Committee letting us know where and when you are going, then submit a list to Faye. She will set up your flight and help with anything else you may need."

"It's that easy?"

"Yep," she says, obviously pleased with herself.

"Alright," I say, standing. "Will do. Thanks again, Shari. I better get home."

"I am sure Kate is wondering where you are," she says, one eyebrow raised.

"As long as I get home before the girls wake up, she won't miss me," I joke. As the door closes behind me, I breathe, centering myself. On to plan B.

"Dad," I hear above me, my eyes slowly starting to focus. "Dad, hey, I think you need to get up," Tal says, his eyes pleading with me.

"Tal, I need to sleep—"

"Dad, you have been sleeping for nearly two days. You've missed your service assignment and I have been stalling for you. I told Kip you were throwing up when he stopped by yesterday. I lied Dad. For you," he admits, exasperated.

"Tal, I'm—"

"You can talk to me when you are up and showered. Go. Now!" he commands and my eyes widen. Without thinking, I force myself up and walk toward the washroom. That. Was impressive.

Closing the door, I brace myself against the sink and move my face close to the mirror. I look like I have aged a year, with deep blue circles under my eyes, almost a week of stubble on my chin, and a general grey tint to my skin tone.

"Get a hold of yourself, Eric," I think. How did this one thing set me over the edge? One ridiculous message and suddenly I am non-functional? But the thought of getting up sounded impossible. All I want to do, even now, is curl up in a ball and close my eyes.

Taking a deep breath, I stand up straight and peel my clothes off, sticky with sweat and dirt from earlier in the week. Dropping them to the floor in an untidy pile, I turn the knob and step into the shower, allowing warm water to cascade around my body. Sighing audibly, I move farther into it, imagining it washing away all of the frustration and hopelessness that has run rampant within me over the past few days.

When the water shuts off, I dry myself and wrap the thin towel around my waist, having forgotten to bring clothes in with me. Exiting into the bedroom, I find Tal sitting on my bed.

"You look—and smell—much better," he says, nodding his approval.

I clench my teeth, trying not to allow my emotions to get the better of me. "I'm sorry, Tal—"

"Will you please tell me what's going on?" he nearly shouts. "One day you are totally normal and then, all of a sudden, you're not getting out of bed. What am I supposed to do with that?"

"Can I put some clothes on first?" I ask.

"Fine, but the bed is off-limits," he teases.

"I promise. I'll change and come out to the kitchen. We can eat and talk, okay?"

"We don't really have any food in the house, but that works," he mutters. "I did pick up eggs yesterday, so at least we won't starve."

As he marches out of the room, I drop the towel and get dressed as quickly as possible. With that attitude, I don't want to give him any other reason to barge in here and make me feel more guilty.

Walking into the kitchen a few moments later, I find Tal cooking up a few eggs on the stove.

"Thanks," I say softly.

"For what?" he asks, unimpressed.

"For the eggs. And making me get up. I feel better now that I've showered."

He nods, scraping the pan with the spatula.

"A few days ago, I got a really weird message. I wasn't able to track the sender, and the next day it was gone. It honestly freaked me out, Tal," I explain.

"What was it about?"

"Kate. It was about your mom."

He stares at me, then, remembering his task, removes the pan from the heat. "What about Mom?" he asks calmly.

"It really doesn't matter," I say. "It wasn't true."

"Tell me what it said, Dad," he says, lifting half of the eggs onto each plate and passing one to me.

I sigh. "It said that she is still alive."

Tal drops his plate, sending egg particles splashing across the counter. Without reacting, I scoop them back onto his plate.

"Do you still want these? I'm not sure if the counter was clean—"

"Yeah, I want them," he answers, pulling the plate toward him.

"Tal. It's not true, and I can't figure out who would send a message like that. When it disappeared from my sensor, I lost it. The emotional side of my brain completely took over. I'm so sorry I wasn't there for you."

"It's fine, Dad. I survived."

"This time, but what if it happens again?" I ask, shaken. "I don't know what to do, Tal. I was completely out of control."

Tal looks at me, his eyebrows furrowed. "What if it *is* true, Dad?"

Taking a bite of egg, I shake my head. "I'm going to run to the distribution center for our weekly portions. Want to come?"

"No, I'll clean up here," he says. Setting my plate down, I pick up a canvas bag and head to the door.

As soon as I step outside, I am lighter. The fresh air seems to heal my soul, cleansing me from the inside out. My walk, while slow in the beginning, gains energy as I near the Center. I'm probably fine? My behavior over the last few days was some strange anomaly. Things will go back to normal. Right?

Moving into the line, I wait, surprised at how busy it is today. What day is it? I realize I have no idea. Tal said I had missed my assignment for two days, so that must put me at the end of the week, though I honestly can't remember when I went last. It feels like a year ago.

Tal's question rings in my mind. What if it is true? I immediately reject the thought. It can't be. As much as I want it to be, it's not possible. And why would she have been taken from me while I was made to believe in her death? None of it makes any sense.

Reaching the front, I scan my sensor.

"Late this week, hey?" the woman asks, smiling.

"Yep, sorry about that," I say apologetically.

"Nothing to be sorry about. Are you doing ok?"

I nod.

"Have you checked in with your health specialist recently?" she questions.

"I don't—I'm not really close to the cutoff, so I don't do that often," I answer.

"Sorry, I didn't mean to pry," she says, handing me my portions. Layering them into my sack, I thank her and retreat to the path.

My mind is blank most of the way home, wandering aimlessly while my body is on autopilot. Suddenly, I am yanked sideways, my sack falling to the ground with a thud. As I whip my head around, something is pulled over my eyes and a sweet, thick scent invades my nostrils. My vision fades as I slump to the ground.

Blinking, I slowly focus on the room around me. My head is fuzzy and movement is difficult, but I begin to take in details. White walls, a low hum, soft light from an open bulb above my head. Movement near the door causes me to move my head quickly to the left, sending my equilibrium swimming and muddying my vision.

"Hey Eric, glad you're awake," a man's voice says softly. "I'm so sorry about the way I had to get you here, but it was the only way to maintain anonymity. I hope you'll trust me on that."

Still clenching my eyes closed, I ask, "Where's Tal?"

"He's here too, safe. Don't worry."

"What is going on?" I ask as something hits my fingertips.

"It's a glass of water," I hear. "Drink some and then we'll talk."

Not hesitating, I raise the glass to my lips and gulp the cool liquid, desperate for it.

"Do you need more?" he asks when the glass is empty.

"Maybe in a minute," I say, my voice hoarse. Opening my eyes, I can see him now. A young man with broad shoulders, handsome. Impeccable bone structure. "Where am I?" I ask.

"You are in a Tier 2 rehabilitation center, not far from your home."

Realization dawns on me. "Is this because of the last couple of days?" I ask. "I have been sick, but I feel much better today. I went down to—oh, I think I dropped my portions," I say in regret.

"We got them, don't worry. They are back at your house," he explains, his voice suddenly warm and kind.

I nod. "Things are much better today. I don't think you need to worry—"

"This has nothing to do with the past few days, Eric, but I do agree that you look like you've been sick. And you are much skinnier than when I last saw you, which doesn't help with my own levels of guilt—"

"Who are you?" I interject, thoroughly confused.

"I am a friend," he says, and instantly my stomach clenches, thinking of the message.

"Did you—"

"I did."

We stare at each other in silence.

"Why?" I plead.

"Because it's true, Eric."

Tears again form in my already tired eyes. "I can't—"

"I know, and you don't have to believe me. I am not going to force this knowledge on you. Too much has been done without your consent already," he admits, running his hands through his hair. "The truth is, I don't have permission to be here, and I honestly don't know how long I will be able to get away with it. Do you know what this machine is?" he asks, motioning to the equipment sitting next to me.

"I think it's a reversal therapy machine."

"Correct. Do you know what it's used for?"

"They use it to eliminate trauma, typically just portions of it—softening it so that people can heal."

"True. It can be used to eliminate anything, really. Even to create memories if desired."

"That's incredible," I say, shifting forward on my seat. "That could do so much good—"

"Always the optimist," he sighs. "You're right, but I have recently discovered that it has been used on unwilling subjects—"

"Sometimes that is necessary, if individuals are unwilling to move forward," I argue.

"Eric, I promise. I'm going somewhere with this," he pleads.

"Right. Limited time. Sorry."

"There are people in Tier 1 who are using this technology for their own purposes. Completely unethically, in my opinion. But regardless of whether you think that's possible, let's talk about you. I'm not going to mince words, so try to stick with me. Eric, you and Kate were split without consent. You are Tier 1 and so is Tal, but you were moved to Tier 2 after your memories were adjusted. Mostly to keep you from seeing Kate again, but also because the Committee knows how hard you work. Kate is alive,

Eric. She loves you. I came here to assess whether you want that life back."

The room seems to shift around me, a million questions darting through my brain at once. I close my eyes again, attempting to calm the clamor.

"I know it's a lot to take in, but we don't have much time. Yes or no?"

"How do I answer that?" I exclaim. "I don't even remember the life you're talking about, let alone know whether I want it. If Kate is alive, I want her. But it's impossible! I don't know who you are, I don't know where my son is!" I shout into the ether.

"Yep, I know. You're going to have to trust me," he answers calmly, ignoring my outburst. "Would you like your memories back?" he asks, his eyes searing into mine. How can I say yes to this? Could this be some elaborate ploy to 'fix' whatever has been going on? Did Tal call the center, worried about me?

"Where's Tal," I ask again.

"Yes or no, Eric. I won't ask again."

My stomach turns. "Yes," I sob desperately.

"Lean back," he commands, and I lower my back to the chair.

Across the field, I see Nick slide a hand around Kate's waist. I watch them as the balloon next to me begins to inflate, breathing hot air across my skin. They talk, Kate's shoulders lifted, obviously tense. Though I wasn't expecting Nick to be here, I can't say that

I'm surprised. Initially, I allowed myself to believe that his involvement was purely out of obedience to the Committee, but seeing the way he looks at her...

Pulling my clenched hands out of my pockets, I begin to make my way through the balloons. The brightly colored canvases against the brilliant orange hues of the sunrise serve to highlight my mood. Today I will be reunited with my family. The seemingly endless days without them are *actually ending*, and I can hardly believe it. Still, there is a part of me that begs to turn around, to stick it out. Ashamed at my weakness. For a long time, that part was strong enough to keep me going, but not anymore.

As I draw closer, I notice Kate scanning the crowd, her hands jammed into her pockets. The boys' eyes are wide in awe of the scene before them. For a moment, I stop, watching them experience the magic. When Kate's eyes meet mine, my heart leaps, making my extremities go numb. My focus shifts to Nick—oblivious—as I walk toward them. As if sensing Kate's emotions, the boys turn and notice my approach, immediately jetting toward me. Tears sting the corners of my eyes, and I stretch my arms wide to embrace them. How did I ever think I could live without them?

"Kate, what's going on?" Nick questions.

"Nick..." Kate starts, but stops short.

"Hey Nick," I greet him, speaking gently, and purposefully keeping my distance. Not wanting to cause a scene, I turn the boys' attention to the nearest balloon.

"Eric, what's going on?" Nick asks quietly. "I don't think you are supposed to be here."

"I'm not," I answer, my heart pounding. "Kate, why don't I watch the boys for a minute and you can have a moment with Nick to explain." I look at her, trying to communicate that I understand. She and Nick, as much as it pains me to admit, have created a relationship. A life. I don't blame her for a second, and I want to give her the space to help him understand. I am here, and the fact that she is also here means that I don't need to know or worry about what has transpired between them.

Nick looks back at her, his face pained. "Explain what?" he asks. Her eyes swim with tears as she begins to lead him away from us.

"I'll meet you at the balloon rides, Kate," I call after them.

"So, what should we do while we wait?" I ask, turning back to the boys.

"Play tag," Bentley suggests immediately.

"Seems a little dangerous with all of this fire everywhere," I tease.

"It'll just make it more fun," Tal says, slamming his hand into my shoulder. "You're it."

The boys scatter and I have to call out the rules above the sound of the fans and burners. "No actual running, only speed walking," I say, and Tal throws his arms up in dissent. "You can still go fast, I promise! And no walking through the balloon prep areas—you have to go all the way around."

The boys nod, and I dramatically begin my chase, goofily swinging my arms by my sides. Bentley roars with laughter, almost forgetting to escape. It proves to be a game of hide-and-seek, rather than tag, as the boys' strategy turns to remaining silently obscured by half-filled balloons. Swiftly turning around each one, confusion sets in. How have I not found one of them yet?

"Bent! Tal!" I call, "I give up!"

No response. Running my hands through my hair, I turn back the way I came and stop short. Shari. And Grace. With Tal and Bentley in hand.

"WHEN IS NICK GETTING BACK?" Bentley asks. He still hasn't said much to me since our conversation.

"He should be home tonight, I think he was only planning to spend a couple of days with his Dad," I answer. "How was conditioning today?"

Bentley shrugs his shoulders, picking up an apple and wandering toward the back door.

"Bent," I call. "What's going through your head? I shared all of that information with you the other day and you haven't said much."

"You haven't said much either," he responds, taking a bite and chewing. He has a point.

"I didn't want to seem overbearing."

"Neither did I," he says. Still chewing. What do I say to that?

"Okay," I nod. "But I'm talking now."

"It's going to be alright, Mom. I know we'll figure out a way to be a family again."

"How do you know?" I ask in disbelief. "How, Bent? This is serious, bud. The Committee is not going to just allow us to waltz out of Tier 1 and join Eric and Tal—"

"They don't have to allow us to do anything," he says, licking the juice as it drips onto his fingers. "Don't worry, Mom."

"Don't worry!? Bent—"

He runs to me and hugs me tightly around the waist. "Nick's on it, remember? You're a team," he says, then runs to the backyard.

A team. If only it were that simple.

Nick arrives late that night, nearly stumbling through the front door in exhaustion. Though I am lying down, ready for sleep, I sit up to greet him.

"You okay?" I ask, laughing slightly at his disheveled appearance.

He looks up at me, not amused. I burst out laughing, not able to hold it back any longer.

"Seriously?" he asks, throwing his arms wide.

"I'm sorry, I don't think I have ever seen you look so out of sorts. I know it's not funny, but...it's kind of funny."

A smile plays at the corners of his mouth as he walks over and slumps next to me on the couch.

"Good visit with your dad?" I ask.

He nods. "Good visit, but travel is exhausting."

"I wish I could commiserate, but I have no experience with it."

Nick pauses, breathing deeply.

"What?" I ask, noticing his hesitation.

"I have to report to the Committee in a few days," he says.

"That's going to be great, right? Show them all of your impressive research and score massive points with the Director?"

"Something like that," he chuckles.

"You'll be great, Nick."

"Thanks, he says, patting my leg. I'm going to get ready for bed before I pass out right here."

"Do you need anything to eat?"

"No, I'm good, thanks though," he says, heaving himself to a standing position. I watch him go, then hit the lights, pulling a blanket over myself and closing my eyes.

As I'm walking home from the outdoor nursery, I see Shari walking down the path toward me. Though I don't have the energy for a superficial conversation, I plaster a smile on my face and slow to greet her.

"Girls are loving this still?" she asks.

"They are. It hasn't gotten old yet," I say. "It helps that they are always bringing in new toys and obstacles."

"I can't believe they are pulling themselves up," she comments.

"You and me both, it's crazy. What brings you down here?" I ask, keeping the mood light.

"I was hoping to find you, actually. With Nick being out of town, I wondered if you could use some help?"

"You didn't have to come all the way down—you could have just sent me a message," I tease.

"Yeah, I know. Maybe I also wanted some fresh air," she says, looking at the ground. "Do you have plans now? Could we take a walk?"

"I actually do need to get a few things done at home, but you can help me if you want," I offer. Something is different in her demeanor today. She seems grounded, more humble.

"Sure, you can put me to work."

We meander home, taking the long way, while Shari fills me in on her most recent trip. I can't remember if I told her that Nick had filled me in on everything, but she must have assumed.

"Have you ever traveled beyond our region?" I ask. So far, she has only described other territories. With everything I have learned in the last few weeks, my curiosity about the outside world is peaking. What if there are other things Berg has decided to keep from us? Things that the various Committees don't feel are necessary for us to know?

"Only once," she answers softly.

"Where?" I ask.

"North. Years ago."

"For fun?" I ask.

"No, it was a recon assignment. At the time, Berg was looking for salt. It is still one of our most limited resources, but back then it was extremely rare within our territories. Before I joined the Committee, I was chosen to go. I remember being terrified. We really had no idea what we were flying into."

"What were you worried about?"

"Everything! Animals, possibly other humans who somehow survived, infection, radioactivity, you name it."

I nod. I have been safely in our Tier 1 bubble for so long, I have forgotten that an entire planet exists beyond our borders.

"So, what did you find?"

"Salt."

"Nothing else?"

She shakes her head. "Nope. The landscape was surprisingly lush, considering the soil toxicity levels. I would love to research that area again someday. Observe what plant adaptations have occurred."

"It would be fascinating," I admit. "Couldn't you go if you wanted to?"

"I could," she muses. "There is always so much going on here, it's hard to justify such a long, dangerous trip."

"Seems like it would be incredibly helpful research," I say and she smiles.

It kills me. I miss feeling close to her. I miss having no wall up, just the freedom to laugh and be ourselves. Will we ever get it back? Can I ever be completely vulnerable again, understanding that she has been privy to my history and isn't willing to be open with me? I may have to try. This could very well be the life that I'm stuck with, and I will have to make the best of it. The very thought causes my chest to sink into itself.

"It would be," she sighs. "Maybe someday."

SHE'S DYING to talk about it. Every move she makes is in some way shifted because of her attempts to hide her desperation. I want to spill everything, but I can't do that to her yet. I have *no* idea if this is going to work or not. There is a very high chance that I won't come home tonight, let alone come home with good news.

Everything shakes. My hands shake as I attempt to eat the delicious food—currently tasteless on my tongue—that Kate has prepared. My legs shake as I force myself to sit still, feigning interest in Bentley's dialogue. My jaw shakes with each bite, nearly causing me to dribble food back onto my plate. Glancing at the clock, I see that there is still an hour before I need to leave. The last few minutes have seemed interminably long. I have to do something productive.

"I think I'll go on a walk. Anyone want to join me?" I say abruptly, cutting Bentley off.

"I will!" he answers excitedly. While I don't love the idea of his chatter in this moment, this is the first time he has expounded on anything in weeks.

"Sure," I say. Beth and Leah begin kicking their legs excitedly, throwing their spoons to the ground.

"Thanks, Nick," Kate teases. "Can we at least wait until after dinner to make announcements like that?"

"I'm sorry, I have to do something. My body is completely hyped up about this meeting," I explain, and she nods.

"Go for it," she says. 'The kids can eat more when you get home. I'll get the stroller and come along—"

"Not unless you actually want to. Otherwise I am fine taking them on my own," I offer.

"I want to," Kate says. Again, seeming to stop short before completing her most pressing thought. After washing her hands, she disappears into the backyard and returns through the front door with hats for the girls, the buggy parked near the step.

Slow down, I remind myself, seeing that Bentley and Kate are lagging behind. My legs burn with pent-up energy and I yearn to run until my body collapses. The cortisol and adrenaline in my body continuously signal for flight.

"Nick," Kate calls from behind. "Seriously, just do twenty burpees right now."

"What?" I ask, turning to face her.

"Twenty burpees. Go."

Without hesitation, I move to the clover next to the path—quickly scanning for bees in the flowers—and drop.

"Feel better?" she laughs, watching the sweat dripping down the sides of my face.

"I feel like I should have changed my clothes," I say, looking down at my rumpled shirt.

"Plenty of time for that before you leave," she says. "Did it help?"

"Yeah, thanks. Sorry, I am really struggling to keep it together."

"Why are you so nervous? Your research should speak for itself," she comments.

"I don't know, it's silly."

"Not silly," Bentley says. "Silly would be underestimating the impact this meeting will have. For all of us."

Kate and I look at each other. Her eyes plead with me, as if asking, "What are we going to do?" for the millionth time.

"What do you mean, Bent?" I ask.

"You're a team right? That means that anything you do well is going to help all of us figure this out. If the Committee likes it, won't that bring us closer to finding my dad?"

My heart sinks. If only he knew.

"Bent, why don't you run over there to the playground. We'll follow. Beth and Leah love the swings."

As he skips happily across the meadow, Kate reaches for my hand. "We have to find him, Nick. I don't know how, and I am sick about what that means for you, but Bent and I—we can't be fully invested here while that hangs over our heads. If eventually we have to resign ourselves, I know we can find a way. But right now...we haven't been forced into that yet. I'm so sorry, Nick," she nearly whispers, wrapping her arms around my waist.

My heart aches and I hold my breath, waiting for the worst of it to pass. How? How am I going to move forward alone?

Suddenly, she whips her head back. "What about Beth and Leah? How will—"

"Kate, stop," I groan. "We can't speculate. This situation is stressful enough as it is—"

"How is it not *more* stressful to *not* speculate? My brain has to do something! I can't sit here doing nothing. I'm basically a walking shell, Nick. I go through the motions, but my brain is working on an entirely different planet."

"I know, I know," I say, rubbing her arms. "I feel the same way. If you asked me what we had for breakfast or lunch, I would have to think really hard about it. It's okay. Bentley, until tonight apparently, has been miles away, too. We are all processing, and I promise, I will have something soon. Just trust me to work on this in my own time, Kate. I'm not avoiding it, but I know this has to be done right."

She nods, breathing deeply. "You're right. I will keep it together, sorry."

Beth and Leah begin whining in their seats. They have been stopped for far too long in front of bushes that couldn't possibly keep their interest in the first place.

"Okay, sorry girls. Let's go to the park," I say, moving toward Bentley who is happily playing in the distance.

After changing my clothes, the time finally arrives for me to head to the auditorium. Tamara sent a message earlier letting me know that our files are prepped and ready to go. All I have to do—my breath instantly stops in my chest. Breathe, I remind myself. It's going to work. *It has to work.* Breathe.

I kiss Bent and the girls on the forehead and hug Kate tightly before walking out the door. My body, ironically, now screams to stay. Forcing each leg to step toward the car, I open the door and lower myself to the seat.

Tal, I think. Where is Tal? Jumping up from the couch, my head spins, and I fall back. I brace myself for a moment while it settles, then attempt standing again. Walking briskly down the hall, I swing his door open and find him lying facedown on his mattress, his legs sprawled into open space.

Relief floods my system as I sit gently next to him, lightly shaking his shoulder. His body spasms and jerks upright. Placing my hands on his face, I force him to look in my eyes.

"Tal, it's me. It's okay. We're home," I soothe, and watch his posture relax.

"What—what happened?" he asks, his voice groggy.

"You tell me," I say. "I know what happened to me, but I didn't see you the entire time. I'm so glad you're safe." I pull his head into my shoulder, embracing him tightly. He doesn't complain. Eventually straightening up, he rubs his face with his hands.

"It's hazy," he admits. "I was here, waiting for you to get back, and the door opened. I obviously thought it was you, but was confused because it didn't seem like it had been very long. Then I assumed you had forgotten something, so I stood up, planning to tease you about getting old, when a man walked in. I froze, Dad. It's embarrassing, but I totally froze."

"Not embarrassing, Tal, completely normal."

"He held something over my face, and then I was in some room—"

"Did you get them back?" I ask, my eyes searing into his.

"All of them," he answers, choking back tears.

I embrace him again, and this time he doesn't let go.

A knock on the door pulls us back into the present. Quickly wiping the tears from my cheeks, I walk cautiously to the front, but relax when I see long, blond hair through the window.

"Eric?" Val calls. "Eric, are you in there?"

I steel myself and open the door.

"Eric," she says in a rush, gripping my arms and pulling me to her. "I was so worried." Scanning my face, her expression changes from relief to concern. "Maybe I still am worried," she admits. "You look awful."

I laugh at the brutal honesty. "Val, I don't—so much has—I don't know where to start," I stammer, whether out of nervousness or exhaustion, I can't tell.

"Can I come in?" she asks, and I motion for her to enter. Noticing for the first time the bag of portions on the counter, I quickly begin to unload while she takes a seat.

"Ugh. It stinks in here. Can I open a window?"

I nod, laughing.

"Please tell me what's going on." she pleads as she pulls the pane open. "I haven't heard from you and you haven't been in the fields. I asked Kip what was going on, and he claimed you were sick, but I haven't ever seen you take a sick day. It seemed off. I probably shouldn't have come over here unannounced—"

I pull her into a hug, cutting her off. "It's okay, Val. I am so grateful that you care." Rubbing her shoulder, we move in tandem to the kitchen chairs. Tal joins us, sitting across from Val and she smiles.

"Val, Kate's alive," I say and her eyes widen. "Tal and I—a friend we know from Tier 1, he...ambushed us today—"

"In a good way, kind of scary. But good," Tal interjects. Val's eyes dart from me to him and back.

"He took us to a rehabilitation center and treated us. I don't know how he did it, but he reversed some adjustments that had been made without our knowledge," I explain.

"What kind of adjustments?" she asks in confusion.

"Memories that were taken or altered. Tal and I—we aren't from here. We are Tier 1, but they needed to keep us hidden after—well, after they decided to take Kate."

"They took her? Why would they do that? And how?" she asks, her eyes wide.

"It's a long story," I start.

"I've got time," she says, leaning back and crossing her arms across her chest.

"So...you have this whole other life," Val says when I finish.

I nod.

"Had," Tal says. "It's gone now."

"Tal—"

"No, Dad. What are we supposed to do with this information? We can't tell anyone, they'll assume we're crazy. And we have no way to find out where Mom is. Or Bentley."

"I know we don't, but don't you think Nick has something up his sleeve?" I ask. "He made it here to us, he must be figuring it out."

"That's a lot of trust you're putting in the man who paired with Mom," he teases.

"Wait, Nick was the one who gave you your memories back?" Val says. "Why would he do that?"

I exhale audibly. "I don't know. I woke up here and didn't have a chance to ask. And Tal, please don't use that tone. Nick is obviously trying to help—"

"Or make us more miserable," Tal says.

"Don't take your hurt out on him," I say gently and see Tal's eyes gloss over. "I am terrified, too. I don't know what to do, but we *will* figure something out. That's what we do."

"I can help," Val announces. "I have some clearance in Tier 1. I can't guarantee that I'll be able to find anything, but I can at least try."

"Val, you don't have—"

"I want to, Eric. This isn't right."

"But it really might be," I argue. "We are in this situation because I was selfish. This research—this pairing—was necessary and I blew it."

"I disagree," Tal pipes in. "If you're right and Nick is trying to help, there has to be something going on in Tier 1. Something that would make him second guess the decisions he made."

Pondering this, I stand to stretch my legs. "It's possible," I admit. "Though I can't imagine what that would be."

"Let me look into it," Val says. "I can send you a message by tomorrow night if all goes well." She stands abruptly and walks toward the door.

"Val," I say, following her. Lowering my voice, I whisper, "I'm so sorry. You mean so much—"

"It's ok, Eric—"

"No, it's not. I know what it feels like to be replaced."

She nods. "I care about you. I'm not going to pretend that I don't wish things were different, but caring for someone doesn't mean that you only 'care' when life goes your way. I'll check into this and let you know," she says hurriedly, throwing her hair over her shoulder and turning before I can stop her.

"Hey, Eric, what are you doing here?" Matt asks, looking me over disapprovingly. "Are you okay?" he asks, stepping out onto the path.

"Are you free for a walk?" I ask.

"Sure, I guess," he answers, his eyebrows furrowed. "Just let me turn off the stove."

"Oh, I didn't mean to interrupt, if you're cooking—"

"No, it's fine, just a second," he assures me, retreating back inside. Maybe this was a bad idea, I think, rocking on my heels. With all of this bouncing around in my head, a disturbing thought occurred to me. Matt has been my mentor since I was a kid. He's been involved in my life every step of the way. Does he know? Was he a part of this, or did they take his memories away, too?"

"What are you cooking?" I ask, smelling herbs. "And how do you have basil this time of year?"

Matt laughs. "I dried some when it was harvested a few months ago."

"Smart."

"Where do you want to walk?" he asks, following me away from his unit.

"Doesn't matter to me. This way?" I point and he nods. "I just wanted to talk and it's easier for me to do that when I am moving."

"I've been trying to get in touch with you, Eric. You haven't answered me in days."

"I know, I'm sorry," I answer. "Some things came up this week and I haven't really been myself." We turn the corner and cross onto a path that leads through a small park behind the distribution center.

"How are things going with Val?"

"Well," I answer. "We are good friends, I think."

Matt smiles. "Nothing more than that?" he teases, nudging my arm.

"Matt, what do you think about the Tier system?" I ask, and he stops walking abruptly. Turning, I face him.

"What are you talking about?" Matt asks.

"I've just been thinking a lot about it. Some friends at work have been talking about their dissatisfaction with life around here."

"Really? Huh. I don't know how to answer that. I guess I haven't thought about it," he says, walking again.

"They talk about wanting opportunity. Have you ever tried to qualify for Tier 1? It seems like you have the numbers to make it happen," I say. "No trauma like I have to hold you back."

"I think I could be close," he answers, "but I'm happy here. I don't feel the need to take on more responsibility."

"You've never wanted to have more variety in life? More opportunities for growth?"

"No, I guess not," he says shaking his head.

I change the subject to his service assignment. I've gotten what I came for. There's no way Matt grew up Tier 2. Completely satisfied with life? Never wondering if there is something better? That sounds like the only other Tier 1 person I know here. Me.

Arriving back in front of his unit, I thank him as he walks toward his door. "Hey Matt, do you really think I should move forward with Val?"

He shields his eyes from the sun, squinting. "What have you got to lose?" He slowly turns and walks through the door, closing it behind him.

Heading home, my mind spins with new information. If Matt is Tier 1, has he been put here to basically babysit me? Help me transition? He is obviously receiving special treatment. That did *not* smell like dried basil. I nearly laugh out loud at the ridiculousness of making an assumption about Matt based on herb possession, and yet in my mind, it stands. It doesn't prove whether he has been involved in any of this, but it definitely makes me suspicious.

Shaking my head, I chastise myself. He would have only been doing what was asked of him, as everyone does. There is no fault in that. Somehow, I am still not convinced that I understand what is going on. Though I remember the order of events, I still can't settle on whether I acted appropriately or not. One thing has been cleared up for me definitively, though: Tal is, and always has been, destined for more. I have to find a way to make it up to him.

45 / NICK

As PROMISED, the presentation is loaded and ready to go in the auditorium when I arrive. Tamara might be the person I feel most guilty about reversing. Though, I only took away information regarding the trials, leaving everything personal intact. Still. She has contributed immensely to our success and now she won't be able to take credit for it.

I am shocked by the number of people already here, milling around, or already planted in their seats. The Director promised a regional audience, but this can't possibly represent only our region. Unless other community members have also been invited?

"Are you ready?" I hear a woman say behind me, and I spin around.

"Oh, hey, Grace. Yes, I think so."

"We are all extremely excited to hear your results. Talking with a few Committee members from down south, it sounds like the side effects we have witnessed are not isolated incidents. Initially, I wasn't sure that other territories were—well, that they had progressed to our same level, using reversal proactively."

Using it to protect yourselves, you mean? I think it, but don't say it. "You feel like other territories are also using reversal more extensively?"

She nods. "Sounds like it. With all of this new research, we weren't the only ones to run into...unwilling participants," she says slowly, a wan smile on her lips.

"Well I hope this will be helpful for all. I would hate to waste anyone's time when they have traveled so far to be here."

"We have representatives from every territory in the union. And —" she pauses, glancing around. "I didn't want to make you nervous, but Carole Berg is here."

My face blanches, the blood rushing in my ears. With eyes wide, I can't make myself respond.

"Nick? Are you okay?" Grace asks, eyebrows furrowed.

I take a deep breath. "Yes, that just took me off guard. Nobody informed me that I would be presenting to *everyone*. The union, really?" Beads of sweat begin to form along my hairline as my mind attempts to process this. "Wait, why would Carole—"

"Apparently she has been very concerned with the reversal reports. She has been hopeful that your research would provide some insights."

"How does she even know about my research?" I ask, incredulous.

"We report every project from our territory," Grace answers matter-of-factly. "Did you think it was off the books?"

"I mean, yeah, I figured it was just my own thing."

"We have to account for resources, Nick," Grace scoffs.

"But if we are utilizing excess—" I start, the wheels in my head turning frantically. "Wait, does that mean that every territory is doing this? Is this change in protocol for Committee members union wide?"

"What did you think? That we were the only region in this situation? Resources are centralized, Nick. We are all in the same boat." She gives me a quizzical look, then laughs out loud.

"Sorry," I say, "of course that makes sense. I think my nerves are getting to me."

"Well, I will leave you be. I don't want to add to it," she says, a smirk still lingering on her face.

"Thanks," I say, my voice disappearing behind her. I push down panic, my fingers and toes numb and cold. In my mind, I had envisioned a very small scale version of tonight. Now, faced with the reality that I will be going for broke in front of the *entire union* leaves me in shock. And *Carole Berg*? I'm a dead man. There is no way that this will fly.

Turning around, I face the back of the stage. This is not me. Again, the Committee has turned me into something I'm not: small, unsure, insecure Nick. Does it really matter how many people are here? How many witnesses there are? Sure, it might exponentially increase the risk of negative consequences for me, but will it really decrease the likelihood of my plan working? Pondering on this a moment, I come to the conclusion that it may actually increase the odds. If everyone is privy to the details, there is less of a chance that someone will reach out with bad information, looking for a more beneficial solution.

Taking a deep breath, I tell myself I am ready. I am ready to make a real difference, not only in the lives of my family, but also, hopefully, for our society as a whole. We can't go on like this. I still have twenty minutes before start time, so I quickly exit for a washroom break. With all of this added pressure, I definitely need to at least feel physically comfortable.

"Thank you all for coming," the Director says, calling our meeting to order. "I know we have all been anticipating this presentation for a few weeks, so I will be brief, but I think it will be helpful for everyone to see some statistics before I turn the time over to Nick." He winks at me, and I want to vomit. The screen lights up.

"This chart is a compilation of information I have been collecting since Nick first reminded us of our reversal conundrum. Of course, we were aware that individuals sometimes suffered from headaches or struggled mentally after some of these procedures, but they seemed very few and far between. Certainly nothing that I was overly concerned about. Curious, I reached out to each of you, asking for numbers and the results were shocking. At least, for me," he adds, pandering.

"You can see here the total number of 'extensive reversal sessions'. For ease of charting, I have lumped all sessions that lasted longer than six hours into this group, regardless of type of reversal event. In the future, we will analyze this more specifically, but you can see, these occurrences have drastically increased over the last year throughout all territories. Next to it, we see the number of individuals who have reported side effects, including headache, dreams, confusion, or lower mental performance."

The room is hushed, everyone's eyes glued to the chart in front of them. The numbers show that nearly eighty percent of patients in that category have reported one these symptoms. My fists clench involuntarily. How did Berg allow this therapy to be used so irresponsibly? How did Committee members move forward into completely uncharted territory without even considering that this could be harmful?

A hand shoots up in the center of the room. The Director, though visibly surprised, calls on the woman. She stands, slight in stature and striking. Her angular face is set off nicely by her soft, auburn curls.

"My name is Jessica Fray. I serve on the Committee for Maine Territory. These numbers are shocking to me as well. In my experience, these extensive reversal sessions are few and far between— used for emergency only. Am I missing something? How are our collective numbers so high?"

Faces glance side to side in the crowd, bodies shifting uncomfortably. Electricity seems to flow through my veins, sending a surge of hope into my being. Not everyone agrees with this, I realize triumphantly. There is obviously at least one individual who isn't currently employing these tactics and many others who don't want to admit to it. I force down a smile, not wanting to betray my feelings. Yet.

"Jessica, great question. Not every territory has progressed equally in this technique, but there will be increasing need in the months and years to come. As each territory is comprised of different population groups, we would expect a different subset of complications from the changes we have experienced. If you haven't personally encountered push-back from our recent initiatives, consider yourself lucky," he says, and I hear a few chuckles rise from the audience. "I am sure Nick will discuss more of this in a moment, but thank you for your concern," he says, diverting his attention back to the group as a whole. Again, I force my face to remain neutral. He has no idea.

"I'd actually like to turn the time over to Nick. As I shared in my briefing, he has been our lead researcher on this subject and I urge you to listen to his recommendations. Nick?"

I nearly laugh with giddiness as I stand, adrenaline overloading my system. Deep breaths, I remind myself.

"Thank you," I say, standing and taking center stage. "Like the Director mentioned, the use of aggressive reversal therapy has been used more extensively and, Jessica was it? I promise I'll comment on that more near the end of my presentation, but first let me share some of my observations. I'd like to get a bit personal. Hopefully that's appropriate in this setting—I think it will give credence to the information I will present tonight." Taking command of the dock, I bring up my first slide. A picture of Kate and Bentley explodes onto the screen.

"This is my pair, Kate. We haven't always been together. You are obviously all familiar with the groundbreaking research completed by Eric Hayes?" Heads nod, so I continue. "Eric and Kate were paired for years before I came on the scene. They had two children —this picture displays only one of them. When Eric's research propelled pairings in each of our territories, Kate and I were one of only eight matches in our territory. I know," I acknowledge the collective, sharp intake of breath. "Many of you experienced fantastic pairing numbers, but we weren't so lucky. Our Committee, based on research and personality analytics, took action to separate Kate and Eric, pairing her with me instead. I am her genetic match under the TSG parameters. Obviously, this was an incredibly difficult transition and both Eric and Kate struggled to make it. This concluded in my first experience with an extensive reversal session—Kate's. Allowing her to move forward without any memory of her previous life. When she began to suffer from all of the side effects that the Director already mentioned, I was troubled and, based on this scan, made the connection that prompted my research on this subject." Her scan appears above me and I stand in silence, allowing everyone to process the horror that was her brain. Sweat trickles down my back, but I ignore it.

"Almost sickening isn't it?" I say, noticing Grace whisper something to the Director in my periphery. "After extensive research, I had a hunch. I began trials, targeting individuals in both Tier 1 and Tier 2 who had reported symptoms. Eventually, I also treated new reversal patients, passed on to me by our Director, using this new technique.

As you know, reversal therapy, when used to alter deep, integrated memories can be extremely challenging. Side effects are caused by what I like to call 'echoes.' These are shadows of the original memory, tucked away in corners of the brain not anticipated by our technology. These echoes are then triggered by random events and experience, but no longer have a framework to shape them. The cognitive dissonance that this creates—both consciously and unconsciously—is incredibly damaging and frustrating for the patient." I click forward on my sensor, showing Kate's 'after' scan.

"After a few initial treatments, this is Kate's brain." Again, I pause, allowing for analysis. Then I pull up both images side-by-side. "Previously, despite being able to see where the damage had occurred, we weren't able to 'release' these echoes and eliminate them. My procedure has proven capable of doing that, not only retroactively, but also for first-time, aggressive treatments."

The next image is a chart, almost identical to the Director's, but with one major difference. The numbers in the second column, representing reports of negative side effects, are all the same. Zero.

Hands begin to pop up across the room. Grace is glowing and the Director has a wolfish grin on his face. My heart races, again making my hands go momentarily numb. Distracting myself, I point to a man on my right, his hand catching my eye first.

"What was your procedure?" he asks. Another voice shouts from across the room, "Has this been tested anywhere else?" I hold up my hands, motioning for silence.

"Let me see if I can answer some of your questions preemptively. Yes, my sample size was fairly small, but the results are obviously statistically significant." This comment pulls laughter from the crowd. "This has not been tested elsewhere. Trials were just recently completed, so there hasn't been time for that. I will comment on the actual procedure in a moment, but first, there is something else I would like to discuss." Here it is. My heart pounds, my mouth becomes thick, and I choke on my last words. Sweat glands prickle uncomfortably under my arms. I close my eyes and envision Kate, desperation on her face, attempting to find a solution to this mess. Bentley, with his absolute confidence in my ability to do so. I can do this, I tell myself. Taking two deep breaths, I begin.

"I promised I would comment on these aggressive procedures, as Jessica brought up earlier. First, let me ask you. In your collective opinion, why has our use of reversal therapy in this way—used to erase memories, sometimes entire portions of patients' lives—increased? This technology has always existed, so why now?" I ask, only to be met with silence. "I know some of you have opinions on this, so I will happily wait," I say, my voice low. After a few uncomfortable moments, a hand raises near the back.

"Yes, sir," I say, pointing.

"I can only speak for myself, obviously, but I know we have seen more pushback, like your Director mentioned. Unfortunately, more Tier 1 individuals seem to be balking at what is being asked of them."

I nod. "Okay, thanks. Anyone else?"

Another hand shoots up. "There have been some incidents in our territory, specifically where a Tier 1 individual has been dissatisfied with a Committee decision. They needed to be dealt with to maintain the peace," she announces shyly.

"These are both things that I have witnessed, definitely," I agree. "Let me ask you two more questions. First, in a society steeped in research and caution when it comes to technology and treatment, why have we begun utilizing reversal therapy in this way, with literally *no* research to justify it? To assure us that there was no harm in our treatment? Second, why do you think, after hundreds of years with zero need for 'dealing' with members of Tier 1, are we faced with conflict?"

Again, people shift uncomfortably in their seats. The Director rises, beginning to move toward the stage.

"Sir, with all due respect, I would ask you to take your seat and let me finish," I command. The room erupts into agitated conversation. Panic again threatens to rise in my chest, but I push it down, staring the Director down. His eyes bore into mine, no longer moving forward, but not sitting down either.

"Stop!" a voice shrieks above the din, and heads whip to the back corner of the room. Carole Berg. As people recognize her, the room again retreats into silence.

"I'll answer your questions, Nick," she offers. "Everyone, please take your seats," she says, pointedly looking at the Director, who obediently lowers himself down again. I breathe a sigh of relief.

"The answer to your second question will explain the answer to your first. We haven't adapted our conditioning quickly enough to accomodate for the changes we are experiencing. Our progress is exponential; this new research by Hayes is only one example of that. Yet our conditioning has remained somewhat stagnant. We are using this technology as a temporary plug. A way to stop the leak until we can better prepare individuals in Tier 1 to meet these expectations willingly."

"And those expectations would be?" I ask gently.

"What they have always been—"

"I would argue that they are absolutely not what they have always been," I interject, my confidence building. "Never before have we had resources in such excess. Never before have we expected individuals to break familial ties for procreation. Never before have we kept Tier 1 individuals in the dark—"

"Oh wake up, Nick," she snaps. "We have always kept Tier 1 individuals in the dark. Absolute chaos would ensue if everyone was included in every decision. We entrust our most intelligent, most committed members to lead us, that's how it's always been."

"And what if our most intelligent, most committed members begin to violate our most basic societal understandings? What if they begin to serve themselves over the collective whole?"

"That can't happen," she argues.

"Why can't it happen?" I ask, incredulous. "It has happened over and over again throughout history. Are we so arrogant to think that we are somehow immune from basic human instinct? You, yourself, just admitted that our conditioning is lacking. Our 'most trusted' individuals have come through that system. Yes, we are still seeing progress, and yes, I believe we are still moving forward, but in which direction? My Director sent me patients to treat without consent. Without my consent, and without the consent of the individual being treated. I have witnessed lapses in judgement that I cannot justify. I believe we are at a crucial juncture that will determine our future as a society. If we continue to allow these small, seemingly innocuous acts to infiltrate our leadership, we will fall. I promise you that. We don't have time for our conditioning to catch up, Carole. We have to act now."

Carole stands, staring at me with steely eyes. The room, again, eerily silent. "And what would you propose?" she asks, causing the Director's face to flush an even angrier shade of red.

"I do not have enough information to propose anything, but I will tell you what I will do personally. I will not give details of this procedure until these wrongs have been rectified—" I am cut off, voices rising in anger from the crowd.

I wait, watching Carole walk to the front slowly, the sound slowly dying as she passes each row. Her shoes click on the stairs as she joins me onstage.

"Please, everyone, silence. What we have just witnessed is evidence that we have adjustments that need to be made. We will work with the research team to make this procedure accessible—"

"I don't think you are hearing me," I say gently. "The procedural information exists in only one place," I say, tapping my forehead. "I haven't kept any information publicly and I have used reversal therapy to remove any pertinent information from my assistants."

"But you can't—" she sputters.

"We do it all the time. Think of the chaos that would ensue if—"

"Don't you dare quote me right now," she hisses. "There has to be a record."

"I assure you, there is not. And as useful as reversal therapy is, we have yet to discover a way to extract information. I recommend you meet my terms."

"We have other means of extracting information."

Addressing the room, I speak up, "If nothing else I have put forward tonight has convinced you that we are in a dangerous situation where leadership is concerned, that statement should do it."

Carole seethes next to me.

"This is not who we are. We don't commit to a trajectory and refuse to adjust when new information is presented. We don't harm our citizens to protect our own assets, our own pride. I have been left with no other choice. I have the key to a therapy that I do not trust our current leadership to use appropriately. I need assurance that our path has been adjusted before I will turn it over."

"I agree," I hear from the crowd. Jessica is standing. A man stands next to her, then another. Soon, at least fifteen people are on their feet.

"Please," Carole says, waving them off, "no need to stand." Nobody moves. Her tone becomes sickly sweet. "I agree that we are progressing quickly and, perhaps we need to realign our priorities. In my defense, we have been in crisis mode—trying to act on new research, integrate new tech, expand our territory and distribution—"

"There's no blame here, Carole. I don't think that anyone actively dropped into these roles purposefully. We are simply misguided— adopting assumptions that are false and avoiding hard truths."

She nods. "Surely we can find a compromise—"

"I have terms that will need to be met. One hundred percent. I'm sorry if that sounds harsh, but I don't see another option that will set things right."

Her lips purse into a tight line and her nostrils flare with each breath. "What are your terms?" she asks coldly.

"I have three. First, this information needs to be made public." As she begins to protest, I raise my hands. "I'm not asking that you expose every resource detail, but you need to allow Tier 1 individuals to understand the situation. I have discovered that many of these reversal situations have occurred due to informational leaks. Open conversation would eliminate the need for these procedures while allowing our citizens to come together and find a solution that benefits all." Her eyes narrow, but she doesn't respond. I take this as my cue to continue. "Second, each person that has been treated without consent needs to be notified and debriefed—"

"That is impossible, it would take months—"

"How could it possibly take that long if this is a 'rare occurrence'? And, as far as I understand it, Committee members have plenty of time on their hands," I say pointedly.

She sniffs. "Third?"

"Third, I want reparations made to my family."

"But you have already eliminated Kate's symptoms—"

"I want Kate to be allowed to re-pair with Eric, and Bentley and Tal to remain with them."

"In what world—"

"Kate has fulfilled her duty. We have two beautiful daughters, genetically primed for tumor suppression. I realize it's not ideal, but neither is living with someone who know would rather be with someone else. I care for them deeply and want them to be happy," I explain, almost forgetting that an auditorium of Committee members is watching our exchange.

"I don't see how—"

"Those are my terms. Meet them or don't," I finish, standing and acknowledging the crowd. "I know we can fix this," I say, my hands resting at my sides, all pretense gone from my voice and body language. "We can't become complacent and slip like every other society, we've come too far." Giving a small smile, I gather my things and exit into the hallway, tears finally allowed to slide silently down my cheeks.

"I TRIED, Eric, I'm so sorry," Val says, hanging her head. "I utilized every tool I could think of, but no Kate came up."

"Do you think they could have changed her name?" Tal asks.

"It's possible," I say, rubbing my face with my hands.

"I'm so sorry—" Val repeats, but I cut her off.

"Val, please don't apologize. It was incredibly kind of you to even try."

"What do we do now?" Tal asks.

"That. Is a great question," I answer, thoroughly exhausted. Though I have been more functional over the last few days, it's still a fight to wake up and get going. I remember everything—or, at least, I think it's everything. Regardless, I remember enough. Enough to make the life I am leading seem truly pointless. Tal was right all along, in his own way. He knew he was destined for something greater, and I...I stifled that. Told him that it wasn't our lot in life.

For the first time in what seems like weeks, I think of Kip. Though seeing some logic in the points he made scares me spitless, I can't deny that he was right about one thing. There is power in belief. Now that I know I am Tier 1, my personal expectations are exponentially higher. Why was I ever satisfied *planting in the fields?*

"Dad?" Tal says, pulling me out of my self-analysis. Focusing on him, I tilt my head, waiting for him to finish his thought.

"We can't stay here." His words drop like solid weights, landing on the floor between us.

"I know, Tal," I agree, leaning forward to rest my elbows on my knees. "We don't have any information to go on. As uncomfortable as it is, I think we need to trust Nick—"

"But—"

"No, I agree with your dad, Tal," Val cuts in. "I think it's your only option. You have been given a gift, having your memories returned. Any misstep, and that could be discovered. I don't understand why any of this is valuable enough to cause Berg so much trouble in covering it up, but I do know that they aren't going to ignore it potentially being let loose. You have to keep up appearances. Eric," she says turning to me, "you have already raised red flags. Missing your work assignments brings the wrong kind of attention. I don't know how long you will have to wait for Nick to reach out, but in the meantime, you have to keep on. Business as usual," she explains soberly.

I nod. "Tal, we don't have to only keep up appearances. There are some things that we could do, discreetly, to prepare ourselves."

"What do you mean?" he asks quizzically.

"You're pretty good with software, right?"

He nods, his eyebrows still furrowed.

"What if you got even better," I say, a conspiratorial grin on my face.

"I think I could probably handle that," he says, unsure, but excited by my energy.

"We may also need to be physically conditioned. New workouts starting tomorrow," I add.

He nods. "I better finish up my conditioning assignments then," he says, moving out of the room with more passion than I have seen in weeks.

When he is gone, I exhale loudly.

"You handled that well," Val says approvingly.

"I gave him false hope," I mutter.

"What has convinced you that it's false?"

"The fact that I have no information. Nothing to go on."

"So finding Kate is the only acceptable outcome?"

I stare at her, not sure how to respond.

She gives an exasperated laugh. "I'm trying to help you understand that one hundred percent success isn't the goal! Life is messy, Eric, as you are now blatantly aware. If you base your happiness on one perfect solution, you are going to miss the beautiful conclusions all around you. Your son has a purpose. *You have a purpose* that was hidden from you before this happened. Yes, finding your family is ideal, but your path isn't dependant on it. If you let it be, you'll be actively limiting your view all on your own."

"If I don't find them, Val, how—"

"You will move on, because you are strong. You are kind, you are intelligent, and you are a father. Stop worrying about how, and commit yourself to doing, Eric."

I nod, anxiety still plaguing my mind, but dissipating slightly. "What if I fail?"

A laugh explodes from her lips. "Fail? What does that even mean?"

Taken off guard, my eyes search the room for an answer that isn't there. "What if I don't get what I want?" I whisper, the words resonating deeply within me.

"Then you will truly be Tier 2, like the rest of us."

"Nick?" I say softly, shaking his shoulder. He stirs slightly. "Nick, I'm so sorry to wake you, but your sensor has been going off all morning. I am worried it's an emergency or something."

At that, he rolls over, throwing the covers off of the bed. "What time is it?" he asks, sitting up and stretching his arms high above his head.

"Almost eleven. I just dropped the girls at the nursery."

"Wow, I'm so sorry. I didn't realize it was so late," he apologizes, standing and reaching for his shirt, hastily tossed on the bedside table the night before. When Nick arrived home last night, I didn't dare ask him how it went. With a pale face and shaking arms, he had collapsed into bed without saying a word.

This morning, he looks like himself, but I don't want to risk upsetting him. Instead, I pick up the comforter and methodically put the bed back in order as he dresses. As I stand, I become aware of his presence next to me.

"Thank you," he says, hugging me, and walking into the hall.

Sitting on the bed in a near stupor, I mull over my possibilities. I know I can't stay here, but other options escape me. Every time I consider a new alternative, I eventually end up in the same place. Memories altered, alone, forgotten. Berg is too tapped into my life, and I can't see a path that leaves me free of them. Is that what I want? To be free of...all of this? No, I silently correct myself. I want Eric, the kids, and, in some ways, Nick. I want him to be okay. To be happy. Again, the connecting links between where I am and the conclusion I seek are missing.

Throwing myself back on the bed, I pull my hair in frustration. Then I hear Nick's voice wafting in from the kitchen.

"...I have been very clear, I won't compromise on that point...Then it doesn't matter, does it? In that situation, the information would be of no harm to anyone..."

A long pause drives me to my feet. Peeking around the door frame, I spot Nick, stooped over, elbows on the counter. I can't make out the words, but I can hear a woman lightly speaking. The voice prattles on, Nick fixated on his sensor.

"Right. I understand, though—"

More nodding, his fingers splaying and then returning to fists.

"Let me talk with Kate, but that sounds reasonable. What are we looking at for timing?"

I walk down the hall, slowly approaching. Nick meets my eyes, a tragic smile on his face.

"Once that occurs and I am shown proof, I will return for the debriefing and demonstration, yes. Alright, thank you. I'll look for it and get back to you within the hour."

His sensor goes dark, and I close the distance between us.

"What was that all about?" I ask, second guessing myself when I see Nick's expression.

"We need to make a decision," he answers, his voice tight.

"About what?"

Nick breathes deeply. "You and Bentley having the opportunity to return to your family."

My heart nearly stops and I stare at him, my mouth hanging open. All of the pent up energy from the stress of the unknown explodes upward, releasing through heat and tears. I collapse in on myself, allowing the sobs to flow freely. Nick lifts me, pressing me to his chest. I hate myself in this moment, for allowing him to comfort me, for being so thrilled when he must be at his lowest. Pulling myself together, I ask the question that is pressing at the forefront of my mind.

"How?" I ask, searching his face.

"It's not important, but—"

"No, Nick, I have to know. I need to know every detail. This has been literally eating at me day in and day out. All I ever think about is how we can possibly fix this—this mess! I can't go one more second *not knowing*," I plead.

He nods. "You're right," he agrees. "You need to know, I just don't want to relive it," he says, running his hands through his hair. "Let's sit."

We move into the living room and sit across from each other on the couch.

"You aren't the only one who has been puzzling this out," he admits. "I know I haven't talked about it, but that's only because I didn't want to get your hopes up. Kate, I didn't think there was anything we could do, and then—well, then I had an idea. I knew it was a long-shot with so many unknown variables that could potentially throw me off course, but I decided to try."

He leans back, stretching his legs out, at least attempting to make himself comfortable. "I have felt sick about this research on reversal therapy. On the one hand, I am obviously ecstatic that I have initialized a new way to administer the therapy. On the other, I am terrified that it will be used to hurt more than help. You understand," he says, meeting my eyes. "These echoes are the only indicator for the patient that something has happened. With the poor judgement I have witnessed, I don't trust our leadership to use it wisely."

"How did they respond to your research last night?"

"I didn't present it," he sighs. "I mean, I did show my tables of results, but I didn't tell them my procedure. My lab assistants actually agreed to be treated—removing their memories of our trials from their minds—in preparation. Tamara...still breaks my heart a little. She was so invested in making sure these trials were successful. One of the only people who I was able to confide in and I can't even give her credit. But I had to be the only one with the information."

"Wow," I say. "Why?"

"Because...I didn't want there to be any possible way for vital information to leak out. Berg has a massive problem with these treatment symptoms and I knew how badly they were going to want this information. My assistants didn't even blink an eye when I told them it was procedure. Last night, I told the Committee that they had to meet my terms in order to have access to anything," I say, holding my breath. "Kate, *Carole Berg* was there," he adds, pausing as if to watch my reaction.

"You told *Carole Berg* that she had to meet your terms?" I nearly shriek, my eyes surely bugging out of my head.

Nick laughs nervously, as if he can't believe it either.

Gathering myself, my brow furrows in confusion. "Wait, hold on. What was this meeting? Why was she even there?"

"It was supposed to be a regional Committee meeting, I thought I told you," Nick laughs. "But representatives from the whole union ended up being there," he admits. "I almost chickened out."

"I can't believe you didn't," I laugh, imagining him telling Carole Berg off in front of who knows how many people. "So what did she say?"

"Here's the thing, Kate. This is so much bigger than us. Our experience, I'm realizing, is just a microcosm of what is happening all over our union. Reversal is being used aggressively, and not justifiably in my estimation. Berg didn't do their due diligence and people are suffering. I can't trust them with my treatment. I can't feel good about handing that information over to people whose priorities are skewed. I explained that in the meeting and garnered more support from other Committee members than I could have anticipated. *That* is worth fighting for. We are a silent minority and we need to stand up for the integrity of Tier 1."

"It's admirable of you, and honestly, I want to hear more about what you have planned, but the blood is pounding in my head so loudly that I can't focus, Nick. I can't force myself to care about Tier 1 right now! Knowing that our family is in the balance somehow...please tell me the terms. Put me out of my misery," I groan.

"I'm sorry, you're right. I've been thinking about this for weeks and it's all new to you. I'm sorry I couldn't bring you into the loop sooner."

I nod, urging him to go on.

"I told Carole that I would be happy to pass on the details of my procedure if they made this information about reversal and excess resources public, informed all patients who had been treated without consent, and—" he pauses, swallowing, "—restored you and Tal to your original family unit."

Heat rises to my face. "Did they agree?" I ask softly.

"That was Carole who has been calling all morning. She agreed. With some caveats. That's what we need to discuss."

I throw myself into Nick's arms, nearly hyperventilating as relief washes over me. No part of me cares that I am being selfish right now. I should care. I should be ecstatic that Nick is holding the

Committee accountable, that he is attempting to correct the pride that has crept into our system, but all I can think of is Eric. And Tal.

Will they even remember me? What if I meet them and they have no idea who I am? Where will we go? What will our life look like? Relief quickly mixes with panic, my mind reeling with potential possibilities.

I pull back, attempting to breathe normally. "Nick, how? And when? What—"

"Take a minute, Kate. Just breathe," he encourages, brushing his fingers through my hair. I allow my eyelids to drift closed, my face pressed against his chest. As difficult as it is to admit, I have come to depend on Nick. I care about and respect him deeply. Watching him parent, witnessing him consistently giving of himself to help others, being willing to make mistakes and try again. Eric is my partner—my pair—but Nick is a dear friend. One that is potentially putting his life on the line for me. What will Berg do with him once they have their information? My hands go cold. This time, the discomfort that pulls at my heart is for him.

"Nick," I say softly, my breathing returning to normal. "What does this mean for you?"

"I haven't thought that far," he answers truthfully. "I know this is right, Kate. That's it. I figure the rest will fall into place, or—they will find a way to silence me," he says with a sardonic laugh. "Either way, I've done what I can."

"Do you honestly think they would go that far?"

"I didn't think they were capable of what they have already done, so in my mind, anything's possible," he sighs. "But, I do have hope. There were enough people who seemed to support me. Maybe we aren't too far gone."

Stretching my neck, I turn over and lay my head in his lap, staring at the ceiling. Streams of light filter in through the back window, creating a juxtaposition of peace and clarity against the muddy unknowns swirling through my mind.

"Okay," I say, finally ready. "Give me the details."

"Let's go outside," he suggests, lifting my head. I obediently follow him to the yard and stretch out on a shaded chair. Nick sits across from me.

"Let me say everything before you jump in, if that's alright? It's not all going to be easy to hear."

I nod, bracing myself. My mind races through the myriad worst-case scenarios. We are put into Tier 3? Wait, there isn't a Tier 3 anymore. Tier 2 then? That wouldn't be that bad. What other options are there? I shudder.

"They have agreed for you to be reconnected with Eric and Tal," Nick begins. "At first, Carole insisted that I treat you—removing all memories of your life here with me—but I rejected that. It is a moot point, given...well, given her other condition." Nick rubs his hands along the arms of the chair, building up to something. "Kate, your family will be reunited, but you won't be able to participate within the Tier system."

My eyebrows furrow. "What does that even mean?"

"It means, you will be on your own."

"On our own—how? Like we can't use any resources?" I blurt out.

"Don't jump in, remember? Let me get this all out. You will be given space in old Tier 3 territory. Abandoned, but safe to use. Soil toxicity will be mitigated, you will have a water source, seeds, some raw materials that have been left there. Shelter, obviously. But you will be opting out of the union. On your own. No communication, no assistance. Berg refuses to support any part of this, but will allow you to go through with it without any repercussions."

"Those sound like some pretty intense repercussions," I mutter.

"Kate—"

"I know, I know, I'm sorry. Go on."

"Your family will be reunited. You, Bentley, Eric, and Tal."

I nod and his eyes seem to be pleading with me. What am I missing?

"Beth and Leah," I gasp. "They aren't going to let me take Beth and Leah," I repeat, my stomach dropping. "Nick, they are my family. They are my daughters. How can they—"

"They are both of our daughters, Kate. And they are Eric's. His research brought them here. And they are Berg's. By creating our pairing and providing the resources, they argue that the girls don't 'belong' to anyone. Do any of us, really? We are all members of this community, privileged to live here, and charged with a responsibility to improve it. Beth and Leah have to stay in Tier 1 so they can procreate and continue to build a cleaner gene pool—" he stops, noticing my distress. My face, despite my attempts to keep it calm, has twisted in pain, tears streaming down my cheeks. I am frozen like this, unwilling to move in case it breaks me. He's right, I know he's right, but I can't bear the thought of never seeing them again. *Never seeing my beautiful girls again.*

"Kate," he soothes, leaning forward. "In the event that you go forward with this, they will be with me. I will take care of them and give them every opportunity. I know it's a small consolation, but it's non-negotiable."

"I know," I whisper, biting my cheeks. "I know. But this is an impossible split. Either option deprives me of people I love—" I gasp for air. "I'm allowed to grieve, Nick. These are my children. I won't ever get to see them walk or talk in full sentences," I cough, clutching my mid-section as if someone punched me in the gut. Nick watches me, his knuckles white against the chair.

"Kate, there's nothing more I can do," he pleads, his voice strained. "This is the best I could do—"

"I'm not accusing you, please don't take it that way. It's just terrible. It's wonderful and terrible and I'm not sure which truth wins. It's difficult to embrace the wonderful when the terrible is attached to it, you know?" I breathe, barely getting the words out.

"Oh Kate. I know," he whispers, his eyes filled with tears. "Don't you think I know? I am giving up half of my family, too. I know you weren't ever really mine, but this is all I've known. *You are all I've ever known.* And I'm giving it up because it's the *right thing to do*, Kate, but there's not much that feels wonderful to me right now."

"Nick, I'm—"

"There's nothing to say, Kate! It's not our fault! That's what kills me. Somehow, it would be easier if I could blame you, or even me. Or Eric, that would be ideal, honestly, but I can't! I can't even blame Berg fully. These genetic pairings *will* improve society in the future. I don't agree with their means, but I understand how they thought they could justify it. So, what is there to do? We live it. We feel it. Yes, we hate it, but we have to move forward." Our eyes are linked, unblinking. "I would normally say something meaningful, like 'I will support you in whatever path you determine to be best' but I know what you need to do, and you know it, too. So, I will assure you that the girls will be cared for. I will love them, Kate. I will tell them stories about their incredible, brave mother, and allow them to grow into strong women just like her. I will—" he sucks in a breath, squeezing his eyes closed for a moment, composing himself. "You and Bentley are a part of me forever, and I will love you enough to help you go. That's it, Kate. That's all I've got."

I nod, still biting my cheeks, the taste of iron in my mouth, my arms squeezing my chest, as if trying to keep it from ripping apart.

"I have to get back to Carole," Nick says. "Do you agree to Berg's terms?"

I nod quickly, still stunned, and see something in Nick's eyes glaze over.

"You need to pack your things. You and Bent will leave on Thursday. I will escort you to your new location, set you up with some necessities, and then I will come home. I will...come...home," he repeats slowly, standing and walking abruptly into the house. Nothing moves. Even the air is still. The pain radiates within me, throbbing rhythmically. Frozen, I stare at the stones of the garden wall, not truly taking them in, just allowing my eyes to rest there. Home. He will come home.

PACKING. What do I pack? What will I need when we have...nothing? I glance at the two storage cubes in the front hall-way. We will need everything. And everything won't fit into those. Robotically, I comb through each drawer and cupboard looking for necessities. Nick assures me that he will set us up with medical and emergency supplies, so I ignore those. He has also promised one year's worth of sustenance so we can get our feet under us. Apparently, that's all Berg could spare. Nick didn't appreciate my derisive comments about excess resources, so I have been keeping them to myself.

Moving into the bedroom, I pull out Bentley's clothes, my body numb. Halfway through his shirts, I hear a rustle in the girls' room next door. Dropping the shirt in my hands, I rush to them. Leah is rolling around, her legs splayed over Beth's back. I want desperately to pick her up, but her eyes are still closed, so I wait.

Her legs twitch, her back arching, as she attempts to find a comfortable position in her sleepy state. Cheeks flushed pink with the heat of sleep, her cherry lips curve around her thumb. Beth breathes evenly, her hair slightly damp against her forehead, small curls forming near her perfect, miniature ears. Try as I might, I can't memorize it. My eyes slowly scan every inch of them, attempting to burn this image—this feeling, this smell—into my brain forever, but I know it's futile. It will fade, and I won't have anything left. Frantic, I begin slowly searching their room. Finding two of my favorite sleepers, I fold them gently and tip-toe back into the hall, placing them in the cube.

Back in Bentley's room, my sensor rings, jolting me from my seated position. Running out to the kitchen to avoid noise near the girls, I answer.

"Hey Kate," Shari says, her voice stilted. "I wanted to check-in before you head out tomorrow."

Head out? As if I'm going on a vacation? Shari doesn't know that *all* of my memories are intact, as far as I am aware. But somehow, we need to acknowledge something real. Leaving this relationship open-ended will nag at me, I know it.

"Shari, can we cut the pretense and have a real conversation? You have been my mentor my entire life. I am leaving—with zero communication—tomorrow and you are *checking in?*"

"That's as real as it gets, Kate. I'm willing to help, even when you are making the worst mistake of your life," she says matter-of-factly.

"Worst mistake? Are you serious right now?"

"Kate, you are removing yourself from a community that has

provided you with everything. Safety, resources, opportunity, relationships. You are walking away from that for one person. *One person*, when you have so many other people who love you and who I know you care about. Because of the agreements our Committee has made, I have to support it. But I don't have to pretend I am happy about it."

"You think I am walking away because of a *person*? You don't get it, Shari," I say, shaking my head. "For you, it has always been so simple to toe the line. You don't question, even when you should! Did you hear Nick the other night? The Director, along with many others, has been way out of line. You have worked shoulder to shoulder with him and, as far as I can tell, have said nothing!" I shriek. "You participated in breaking my family apart, as if it was nothing. And even if I could convince myself that that part of it was justifiable, you have been party to countless treatments of aggressive reversal that is not. How could you?" I accuse, my eyes burning. "I am not leaving because of a *person*, I am leaving because Tier 1 has failed me and I have built a life with people that mean more to me than this system," I finish, my nostrils flaring with every breath.

Shari stares at me. "I don't expect you to understand," she says, her voice even. "I have done what I had to do—"

"To protect yourself and your lifestyle. You have spoken to me about sacrifice, yet you know nothing of it, Shari," I spit.

"Kate, don't think that my sacrifices haven't been as difficult as yours because they aren't as dramatically visible," she fumes. "*We are different people, Kate—*"

"Please, explain that to me! How are we genetically similar enough to be matched for mentoring, and yet conveniently different enough to justify your actions?"

"Our lives have taken very different trajectories. While genetically similar, our social experiences have been significantly different. You judge me, but you don't understand my life just as I don't understand yours," she says softly. "I wish I understood—I've tried, but...you and Eric. The way you feel about him. It's so impractical, Kate. Look at the mess it's caused. Can't you see the negative impact—"

"Shari, you don't understand," I sigh, the anger rushing out of me. How could she? The closest thing she has had to a relationship of that magnitude is...me. And I am leaving. Shari is hurting, too, I realize. And I am berating her.

"Remember our weekly lunches?" I say, a sad smile on my lips. She nods, taken off guard. "You helped me figure out the software before my first health consultation. I was so frustrated," I say, a small laugh escaping my lips. "You watched Tal and Bentley more times than I can count. You held me when my mom died," I say, scrunching my nose, trying to hold back tears.

"Kate, I—"

"No, it's okay, Shari. I don't get a lot of what has happened recently, but I want you to know that I'm grateful for the impact you have had on me. Thank you for always being there for me."

She nods, emotion uncharacteristically present on her face.

"I love you. I wish things had gone differently," I say, tears stinging the corners of my eyes.

"Me too," she whispers, looking down. For a moment, neither of us moves, and then the display goes dark. I am left staring at the cupboard facade.

The door opens and Bentley walks in, hanging his bag on a hook and peeking inside the cubes.

"Are those my clothes?" he asks.

"Most of them," I say. "You can go check and see if I missed anything important."

As he bounces off to his room, I resume my game. Leah waits patiently to see my head peek around the corner of the cabinet. On my hands and knees, I slowly creep forward until I catch her eager eyes, then quickly retreat, sending her into a fit of giggles. She crawls as fast as she can toward me, drool dripping from her bottom lip in her excitement. As she rounds the corner, I laugh and cheer for her to get closer, then scoop her up into my arms and tickle underneath her chin.

Not to be left out, Beth squeals in the other room. She isn't as adept at getting around, but I know if I tease her enough, she will follow. I crawl her direction with Leah following close behind, grabbing my toes when I pause. Leah's frustrated expression quickly gives way to a broad smile when she sees me. Sitting squarely on her bottom, she scoots, refusing to move to her hands and knees at first. Such a stubborn thing. She'll pull herself up all day, but avoids crawling with everything she's got. Slowly, as I mime crawling and point to her hands, she leans forward.

"You can do it," I coo. "C'mon!" As if on cue, Leah rockets around my legs, energizing Beth with a little sibling rivalry. She pinches her lips in determination and moves her arms, allowing her knees to follow. I cheer and urge her forward while Leah looks at me, attempting to confirm that the celebration is actually for her.

"Mom, I put my hat in the cube. That's the only thing you missed," Bentley says, sitting next to us. I sit up, looking at him.

"How are you doing, bud?" I ask.

"Good," he sighs. "I am really going to miss Beth and Leah."

My throat tightens. "I know, me too."

"Why can't we take them?" he asks for the hundredth time.

"I—"

"I know, Mom. You don't have to tell me again. I just like to ask it," he says, leaving my side and chasing them around the room.

"Do you see it?" I ask Bentley. His face is pressed against the window, eyes searching the landscape. A tiny circle of fog appears in front of his lips.

"No," he whispers.

"Keep looking," I say, smiling. It should only be a few seconds more, considering that my eyes hit a foot higher than his.

Suddenly, he gasps. "That's it," he says softly. "I can't believe how big it is. Is that really it?"

"It is. The Pacific Ocean," I answer. Kate watches us, sitting quietly in the seat next to Bentley. I catch her eye and a small smile lifts the corner of her mouth. It's something.

"Is that where we are going?" he asks.

"Close," I say. "We still have another hour or so." His shoulders slump. "Bent, when we arrive, you will only be a fifteen minute walk from the coast. We're going south, not further inland." His energy returns at this revelation and I can't help but laugh. Movement catches my eye and I notice Kate twisting and untwisting her fingers.

"Nervous?" I ask and she nods quickly. "There's nothing to be nervous about," I assure her. "The hard part is already over."

At that, she turns her head and looks out the window. I sigh, regretting bringing it up. Hours earlier, Shari and I loaded up supplies into this transport vehicle while Kate and Bent spent their last moments with the girls. My heart aches, envisioning her face as she hugged them goodbye. Holding their pudgy fingers in her hands, kissing their round cheeks. Beth and Leah laughed and kicked, unaware that today was anything but an ordinary day. She hasn't said two words since getting in the car, and I don't blame her.

I stare at her, unabashed. Watching her touch Beth and Leah, feeling every inch of them as if committing their arms, their ears, their hair to memory, resonated with me. Because that's all I want to do: memorize every part of her. The way her eyelashes curve, the line of her jaw against her slender neck. The way her hair falls along her collarbone, brushing the edge of her cotton shirt. Her fingers, perched on the seat, arms long against her side. Her chest, rising and falling. Alive. Here. With me.

As if understanding my thoughts, her head turns and our eyes meet. We stare at each other, unblinking.

"Some of it is really dark blue and some of it is lighter," Bentley says, still fixated on the expanse of water in the distance.

"It's pretty amazing, isn't it," I say, looking away and clearing my throat. Kate leans her body across the seat and shifts, moving next to me. Bentley doesn't notice as she wraps her fingers around mine.

"I've been avoiding saying goodbye to you," she says softly. Almost immediately, I can't breathe. Tears fill my eyes, any strength I previously thought I had evaporating.

"Kate, I can't—"

"I have to, Nick. I can't leave forever without telling you how I feel."

"It doesn't matter at this point," I choke out, "and I don't think I can take—"

"You don't have to say anything," she assures me, turning my face to hers. "But I need you to hear it," she whispers, her eyes pleading. My heart squeezes and a tear drops, hitting the collar of my shirt.

"Nick," she says smiling, "when I first met you, I was impressed. You expressed yourself in a way that belied your age and experience. Your body and mind are intimidating, to say the least," she laughs, glancing down at my chest and I can't help but smile. "Over the last month, something has shifted in you. You went from being unsure of yourself—trying to prove your worth in our home, in your work—to becoming this pillar of strength. You moved forward with research you believed in. You stood up to *Carole Berg*, knowing it could literally cost you everything, because you felt like it was the right thing to do. You are giving up people you care about because you feel like it's the *right thing to do*. This is Tier 1, Nick. You are it."

I shake my head. "No, Kate," I say, my face twisted. "I did it for you. I wanted to help you, to fix the problem I created. It wasn't altruism, it was guilt," I choke out.

She smiles. "It isn't true, Nick. Sure, it may have started out that way, but you figured out how to help me a long time ago. You could have administered treatment and none of this would have happened, but you didn't. You questioned the Committee and didn't turn a blind eye like so many others have. That had nothing to do with me and you know it. At this point, I am simply a representation of the many poor decisions the Committee has made."

I stare at her, tears still streaming down my cheeks.

"I tell you this," she continues, "because I want you to know what I see. A man who is solid, a force. You have started something, Nick, and it isn't going to stop here. You have to see this through. *You don't need me.*"

I look down, gripping her hand.

"I am so grateful," she says, her eyes brimming with tears, "that we were here for each other. Thank you for agreeing to pair with me, even after I hurt you that day. Thank you for fighting for me, even at great personal loss. Thank you for building a family with me, even if only for a short time, and thank you—" she stops, pulling in a few staggered breaths, "—for taking care of Beth and Leah when I can't." I pull both her hands close to my chest. "Nick, I love you. It's different than the way I love Eric, and I know that probably sounds pathetic, but I can't describe it any other way. If there was some way to keep us all together in some weird family, I would do it!" she says, laughing and I snort. I get it. Tragically, I understand now. Because letting her go, I imagine, feels—in some small way—comparable to what she felt leaving Eric.

"I love you, too," I say. She slips her hand from beneath mine and touches my jaw, lifting it toward her. Moving close, she kisses me. Wrapping my arms around her back, I pull her close and kiss her back, gently. Though it only lasts for a moment, I cling to it. Laying her head on my shoulder, I wrap my arms around her and hold tight. One last time.

Something shakes and my eyes fling open. Lifting my head from Nick's chest, I see that we have stopped. Bentley is passed out on the seat next to us. I shake Nick's shoulder gently and smile as his eyelids flutter open.

"We're here," I say, keeping my face still, though excitement builds within me. Having done all of the hard things, there's nothing left to do but see him. See them. Finally, something good.

Nick lifts himself off the seat and stretches. "Should we let him sleep?"

"I don't know. What happens now?"

"It will be a bit before Eric and Tal arrive," Nick says nervously. "I wanted to have everything unloaded so that we could—"

"Are you trying to avoid seeing them?" I ask, incredulous. "Nick, that's not an option. Eric will want to see you—"

"I don't know if that's true, Kate. I have been keeping him from you all this time."

"Eric won't see it that way. Does he—" I stop, eyes wide, my fears suddenly rushing back in full force.

"He knows who you are, Kate. He remembers everything," Nick says softly.

"Did Berg give them back?" I ask.

"Something like that," he says, moving past me to unload.

As I step out of the vehicle, I scan the location, taking in my surroundings. It is definitely overgrown, but there is vegetation everywhere. The soil must be good. The shelter is small, but isn't as dilapidated as I had imagined. Not knowing what else to do, I follow Nick into the holding compartment and begin hauling boxes.

When we are finished, I wake Bentley. He practically bounces to the ground, exploring the area immediately. Before he can escape, Nick hands him a sandwich, passing one to me as well. Taking a bite, a low hum in the air sends my eyes skyward.

"What is that?" I ask.

"Eric," he says, standing and closing the doors to the compartment. "That's my cue," he says.

"Nick, please," I beg. "Please stay, just for a minute." Though he doesn't agree, he moves a little less hastily.

Slowly, the hum grows in intensity and Bentley points at a black shape in the distance.

"What is it?" he asks.

"A helicopter," Nick states, and Bentley's eyes go wide.

"We have those?" he yells in excitement. Nick laughs with his mouth full, nearly spitting out his bite of sandwich. He moves next to Bent, wrapping his arm around his shoulder. The noise is loud enough now that I can't hear what they are saying, but Bent is fixated on him. Suddenly, he throws his arms around his neck and holds tight. I look away, not wanting to interrupt their moment. When a hand touches my back, I turn to see Bent's face staring into mine. He reaches for my hand and pulls me closer to the shelter.

We watch as the helicopter draws closer, holding our ears as the wind whips around us. It touches down in a clearing and, with blades still spinning, the door opens. Two figures climb out and reach up to retrieve duffel bags. Everything and everyone safely on the ground, the helicopter lifts back into the sky and heads back in the direction from which it appeared.

I stand, fixed to the spot, alert. The two figures pick up their gear and begin trudging toward us. My eyes squint, trying to make out their faces. Suddenly, the taller figure stops, dropping the bag, and begins to run. Without thinking, I drop my sandwich and sprint toward him. Breathless, with legs pumping, I finally get close enough to make out his features. Though I knew it was him, seeing the familiar outline of his face sends electricity flooding through my body. I run faster, my shoes flying through the grass. When we meet, he swings me into the air and I grip his shoulders, surprised at their strength. His body is thicker, fuller somehow. I kiss his face through my tears, squeezing so tight I think I might burst.

Noticing someone next to us, I stop and gasp. It's Tal, but he's...tall. And masculine. I fling my arms around him, sending him backward. He catches himself and sobs into my shoulder. Something hits my waist, and I glance down to see Bentley gripping us tightly. I laugh at the impossibility of it all. We are here together. After touching Tal's face, I turn, remembering Nick. He stands awkwardly next to the shelter, kicking the dirt with his shoe. Meeting Eric's eyes, I grab his hand and walk speedily toward him.

"Nick," Eric calls and he looks up. Without saying another word, Eric moves toward him and pulls him into an embrace. "Thank you," he says, loud enough that I can make out his words. Nick claps him on the back, eventually stepping back.

"Eric, I—" he stammers.

"I owe you everything," Eric cuts him off. "How did you find us?"

My eyes flit between them, not understanding.

"It wasn't hard," Nick says. "I'm sorry it had to be so abrupt."

"Thanks, Nick," Tal pipes in.

Nick looks at both of them and nods. "I have to get going. I've unloaded your supplies and enough medical essentials to last all of your lifetimes—" he pauses, grinning, then thinks better of it. "Good luck," he says, giving a small wave and moving to the door of the transport.

"Nick," I say. He stops, but doesn't turn. I can't finish my sentence. I've said everything I wanted to say, but somehow it doesn't feel like enough. He walks forward and lifts himself inside the vehicle. We watch, entranced, as it drives down the road.

The weight of our situation hits me in the silence. My body is paralyzed momentarily, fear coursing through me. What have we done? Our children will have nothing. *We have nothing*, I think, glancing around at the empty landscape.

"Kate," Eric says softly. I turn, taking in his face, strange and familiar all at once. "Welcome home," he says, his voice tight with emotion. The boys embrace and Bentley follows Tal into the shelter. Eric pulls me close and we stand there. We could stand here forever, I realize. We have nothing pressing, no assignments to report for, nobody to check in with. Tears spill across my cheeks, the immensity of it—all of it—simultaneously lifting from my shoulders and settling in.

As Eric presses against me, something hard hits my ribs. Pulling back, I look down. Not seeing anything on Eric that could have caused the sensation, I reach into my jacket pocket and pull out something familiar.

"Did you forget to turn in your sensor?" Eric asks, and I look at him, my eyebrows furrowed. "It's ok," he assures me, "it won't work here anyway. We can keep it as a memento."

"This isn't mine," I say softly, turning the small, blue indicator light toward him.

ABOUT THE AUTHOR

 Cindy is first and foremost mother to her four beautiful children and wife to her charming and handsome husband, Scott. She is a musician, a homeschooler, a gardener, an athlete, a lover of Canadian chocolate, and most recently, a writer.

Cindy grew up in Airdrie, AB, Canada, but has lived most of her adult life between California and Colorado. She currently resides in the Denver metro area. Cindy graduated from Brigham Young University in 2005 with a B.S. in Psychology, minoring in Business. She serves actively within her church and community and is always up for a new adventure.

facebook.com/cindygwrites

instagram.com/cindygwrites